SO SMART YA STUPID

A Novel

by

J.GAIL & EL WIL

Brought to you by Truth Hurts Publications
an imprint of Jazoli Publishing

TRUTH HURTS
PUBLICATIONS
*"Gritty Urban Tales That
Inspire and Excite You"*

Sometimes the truth hurts, but it can set you free.

Truth Hurts Publications
P.O. Box 1316
Brookhaven PA 19015

So Smart Ya Stupid
First edition
Truth Hurts Publications (an imprint of Jazoli Publishing)

ISBN13 (paperback): 978-0972697880
LCCN: 2012949148

Cover model: Mont (Recording artist and producer)
contact him at montmusic103@gmail.com

Cover photo by Michael Knight Fotografia

*A special thank you and shoutout to Miss M.W.,
L.W., S.W., El Wil's children, grandchildren,
cousins, nieces, nephews and the entire family.*

Dedicated to El Wil
OUR HERO and the true definition
of a **MAN**
We ride with him 'til the wheels fall off!

Prologue

"...damn... he got me," he said weakly. He clutched his chest tightly as he struggled to make out his last few words. Blood spurted out from between his fingers and stained his white polo shirt...

Everyone at the party rushed toward the door and looked on in horror as he dropped to the ground and slowly rolled down the hilly sidewalk.

"Somebody call an ambulance, quick!" someone screamed.

Prologue

Part I – The Old Life

Chapter 1
Beezy

Dear Jerome
It's me, your son Shawn. Remember me?
Remember when you threw me in that pile of snow
when I was a kid?
You was proud of your little peanut-head son...
I laughed so hard I couldn't breathe...best night of my life!
Pop, I am not an angry man nor am I a bad person. I am just me.
And you... well you just you. You that nigga Pop!
Are you listening? I'm talking to you Jerome!
Why the fuck you so quiet?

"They call me Beezy! Smile always cheesy. Face stay greasy!!" Shawn said and then laughed like he had never heard anything funnier in his life. He was known to kick his little spiel when he was feeling really good and on his level.

"Head stay peasy!" his boy Tino joined in and laughed along with him.

Shawn Karlson was addicted to tight gear, flossing, making money and of course the ladies. He was a good-looking brown-skinned brother standing at just under six feet tall. He had a solid medium build with a physique somewhere between a basketball player and a football player. He always sported a low cut Caesar haircut along with a close cut beard and trimmed mustache. He had a perfect set of white teeth and no matter how much he ate he couldn't get fat—it was in his genes. He proudly donned a large tattoo on his arm that said "Real Nigga" in script letters. It was a tattoo that he got done while in the military as a way to give a middle finger to everybody who didn't respect where he was from.

Shawn's laugh was infectious. It started off as a comical chuckle then grew to a mischievous and obnoxious cackle then slowly developed into a full blown laugh with his mouth wide open that could either make your day or make you want to strangle him on the spot. He had no problem laughing right in anyone's face.

Shawn could best be defined as a block hugger—he was raised on the streets. He could usually be found posted up in front of the local Chinese spot, holding an ice cold can of 211 in a paper bag, politicking and intimidating the weak-minded corner boys he knew had no business being out there. He picked on them partly because he enjoyed it, and partly because he wanted them to go try something else—especially the younger ones. Not everyone was cut out for that life. Things could go very wrong very quick and you had to stay on your toes.

"My head might be peasy but that's cuz this life ain't easy!" Shawn continued. "I'm a real nigga. The rest of these niggas out here is fake and phony fraudulent bitch ass muthafuckas!"

"Yup!" Tino agreed with a nod and took a long guzzle from his beer.

"T these niggas out here snitchin' like a mufucka! Show and tell niggas, runnin' they mouths gossiping and shit! They got us all fucked up in the game," Shawn said, shaking his head. He looked over at one of the brothers who hung out in their circle and winked at him as if to say he knew something.

The accused person looked away, trying to look cool and silently praying that Shawn wouldn't call him out on the spot as a snitch.

"All about a dollar but ain't makin' no sense," Shawn commented and then took another swig of his beer.

Shawn was an asshole, and he would be the first to admit it. He didn't care—his whole life was about taking risks. At 32, a black man living in Philly, he knew that statistic-wise he wasn't even supposed to be alive at that age when you're "about that life." Sometimes he felt like he was living on borrowed time.

"You always spittin' the truth Beezy, and that's why I fucks with you," Tino said and glanced in the direction that he was looking. Everyone else was too far gone at that point, high off some good weed, to notice what he was doing. After a few minutes the accused person slowly slid away from their group. Shawn watched him, feeling satisfied that he'd run him off. He hated weaklings and snitches with a passion.

"Yup, me too," Ron, another one of the regulars said and nodded eagerly. He was "me too" dude. Every time somebody who was talking made a statement he said "me too."

This dick-riding pussy, Shawn thought of Ron as he took another long puff of his Newport. *Man I gotta get off this island before they drown me!*

"Nigga, I bet if I told you DEEZ NUTS made of solid gold you'd say 'yup, me too'!" Shawn quipped at Ron as he grabbed his crotch disrespectfully.

"Fuck you SB."

"No fuck *you* nigga," Shawn replied.

Shawn was from North Philly—born and raised in the projects. Even if he moved outside the projects, he would represent his block from the cradle to the grave.

They called him SB in the hood because he never stepped back. "Always moving forward": that was Shawn's motto.

Nobody liked to challenge Shawn because they knew he was a little "thrown off" at times, especially after a few drinks, and when inspired he could fight like a champ in the ring. He was vicious with his fists. If someone got into it with Shawn he knew he'd better be prepared to throw down and possibly make a hospital visit.

Shawn drank a lot—that was one of his vices and it got him into plenty of trouble. The first time Shawn drank an entire fifth of vodka by himself was at the young age of 19 after hearing his dad had been killed. Shawn was serving his country overseas when he got the word. He was angry that he didn't get a chance to say goodbye. No one really knew exactly who killed his father and why, but whoever did it took him by hitting him in his head with something hard. The doctors blamed his father's death on an aneurysm.

Shawn's dad Jerome was a thorough cat—the son took after his father in many ways. He slipped and slid through many a gathering and wherever he went he was always welcomed. Everybody wanted to be around Jerome because he kept the party live. But at the same time nobody wanted to be on the receiving end of his rage if he got into one of his moods.

Shawn was granted leave to attend Jerome's funeral in Philly that year. With a brown-bagged vodka bottle in hand he found his way to the front door of his favorite childhood hangout—the Chinese convenience store. He took a milk crate away from a bum and sat down in his place. Within an hour the entire bottle of cheap vodka was gone.

He got so drop-down drunk that day that he blacked out and couldn't remember what had happened. It couldn't have been good though because he woke up with a swollen eye and a cracked tooth.

A few years later when Shawn was discharged from the Army, he found himself right back out there doing what he knew best: slanging and hanging on the block. His first civilian job just didn't work out and it was right back to the streets.

But Shawn was no dummy. Even though he went to some of the roughest schools in Philadelphia, he still got good grades. Before going to the Army he was so on point with both his studies and athletics in high school that he got a scholarship to play football at a school in the south when he was just 16. Everything was going so smooth until he had to watch Mike, his dorm mate in college, get shot to death—he had been sitting five inches away from Shawn.

Some drunken kids at the party were playing with a gun. Malt liquor, gin and killer hydro was involved. One of them pulled the trigger not realizing that a bullet was in the chamber. Mike died almost instantly of one shot to the forehead as he was leaning forward to grab his beer.

Shawn was so spooked that he dropped out of classes the very next day and high-tailed it to the Army. When they told him he would go overseas he was sold—he wanted to get as far as he could from that school.

He felt that Mike was haunting him. A few inches to the left and it could have been him, right in the heart. Right there Shawn's paranoia was birthed...

After serving his time in the Army Shawn had the skills and knowledge to kill a man with his bare hands if necessary. He also learned not to take shit off of anybody.

"Hey SB, you know I knew your dad. That was a real thorough brotha right there."

Shawn turned his head slowly to the left and his eyes fell on Jimmy "Crack Corn," one of the neighborhood's most infamous crackheads. He turned his nose up and looked Jimmy up and down with a fresh unlit cigarette hanging from his lips.

"What?"

"We used to hang tight back in the day SB, you know."

"I know you didn't just interrupt my thoughts on that bullshit. Disrespectful ass! And keep my pop name out ya mouth!"

Jimmy started doing his little shuffle from side to side. He was getting more and more nervous as each second ticked forward—he knew that he was playing with fire bothering Shawn when he was on a mission. But that stuff was calling him.

"Can you help a brother out SB? You know I got you next time boss. Hit me off with a dub? I just need a lil something something til I get my check in a few days."

"Hell no."

"A dime?"

"Fuck no!"

"A crumble…"

"No. Beat it Jimmy!"

"Come on SB help a brother out here, just a lil piece of somethin'…" Shawn looked at him in disgust and disbelief. He snatched the cigarette out of his mouth and then snapped.

"Nigga I ain't got no brothers, all I got is sisters! You probably a sissy but you damn sure ain't my sister! Nigga if you don't get the fuck out my face wit ya beggin' ass self! Talkin' 'bout 'my brother'… just keep talking, I'll DDT your ass off this curb!…"

Jimmy started shuffled away talking to himself, as Shawn kept going off on him. Tino just laughed. Shawn had a way with words and he could go on for hours ranting when he was really pissed. He hocked and spit behind Jimmy as he walked away. Shawn didn't have much respect for drug users, especially when they begged for crack. He would help someone out with a sandwich if they asked, but never a free rock in a million years. When Jimmy got a few steps away he turned back to Shawn.

"A cigarette?" he asked.

Shawn made a motion like he was going to backhand him and Jimmy continued on his way. Only when he was across the street did he start talking back.

"But you ain't have to call me no sissy SB, that was uncalled for," Jimmy said and kept mumbling as he kept walking down the block. "That weren't even right!"

"Nigga take your country ass on down the street!" Shawn yelled.

"You ain't have to do that to old Jimmy, give 'im a break," Ron shook his head and chuckled. "Jimmy can't hurt nobody."

"Nah, fuck that. I give him a break all the rest of them gonna want one too," Shawn said as he pulled up his slightly sagging jeans and finally lit the cigarette in his mouth.

"Yup I feel you, that's the problem with niggas today. Always wanting a handout," Ron suddenly started agreeing again. Shawn hated that. He wanted a good argument some times, someone to stand up to him, but most of the dudes around him were "yes" men and they didn't want to disagree with him. Shawn could see right through it; he knew that they were either scared or plotting. He didn't like Ron—he tolerated him.

"No, these niggas out here that act like groupie bitches: that's the real problem. Groupie ass, thirsty ass 13th street hooka ass niggas on the stroll!"

"Yea, I hear you SB! Speak on it," Ron nodded, not even realizing that Shawn was talking directly about him. "They on the stroll down 13th street like a mufucka."

10

Shawn looked at him sideways with his eyes slitted as he puffed his cigarette and it made Ron nervous. He quickly tried to change the subject, not wanting to get Shawn started. Tino was amused and just stood by watching—he enjoyed watching Shawn when he was in trip-mode.

"What the fuck up with this drought though," Ron suddenly said to Kidd, who was staring down the block, in his own world as usual. Kidd was half Puerto Rican, half black and 100 percent hustler. He was one of Shawn's most reliable connects; they had known each other since kids. He and Shawn were a lot alike and if there was anyone more paranoid than Shawn it was Kidd—he always thought someone was out to get him. Shawn acted somewhat as his personal bodyguard when he was holding a lot of product in exchange for deals. Kidd smoked wet on the regular. This particular night it was clear he had one too many puffs because he was really edgy and anxious.

Kidd didn't answer, putting Ron in an even more awkward position. Shawn kept glaring at Ron and smoking his cigarette. He loved this: making the weaklings uncomfortable, because they should be at home but always wanted to run with the big dogs.

"Nigga did you hear me," Ron tried to be tough while plotting an escape route from Shawn's clutches. He had witnessed first-hand how things could go so wrong so quick messing around with SB. Shawn didn't care—when he went there, he really went there.

"Yo, Kidd," Ron said again, louder and sounding even more nervous.

"He heard you, he just don't wanna speak to your ass," Shawn answered for Kidd.

Tino, always the observer, chuckled and slapped hands

with Shawn. "Look partna, Imma holla. Got daddy duty in the morning. Taking my daughter to Dave & Busters."

"Aiight nigga, stay up," Shawn said with a nod as Tino left. He threw his cigarette down and walked over to Kidd to tell him something in private, which made Ron even more nervous. He liked to be a party in every conversation.

"Who you looking out for K?" Shawn asked him.

"Man I 'oun know, I just got a feeling 'bout something, you know," Kidd answered. "Gotta stay on point."

"Well you making me nervous. I told you stop smoking that shit," Shawn advised. "And what's up with the dude, you know I'm running low."

"This week. I got you my nigga," Kidd confirmed.

"Aiight, and you bet not let this bitch ass nigga Ron get a new pack before me. I will fuck both you and him up," Shawn told him seriously.

"Naw, I got you my dude," Kidd reassured his friend with a little laugh, never looking him in the eye.

Shawn flicked his cigarette ashes down on the concrete and shuffled around. "Fuck it. It's the end of the month and these broke ass feigns on that beggin' shit. I'm going down to the spot for a drink."

"Aiight man, Imma get up soon too. One," Kidd said and gave him a pound. Shawn started his stride down the block and almost immediately his cell phone started ringing. It was Kay, his on-again off-again fiancée who he lived with. The last time she agreed to marry him he went and got her a ring to make it official so that she couldn't take it back again. He liked having a woman at home waiting for him.

Shawn hesitated to pick up Kay's call, but decided to get it at the last moment.

"What's up babyyy," he said like he knew he was in trouble.

"Where are you?" she asked. "It's already midnight."

"I'll be home soon, I'm about to get on the bus right now," he lied.

"Well you better hurry up. You know the buses stop running after one."

"I know baby, I love you, I'll see you soon. Hold up, there go the bus right now," he continued lying and hung up the phone.

Pop. Pop. Pop. Pop. Pop.

Before he had a chance to put the phone back in his pocket he heard shots ringing out nearby and started looking everywhere to watch his back. He quickened his stride and crossed the street right into his favorite neighborhood bar. Hearing gun shots was almost like hearing a truck go by those days in the neighborhood.

* * *

"Shawn! Leave me the fuck alone! I'm serious!" Kay shouted and smacked his hand from her ass.

"Come on baby…" he pleaded. It was after seven in the morning and Shawn had just come into the house. He was very drunk, even at that hour, and horny of course.

"No, get the fuck away from me Shawn!" she screamed. "You can't just come in here any time you want and think you're getting some! It's almost eight o'clock in the fucking morning!"

"Aw, come on baby. I got stuck down there handling some business. Cage and Tino got me held up into some bullshit baby," Shawn slurred. "But I promise you it won't happen again!"

The truth was that *Shawn* was the true nucleus of all the

bullshit. He was like the sun and all the hood shit revolved around him. He helped keep things moving, even if he wasn't directly involved. He had the power to say when it was time to go home, but he just chose not to.

"I don't care," Kay shouted back. "Just go to sleep and get up when it's dark like you usually do."

"Kayby, Kayby, Kayby," Shawn slurred his nickname for her and sat back against the headboard. "You know I can't sleep and I can't cheat. So why would you use sex as a weapon? You supposed to take care of your man. I am still your man ain't I?"

Because she had refused sex she was now sentenced to a long morning of Shawn's ramblings. And if she didn't respond to his questions promptly he would just shake her until she did.

"Hey, hey, did you hear me?" Shawn shook her shoulder. "Look at you you're living like you're in hell. Your dirty hot ass probably ain't take a bath for days and think you're the shit. You got to be fucking kiddin' me!"

"Shawn I need my sleep!" she protested. But she knew he didn't care—he was going to keep talking until he finally passed out. She zoned out.

Kay was slim and medium height with dark brown skin. In her younger days she was hot and popping, but those days she was a plain Jane type who preferred the boring quiet life. She had left behind most of her partying ways in college and stopped caring about getting fly once she got into a relationship with Shawn.

She was a passionate artist who loved to draw and had sold a few of her works at Philly social events, but couldn't manage to make a living from it. She was too distracted and depressed.

Shawn and Kay met at a club one night on Delaware

Avenue. Shawn walked right up to her and claimed her on the spot. They went home together that same night, split a classic roast beef hoagie from Wawa and hadn't separated since. They were both going through issues at the time and feeling lonely, so they quickly bonded. They met each other's needs—or so they thought at the time.

But it didn't take Kay long to realize that Shawn was troubled beyond what she had ever imagined. He had two personalities—SB was mean, cruel and impossible to reason with. He came out when Shawn was drunk or high. Meanwhile the real Shawn was kind-hearted, helpful and fun to be around.

Kay thought that his split-personality was due to his environment and wanted to take him far away from it so they left the city for the 'burbs, but he was still very much about that life. It was as if he was tethered to the hood—he just couldn't leave the streets alone. Meanwhile Kay was one of those sisters who thought she could change a man. Unfortunately she learned a lesson the hard way that she could take a brother out of the hood, but couldn't take the hood out the brother.

Shawn would regularly come home very early in the morning, even on weekdays, straight tripping. He always thought she was cheating on him, though she wasn't.

At times she felt trapped, like she was living in a prison, and it was driving her crazy. Shawn was putting her through the ringer and she was starting to plan a way out of the relationship.

* * *

"You heard about Kidd?" Shawn clutched the phone to his ear as he lay on his stomach in bed. It was almost 6pm and he was just now stirring. He had 15 missed calls.

"Naw, what happened," he grumbled into the receiver. It

was his best boy Cage.

"Nigga dead and gone," Cage confirmed. "They shot 'im down right in front of the store last night!"

"Uh uh. I was just with the homie last night!"

"Got 'im in the head and the stomach," Cage said as he shook his head. "Cold-blooded. He was dead at the scene."

"They know who it was? Shawn asked as he started to sit up in bed and look around for Kay.

"They think it was over some shit with Q and them," Cage explained. "But you know nobody seen shit."

"Aw shit, Q? Why Kidd gonna lie like that, he told me everything was straight," Shawn said as he held his forehead in his hand. "Damn!"

"I guess not."

"What about that nigga Ron? He was still down there when I left 'im at the store."

"I 'oun know. Nobody know where Ron at. You know that sneaky nigga slide his ass in and out so smooth."

"Dammit! Shit," Shawn said and shook his head for a while in thought. He thought about how it could have easily been him instead. "That was my nigga. RIP. My man was under a lot of pressure."

"Yea, he was a good dude. His family's fucked up."

"I bet...let me holla at you later Cage," Shawn said and hung up the phone before he got an answer. He pulled himself up out of bed and dragged himself into the bathroom.

When Kay walked into the house and smelled the aroma of shit coming from upstairs, she knew Shawn was finally up. He could blow up a bathroom like nobody's business. She tried to stay quiet as she went into the kitchen to put groceries away. She didn't want to say a word to him after he kept her up all morning.

I don't care what he says, I'm not talking to him! she said to herself, trying to prepare for the "sorrys" that were sure to come. Shawn was extra witty, had a way with words and could make anyone laugh when he wanted. He knew that if he could get Kay to laugh, all would be forgotten from the night before.

Like clockwork, Shawn came downstairs and walked right into the kitchen as if nothing had happened.

"Hey baby," he said and walked right up behind her to give her a hug and a kiss on the neck. He was about to tell her about Kidd, but she bristled when he touched her and didn't say anything.

"Hellooo," he said again. "What you ain't talking to me? Baby come on, don't be like that."

She didn't respond so he started following her around the kitchen, everywhere she went. She sighed and finally left the kitchen to go to the living room where she sat down to watch television. He sat down almost on top of her and stared right at her face, smiling.

She continued giving him the silent treatment and tried to think about anything except him sitting there in her face.

"I love you boop booooop," he said drawing out the last word obnoxiously. "I'm sorry. You know I'm your lil' asshole!"

Kay sat stone-faced watching the screen and started flipping through the channels.

"Come on baby," he said as he poked her in the side playfully. "Talk to me."

"Stop it Shawn!" she finally broke and spoke to him. Then he started to tickle her and got that giggle that he wanted.

"Quit it!" she shrieked and laughed. "Uggh, I hate you!"

"I know you love me," he said and grabbed her up into a hug. She struggled to get loose and broke out in a fit of laughter when he started kissing her all over her neck and face.

"You told me you weren't going to stay out all night anymore," Kay said when she finally gave up trying to fight him. "You promised."

"I know, I know. I'll be good from now on baby! I promise."

"Yea right, you always say that," she rolled her eyes. "And you're not going out tonight so don't even think about it."

Shawn sat up and started scratching the back of his head. "I don't know... I might have to though."

"No."

"Sorry Kayby but I promised my daughter I'd go see her today," Shawn said, telling a little white lie. He did plan on seeing his daughter Mya but the main reason he was going back down the way was to find out more about what happened to Kidd and to figure out how he was going to make some money. It was Saturday, the first of the month and there was no way he could afford to stay in the crib.

"Well look Shawn, I gotta go into work tomorrow afternoon so you can't be coming in late tonight on that bullshit!" Kay said, getting annoyed again.

This had been their life for four years. She was exhausted dealing with his antics, but she loved him and knew he was a good person at heart. She put up with him in hopes that one day he would change.

"I'm gonna come in by midnight babe, I promise," Shawn assured her, knowing that was a bold-faced lie. On a Saturday night things didn't start popping off until *after* midnight! He also knew that everyone would be buzzing about Kidd. They would probably be politicking, drinking and playing cards all night long, talking about what happened.

"I'm serious Shawn! Don't play with me. I will lock your ass out the house tonight if you come in late!"

"Whatever," he said under his breath, brushing off her threat and stood up from the couch.

"What was that?"

"Nothinggg! Love you baby! I gotta go hop in the shower."

Kay crossed her arms angrily, feeling duped. Shawn had not only gotten his way, he was going to go out yet again that night and would probably do the same exact thing in the morning. She didn't even know how he did it, but he did it every time, for years. She had to admit that she was weak for him — even if she had an open opportunity to leave him, she probably wouldn't take it… at least not yet.

When she thought back on her life, Kay couldn't really understand how she had gotten into the position she was in. She went to college, got a degree in legal studies and was on the track to becoming a lawyer. On the side she pursued her art. A few years later she was working at a data entry job making $13.60 an hour and engaged to be married to one of the most notorious thugs that probably ever came out of North Philly. She wasn't sure when she had stopped looking to the future.

She had always been attracted to bad boys, but this one just took the cake. Shawn just didn't give a fuck, and she knew it. She liked his attitude about life. The problem was he didn't give a fuck about *anything*, including their relationship.

But she also knew the other side of Shawn. The real Shawn. The Shawn who would carry every bag from the car into the house, no matter how many there were and tell her to go on inside.

The Shawn who would chase her down the aisles at Home Depot and argue with her about paint colors.

The Shawn who mowed the lawn every Sunday and took out the trash twice a week without ever being asked or reminded.

The Shawn who cooked her chicken wings, macaroni and

cheese and string beans for dinner.

The Shawn who would encourage her to go back to school and become a lawyer.

The Shawn that made her laugh until she could hardly breathe. The Shawn who would travel to the end of the earth for her if she just asked him.

She loved that Shawn and she didn't want to give up on him.

"Aiight baby, I'll see you later," Shawn said as he jogged down the stairs and to the door.

"Be safe, smart and responsible out there Shawn." He came back into the house, checking himself, and reached down to give Kay a kiss on the lips.

"I'll be back in a few hours, I promise."

* * *

While walking to his daughter's house, Shawn couldn't get Kidd off of his mind. This was yet another example of a close encounter he had with death. If he had hung around Kidd any longer that night he might have been shot down right along with him. Was God trying to tell him something? He brushed off the thought as quickly as it came.

Kidd had been nervous and Shawn had assumed it was just the wet he smoked. But it turned out that it was a real threat out there that he just wasn't speaking on.

"Daddy!" he heard that beautiful voice call out and snapped out of his thoughts. His daughter Mya ran up to him. She had been playing with her friends outside her house and spotted her Dad from a block away—it was hard to miss Shawn's familiar confident gait, which was a cross between George Jefferson, Tupac and DMX.

"Hey, baby girl." He smiled and took a last puff from his

cigarette before throwing it down on the ground. He opened his arms and grabbed his daughter off the ground just as she ran into them.

"You out here playing with those little bad ass kids again?" he asked her as he adjusted her on his hip and kept walking. "What I tell you 'bout that. You supposed to be in the house studying!"

"They ain't bad Dad," she assured him. "That's my crew, and they do what I tell them to do!"

"Oh yea? That's your crew?" Shawn asked, always impressed with his daughter. She had taken after him in almost every way. She was strong, witty, extra-smart and could analyze a situation from top to bottom before anything even went down. However unlike him, she thought before she spoke. He had taught her how to fight and she took it to another level. Mya was getting called out of school for beating up both boys and girls who messed with her.

"Yup, they go get me my French fries when I tell them to," she said with a nod.

Shawn stopped at the corner store for a beer, then walked her down to the park and let her play on the swings and monkey bars while he placed a phone call.

"Where you at?" he asked Cage. Cage was a good looking, tall dark-skinned brother. He was a loyal dude—he and Shawn had grown up together. Spray painted murals together. Robbed hoodies out of the department store together. Played in the sewey holes together.

Even though he had a house in West Philly where he rested his head now, Cage was Shawn's link to what was going on down the way. Cage spent more time down North Philly than Shawn even did because he had a girlfriend that lived there.

"Down at the store. Yo niggas irkin' over this Kidd shit.

They worried 'bout where they gonna get their shit," Cage said. Shawn could hear multiple voices talking and arguing in the background on the line. The natives were getting restless— Kidd was everybody's connect during the drought and he started to make a lot of cash, fast. Shawn assumed that alone was probably what put the spotlight on him in the first place and got him killed in the second place.

"Oh yea?" Shawn confirmed as he scratched his chin in thought. "I'll be there. Don't tell nobody shit yet, but I'm the man with the plan."

When Shawn finally walked up to the store later that evening, he saw at least 10 people he knew involved in heated discussions. He could tell that everyone was seriously pressed by the vibe emanating from the group.

"What up," he said as he greeted Cage, who was just coming out of the store with a beer in hand. "Niggas look stressed."

"Yea, half these mufuckas broke down. These niggas scared to spend what little they got even on a beer. They mad as shit," Cage said in a low tone. "They might as well go home, but they worried 'bout what they baby mommas gonna say if they come home broke. You know!"

Shawn scanned the scene one more time as he bit his lip in contemplation. He had money on his mind. Fast money. He walked away, grabbed his cellphone and placed a call.

A few minutes later he came back to the group and stood right in the middle of everyone and made an announcement.

"Any ya'll niggas need the hook up holla at ya boy."

By 8pm, Shawn had over $700 in his pocket and he didn't have to do a thing other than broker a few deals. He had called in a favor from one of his old running partners Cee who now lived all the way up in Reading. Turned out Cee had just enough product available to cover everyone who needed something for the week. If the drought continued he promised he could do it all over again. Shawn knew he could easily become the connect, but he preferred slower money over the high risk of dealing with major weight on a regular basis. With slower money he knew he'd have a better chance of living another day. Kidd getting killed just reaffirmed his theory. He was even more paranoid now.

Shawn had enough money that he could retire for the night, go home to Kay and be good for the week with money. But that wasn't in his nature—instead he took his cash right down to Atlantic City to play cards. He ended up winning another $1,500 in a few lucky games of blackjack. When he came back to Philly, riding in Cage's truck, it was a little after midnight and he was popped. They ended up at a popular little hood spot down near Broad Street where Shawn used to take Kay when they first started dating.

When Shawn got some money in his pocket he didn't know how to act. He would just shit on everyone around him—especially people he didn't really like.

"Nigga why you always wearing those tight ass busta browns!" he taunted Brian, a rival he knew since high school. "Where you get those? Don't they be hurtin' your feet? I bet they hurtin' your *soul* right about now ain't they?"

Brian notoriously had very bad breath due to halitosis so they quietly called him DBB; short for Dick Breath Brian. He also had a serious attitude problem—he and Shawn were constantly competing to see who was on top. This particular night, with a pile of money in his pocket while Brian could barely afford to pay attention, Shawn had the crown.

"Shut the fuck up nigga, while you got on those Tripperlands. Prolly paid 2 for $59.98," Brian shot back.

Shawn smirked and pulled out a stack of bills. "I guess that mean I can get me 200 pair!"

Brian's face looked hurt—it could have cracked into a million pieces from envy when he saw all that money.

"How much money you got nigga? Bet you got an old button, a tic tac and an expired condom in that pocket. Ain't none of 'em workin' for you! Hahahahahaha…"

Shawn cackled so long that it started to keep time with the beat coming from the juke box. Slick Rick's *Mona Lisa* was playing. Everyone around him laughed too.

Brian's feelings were hurt, especially when other people around him started to laugh along with Shawn. They knew Brian wouldn't dare reach into his pockets to show what was in them.

Out of nowhere, Brian took a wild swing at Shawn, thinking he was catching him off guard.

But never that—Shawn was a pro. He knew that Brian was the type to swing first and was just waiting for him to do it. He ducked back just in time and hit Brian with a quick uppercut to the chin so hard that blood immediately splattered everywhere from his nose. He came after Brian with a vengeance like it was a prize fight and within minutes had him on the ground. Shawn stomped him hard in the chest with his boot before someone pulled him back. When Shawn really blanked out he could easily send someone to the hospital. He talked shit and was prepared to back it up.

"How you like those Tripperlands now pussy!"

Brian was on the floor holding his chest, trying to catch his breath. Blood was smeared across his face and he looked dazed and confused. Shawn and his boys left and jumped into Cage's truck.

"Damn, you laid that nigga out," Cage laughed as he

whipped around the corner toward his house. "But hey, he asked for it!"

"That nigga couldn't never fight, not even back in high school. Just like to talk shit."

"You want me to try to get you back to the crib?"

"Naw," Shawn said as he stretched out his hurting hand. He reached back into his pocket to check for his money—it was all there.

Shawn decided to stay over Cage's house in West Philly for the night. As he lay on Cage's couch in his drunken stupor he managed to turn his phone off to avoid the guilt of seeing any of Kay's missed calls.

Chapter 2
Why Kay Stays

"What the hell happened to you?"

Kay was just opening the door to leave out to do some errands at four o'clock in the afternoon as Shawn was walking up on the porch with his khaki button-down shirt draped across his shoulder. His white t-shirt had blood splatters on it but he didn't seem to have a scratch on him.

"Heyyy baby," he crooned with his trademark bright white smile spread across his face—it could light up a stadium.

Kay couldn't even be mad at him at that point, especially not after seeing how happy he looked. She was just happy that he was alive and that he hadn't come home the previous night to stress her out. It had actually been a very peaceful couple of days for her.

"Why is your shirt bloody like that?" she asked and started checking him from head to toe. His fist was a little busted up, but otherwise he was fine. "You okay?"

"I'm fine baby," he answered, enjoying the attention, and gave her a kiss on the cheek. "Where you headed?"

"Down to the supermarket, the home store and a couple of places," she answered and started to walk around him.

"Can you wait for me? I wanna go. Gotta get me some Newports anyway," he looked at her for an answer. She looked back at him, wondering if he was up to something.

"Sure, hurry up though. I wanna catch my show at 9."

20 minutes later Shawn was all cleaned up and sitting in

the passenger seat of Kay's Camry.

"So you gonna tell me what happened or what?" Kay asked as she pulled off.

"Niggas just be trippin'."

Kay rolled her eyes and kept driving. There was no need to dig deeper—this was just how Shawn rolled. She knew what it was when she first started dating him. The fourth night she knew him she had to go down to the projects to pick him up after rumbling with some other trouble makers.

Her thoughts drifted off to what she had to buy at the store and how she was going to pay for it while still covering her bills for the month.

"Here," Shawn suddenly said as they were sitting at a light as if he was reading her mind. She looked down at his hand and saw five hundred dollar bills. He folded them in half and shoved them into her purse.

"How..." she started.

"Don't even say it," Shawn scolded her. He hated when she questioned where he got his money. "Just take it."

Kay was quiet and then just nodded.

All afternoon Shawn was patient as Kay went from store to store. He even went in with her when she did business at the bank and post office. When they got home he grabbed all of the bags from the car and trudged up the steps with them.

They put the groceries and supplies away together while Shawn talked about some of the stuff he had coming up. He was due to show up for child support court later that week—if he missed the court date they would put a warrant out for his arrest. Kay told him about a female on her job who was trying to get her fired.

"If she doesn't stay out of my business I will kick her ass

first and then I'll quit. I want to get paid for that beating!" Kay said as she watched Shawn fry up some chicken wings and cook Spanish rice. He was the chef of their little household.

"Girl please, you can't fight," Shawn teased her.

"Oh yea? Well why don't you teach me some moves then Chuck Norris."

Shawn thought about it for a moment. He put down his spatula and brushed his hands together.

"Let me show you how to disable somebody so you don't even have to break a nail," Shawn said and then grabbed her hand. She stood up from her seat in the kitchen.

"Aiight, attack me like if you was gonna punch or slap me," he told her.

"You ain't gonna hurt me for real are you?" Kay asked with a little smile.

"Naw, come on, quit bitching," Shawn told her. "Just put your hands up like you're coming at me."

Kay made like she was going to punch him in the chest. Shawn quickly grabbed her hand with his thumb in a way that caused her arm to twist up so that she could barely move.

"Ow ow ow ow ow…" Kay complained until he finally let her go.

"See? You can't move. Try it on me."

They practiced a few times until Kay had it just right. He then showed her a few more defensive and offensive moves.

"And you better not try to use that shit on me!" he told her when the food was ready.

"Mmhmm."

When they finally settled in on the couch after eating Shawn's delicious home cooked meal they caught the end of Kay's favorite television show and then watched one of the movies they rented at Blockbuster. Kay lay back in the nook of his arm. They drank ice cold Yuenglings and enjoyed a nice fat blunt. It was moments like these that reminded Kay of why she had stayed with Shawn for four years in spite of his ways.

When Shawn reached down for a kiss Kay didn't turn her head with an attitude like she usually did. She kissed him back, deeply. He took that as a cue and stood up to lead her upstairs.

"The movie Shawn," she protested and pointed at the screen.

"Fuck that movie," he said and reached over to switch off the television. He then grabbed her up in his arms and carried her up the stairs.

It wasn't often that Shawn got any loving from Kay those days, so he was eager to get started. If he got some it was usually pity sex or "go to sleep already" sex. When he reached the bedroom he tossed her on the bed so high that she rolled over twice and nearly hit the floor.

"Damn Shawn!" she complained as she caught herself.

"Ooo, my bad!" he said. He stripped down to his boxers in a matter of moments.

Kay rolled over on her back and started pulling off her pants. "You got a condom?"

Shawn's heart sunk. He knew she wasn't on the pill. "I don't know... I don't think so."

He started frantically searching the room for a condom in drawers, under the bed and in the closet. Finally, just when he was debating the possibility of making a mad dash to the grocery store, he spotted a condom peeking out from under a few papers in a shoe box where he kept receipts.

"Got one!"

"How old is that?" Kay asked.

"It's good!" he yelled as he tried to hurry up and get in the bed. He was nervous and eager since it was very rare that they had sex those days.

"Shawn that shit better not break!" Kay said and started to get agitated. Shawn flipped her over on her stomach.

"Damn, chill out! Calm down!" she grumbled. As he was trying to position her just right he caused her to bang her head hard on the headboard.

"Ow! Shawn!" Kay yelled and rubbed her forehead.

"My bad!" Shawn said and put a pillow up as a buffer.

"Never mind Shawn, this ain't gonna work!" Kay started to protest and held up her hand. "Just ain't gonna work!"

"Like hell it ain't," Shawn said and flipped her back over to face him. He looked at her in the darkness for a moment as she held her forehead and started laughing. She laughed back and relaxed. They kissed deeply and hugged, then got back down to business.

Chapter 3
Decisions

The next day Shawn went down to Jeweler's Row to pick up something for his mother with some of the money he had left. He knew money didn't stay in his pocket long, so he made every attempt to buy everything he needed as soon as he got it and before he went out drinking with the boys.

He hadn't seen his mom in a long time and wanted to give her the idea that he was doing well. He didn't want her worrying about him. He felt that giving her an expensive gift was the perfect way to let her know he was on the right track so he picked out a nice pink diamond pendant necklace, paid for it in cash and then hopped on the bus to her house.

"Ay ma!"

"Shawn, that you?" his mother called out.

"Yea ma, where you at?"

"In the room son."

Shawn loved his mother dearly, but they mixed like oil and water—they both had very strong personalities. They were a lot alike in many ways.

Shawn wanted his mother's approval. He cared about her opinion. All he wanted was to make her proud. Her words had the power to either soothe his soul or cut him so deep.

Every move he made was to make his mom proud; from going to college at the young age of 16 on a football scholarship, to heading off to the military. But she didn't like that he ultimately chose to run the streets.

Shawn slid into his mother Rhonda's room furtively with his hands behind his back—he had a mischievous smile spread across his face. That smile alone could get him just about anything he wanted. He saw his mother sitting up in bed reading her bible.

"What you up to boy," his mom asked immediately when she saw the look on his face. She knew her son better than anybody, when he was up to something, when he was stressed and when he was troubled.

"Why I gotta be up to something? I got something for you," he said as he pulled his hand from behind his back, revealing a small white gift box. He sat down on the edge of her bed as she held the box on her lap.

"What's this?" Rhonda said as she started to open the box carefully as if a snake was going to jump out. She couldn't stop smiling when she saw a beautiful necklace inside.

"How much was this? Where you get it, it ain't hot is it?" she asked out of habit. It seemed like Shawn was always into something.

"Come on ma, can't a son get his mother a gift? Don't play me like that," he said and started to get upset. He sucked his teeth, got back up from her bed and started to walk toward the door.

"Thank you son, this is really nice," Rhonda said quickly before he went off on one of his tantrums.

"Fuck ever," Shawn said with an attitude under his breath as he huffed out of the door.

"Now don't go being disrespectful Shawn, I just asked you a simple question!" she called after him.

"Speak to you later!" he yelled back. Before she had a chance to respond she heard her front door slam closed.

Rhonda wanted nothing but the best for her son but she

couldn't control the choices he had made in his life. She told him almost daily to stay off the streets and go back to school — he had always done well in school, getting As and Bs. But something kept drawing him back to those street corners. He was regularly in the company of killers, thieves and people who made a career out of making trouble.

* * *

I can't do this anymore, Kay thought as she sat in front of her computer with a pen, pad and blank screen in front of her. She was trying to brainstorm ideas for artwork she could draw up for her portfolio but only drawing blanks. Kay had won awards in school for her digital designs and illustrations, but for some reason couldn't seem to break into the business as a serious paid professional.

Shawn was sitting on the couch watching television. In the past week he had come home after seven in the morning almost every day. One time he didn't come home at all for two days. She was really starting to feel like not just a fool, but a damn fool.

What woman in her right mind allowed her man to come into their house after 7am on the regular? She felt weak and stupid.

Kay glanced at the diamond ring that they had both gone downtown to pick out. It was pretty, but when the tiny stones kept falling out of their placement it made Kay start to rethink things — maybe getting married wasn't the right move at the time.

She remembered how she got with Shawn in the first place. When they first met he was going through drama and so was she. They fed off of each other's energy. He also helped cure her loneliness and boredom. Kay had been living alone and going stir crazy by herself.

On the first night they met, Shawn was fun and witty. But he also had this troubled look on his face that made Kay's "cap'n save a bro" side kick into full gear—she wanted to help him out. Their relationship was the classic case of a woman trying to change her boyfriend and mold him into what she wanted. She tried to help him get his license back, find a legitimate job or go back to school—anything to make him an honest man.

But Kay quickly learned that Shawn was more than just a work in progress—he was more like going "back to the drawing board." He was stubborn as a mule and a real piece of work when he wanted to be. Nobody was gonna change Shawn—he made his own decisions on his own time and if anything, he was changing *her*.

As the days ticked on Kay became more and more miserable and unhappy with the way she was living. She never pictured herself in this type of situation but there she was...

Kay Lynn Collins, this is your life.

"So Kay when you gonna get those beady beads under control?" Shawn suddenly asked out of nowhere, breaking her out of her thoughts. He was bored with what was on television and scratching his balls, so he decided to start picking with her instead.

"Huh? Shut up Shawn, I'm not in the mood."

"Seriously Kay, you need me to go get my clippers? You need a shape-up back there!"

"Why are you so concerned about my fucking hair?" Kay snapped, starting to get defensive. He made a sport out of picking on her and it had played on her insecurities for a very long time.

"I just don't want my girl walking around with beady

34

beads sitting up on her neck. I'm just lookin' out for you, so don't get no attitude with me," he replied. Whenever Shawn knew that something bothered Kay he would go in even harder, just like he did with his friends on the streets. In most cases he did it to start a fight so that he would have an excuse to leave the house.

Kay took a deep breath and let it simmer... until he continued.

"Boy I can't stand a woman with beady beads, buckshots and peasy peas!" he said again as he flipped through the channels. Kay gritted her teeth, squinted her eyes and then snapped on him.

"You know what?" she said as she threw down her pen and pointed at him. "If you were to grow *your* hair out there would be a whole GARDEN of peas back there to pick! In case you forgot you got African roots too you asshole!"

"Oh!?" Shawn said and turned his head to look at her with his mouth open.

"But you *won't* grow your hair out because if ya did it would like you got the letter 'W' etched on your forehead. 'W' for 'where my hairline go?'" she quipped.

"Ohhh, shit!" Shawn said as he ran his hand over his forehead self-consciously. He had never heard Kay with a good comeback in all the years he had been with her. He stared at her silently—she stared right back waiting for him to say something. He could tell she had more jokes. All he could do was begin to laugh hysterically.

"Damn baby! That was a little funny!" he said with a smile like a proud dad. "That's my girl! Now that's how you handle a muthafucka."

Kay shook her head at him before picking her pen back up. "And for your information, I'm thinking about going *all* the way natural, so if you love me you'll love all my naps and beady beads too! Now leave me alone."

"Alright, alright. I gotta roll soon anyway," he said and got up to go upstairs. He stopped on the way and kissed Kay on the side of her head. "And yes I'll love every single nap on your pretty little head baby."

Going out again? Kay thought but instead she just said: "Fine, whatever."

Shawn was a little surprised that she didn't protest as she usually did. But he just went upstairs to get dressed. He came back down an hour later dressed in a blue polo shirt, black jacket, black khaki pants and black Gucci boots he had purchased the last time he was in Atlantic City. He had on a New York Yankees cap that was tilted slightly to the side and pulled down ever so gently on his head.

"So you really not mad? I'll be home in a few hours."

"Yea, whatever man," Kay snapped back as she typed on her laptop. *Fucking liar,* she thought.

* * *

The club was dangerously packed. Anytime a North Philly hood spot was that tight it was bound to be a fight, an argument or probably a shooting. Everyone was just getting their jig on for as long as they could before shit hit the fan.

Shawn and his crew were celebrating their friend Joe's birthday. Even though it was Joe's birthday, Shawn was popping bottles of champagne as if it were his own.

Shawn started laughing to himself as soon as he saw Tammy, a girl that he had messed with some time ago, squeeze her way through the crowd toward him.

"Hey SB, what you been up to?" Tammy said with a

crooked smile.

"Minding my business and getting this money," Shawn responded and took a swig from his bottle. He had been smoking blunts all night and was twisted.

"Well you sure lookin' like a bag of money!" she commented with a nod and a chuckle as she glanced down at his Gucci boots. "What you doin' after this?'

"Minding my business and getting this money. Excuse me," Shawn repeated as he rudely pushed her shoulder aside and moved over to another group of his friends. Tammy followed him.

"Damn you rude nigga! Why don't you stop fronting in front of your friends and come holla at me?" Tammy said boldly. "You know, I got my own place now."

"Uh uh, no sir. SB don't never step back," Shawn answered with a frown. "Bitch you ain't heard? I'm always moving forward."

"Muthafucka, why you always actin' brand new?" Tammy asked. "Every time I see you you trynna play me."

"That's *fly* muthafucka to you, and I ain't even in ya atmosphere," Shawn replied nonchalantly and then took another sip of his champagne bottle with his pinky in the air.

"Come on Shawn I just want to talk to you," Tammy tried again, trying to sound sweet. *Warning* by Biggie Smalls started blasting through the speakers in the club.

"Yea nikka what!" Shawn turned away from Tammy and shouted when he heard his song come on. He held his bottle of champagne way above his head, did his little two-step and just ignored her from then on. Tammy just shook her head and walked away looking dejected. She couldn't take the feeling of all those laughing smiles around her from Shawn's boys—they were probably going to talk about her like a female dog as soon as she stepped away.

"That chick was kinda nice," Ron said as soon as she went away.

"Her pussy stink!" Shawn said bluntly. "Excuse me, but step aside my nigga, you in my space as well."

"Damn, SB you a asshole," Cage said with a chuckle as he took a toke from his blunt.

By the end of the night Shawn had spent every dime of the money that was in his pocket on bottles of champagne.

Later that same night Shawn and Tino stumbled into the Chinese store, which was still open at two in the morning. They saw their friends C-Rock, Big Tone and Pat, who was a functioning crackhead, in there politicking and drinking beers.

"Yooo," Shawn said as he gave C-Rock and Tone a pound. He gave Pat a head nod.

"Where ya'll coming from?" Big Tone asked.

"The new spot down on Erie, that shit was poppin'!" Tino answered.

"Oh yea? I heard that place was nice, how come ya'll ain't come and holla at a nigga?" C-Rock asked as he placed some cash down on the counter for another beer. Big Tone pulled his coat to show him a text that just came through on his phone.

"That shit," is all he said.

"Oh, aiight…" C-Rock said with a knowing nod. Even in his tipsy state Shawn had his ears and eyes open wondering what they were talking about.

C-Rock turned back around to the counter. "Yo where my beer at bitch? Hop to it!"

The Asian lady behind the counter went into the freezer and pulled out a can of Steel Reserve. She held it behind the glass.

"Two dolla," she said.

"I just gave you money, give me my fuckin' beer," C-Rock demanded. "And my change."

"You no give me no money," the Asian woman protested. "Two dolla!"

"The fuck you talking about, I just gave you a fucking five dollar bill!" he shot back and turned all the way around, ready to start some shit.

"You give me nothing!" the Asian clerk said as she slapped her hand down on the counter. She was no pushover—to do business there you couldn't be a punk. Her brother, who was also behind the counter, noticed that things were about to escalate and tried to calm things down.

"Hold on, hold on!" he shouted with his hands up. "I got the tape, let me play it back!"

As soon as he said that, Pat started to make a movement toward the front door. Shawn immediately noticed this and went over to stand in front of the door to block him from leaving.

"Where you headed Pat?" he wanted to know.

Pat looked nervous.

"Go back over there!" Shawn told him and pointed back at the counter. Pat reluctantly did as he was told.

C-Rock was more concerned with the tape at the moment. The male clerk rewound the tape on their little bootleg surveillance system and played it back for them all.

There it was—Pat had snuck the $5 right off the counter while nobody was looking. It was so slick that even Shawn was impressed.

C-Rock squinted as he grasped the counter and looked closely at the black and white screen to make out the figures. He asked the clerk to play it back one more time.

"See I tell you!" the female clerk said.

As soon as he saw it for the second time he didn't even say a word—he just turned around and floored Pat with a one-hitter quitter. Pat fell back to the ground and laid there motionless. He played dead.

Shawn immediately started to fall to pieces. He crouched over and laughed so hard and long that he could barely catch his breath. The entire store broke down in laughter. Even the store keepers started laughing.

C-Rock snatched his $5 out of Pat's pocket, calmly paid for his beer and left.

"Damn nigga, you got knocked the fuck out!!" Tino said as he stood over Pat and pointed. "Fuckin' thief!"

Chapter 4
Fam

"I'm gonna kick his ass!" Kay yelled and pounded her fist against the wheel. "He must think I'm a straight up sucker!"

Her heart was pounding inside of her chest as she drove down Route 95 in her beat up back up minivan. She was forced to drive the van because Shawn had stolen her Camry and went down to the hood with it.

Kay was so heated that she didn't even bother to take the rollers out of her hair. While she was in the shower she had told Shawn *hell no*, he couldn't take her car down to the projects. He was always trying to borrow her cars, her nice Camry in particular, even though his license was suspended.

She finally got out of the shower, roller-set her hair and then nodded off under her bonnet dryer.

A half hour later she woke up and the house was quiet—way too quiet. She immediately ran to the window to take a look at the cars as she clutched her robe closed.

"No that motherfucker didn't!" she screamed at the top of her lungs. All that was left of her Camry was a few oil streaks on the concrete. When she called him the line went right to voicemail.

That was when she blanked out. She frantically put on a mismatched outfit and the first pair of shoes she could find—the same sneakers Shawn used when he cut the lawn. She snatched the minivan keys off her dresser and made a beeline for the door.

41

She knew exactly where Shawn would probably be—outside of his friend Ray's house, drinking beers and bullshitting; either that or at the Chinese store. She was almost having an out-of-body experience—she could see herself looking like a hot ass mess, but she just didn't give a damn anymore. She was fed up with Shawn's antics and wanted to embarrass the shit out of him.

Shawn was laughing heartily at something with his head thrown back when he heard a car's tires screech up behind him.

"Oh shit, whose girl is that?" someone whispered.

"Shawn!" Kay shouted. "Give me my fucking car keys!"

Shawn slowly turned around and there she stood, huffing and puffing. She was wearing big colorful magnetic rollers in her hair, a green button-down shirt with the buttons in the wrong loops, a pair of brown sweatpants and his busted down blue sneakers.

Shawn was so horrified that he could barely make out words. "Damn baby, why you—?"

"Where's my keys? Give them to me now!" she shouted again.

"Shawn, that your girl?" someone said and Shawn shot him the look of death. When he turned back around he took a good look in her eyes and could tell that she wasn't playing. He just dug into his pocket and gave her the keys as she requested.

Kay threw the minivan keys at his chest. "Bring my van home tomorrow! Where's my fucking car?"

Shawn pointed in the direction and she stormed off without saying another word.

Tino broke down laughing after she left and patted Shawn on the shoulder.

"Shut the fuck up man," Shawn said, still in shock.

"You have just inspired me to take my ass home," Tino said with a smirk.

* * *

Tino had always been a family man. All of the men in his family had taken care of their kids. His dad wasn't married to his mom but he was always around. Tino married his young girlfriend Elisha after two kids and three years together.

Tino was light-skinned and short, standing at 5'8 but stocky and solid. Even though Tino still did his thing on the streets from time to time, he had a job during the day. He managed the stock room at one of the biggest warehouse stores in Philly.

Before he got married he had the mentality of a lot of brothers on the streets—that getting married was for suckers and it would only lead to heartache and pain.

But he had been married now for almost five years and couldn't be happier with his decision.

He and his baby's mother Elisha had their issues like anyone else, but they dealt with them differently. He chose well when he chose her. She was born and raised in the hood but overcame the negative mentality of her peers early on. She was a hard-working level-headed woman at the young age of 27 and had been that way since she was a teen. They communicated with each other—if there was a problem they hashed it out and then squashed it. They didn't bring up old beefs. They had an understanding to always show respect for each other and put their family first, and it had been working out just fine. Because they were married they pooled their resources, had a nice paid-for little house and some money saved up. They already had enough set aside to send their kids to the best private schools in Philly if they wanted.

Tino couldn't understand why some of his friends kept

making baby mothers and then leaving them to fend for themselves. Then they complained about child support and "the man" keeping them down. He once told them all they should marry their baby's mothers to make them into honest women and take control of their households so that they would have a normal family and not have to pay child support. They all just laughed at him and started telling stories about how crazy their baby's mothers were.

On some of his off days Tino helped out at the local boys club, helping them out with homework and providing a strong male role model for them to follow since most of the boys in the program didn't have fathers around. He didn't really tell any of his friends about his personal business because he knew they would either make fun of him or try to mess up his happy situation—misery loves company.

The only person who he talked to from time to time was his boy Shawn. Shawn had proposed to Kay not too long after they met because he really wanted a family like Tino's. As bad as Shawn could be out there on the streets, he knew that he needed a home base.

There were suspicions that Shawn and Tino were somehow related—distant cousins either through blood or marriage from way back. Whether or not they were related by blood, they were tight like brothers and would die for each other if necessary.

"Elisha, I'm home!" Tino called out and tossed his keys on the table.

"Hey baby! You're in early," Elisha called back. No matter if it was five o'clock in the afternoon or in the morning, Elisha greeted her husband with love when he came in the door. That was because he very rarely disrespected her by coming in extra-late and when he did he called to let her know what was going on. He knew the importance of showing her the utmost respect.

"Well I missed you," he told her.

Tino loved his home. It was quiet, peaceful and clean. He never had to be coaxed to come home—in fact, more and more he found himself coming up with reasons *not* to go out and hang with his friends. Elisha didn't have to work but she chose to in order to help them build up wealth to pass onto their kids. They both knew they had to make contributions and show respect for each other in order to keep the household functioning. There was nothing and no one Tino put ahead of his family.

"Aw, I missed you too bae," she came out and threw her hands around his neck to give him a kiss. "You hungry? I'll heat you something."

"Naw," he said as he felt her up and grabbed her butt. "The kids sleep?"

"Yea I put them to bed hours ago."

"Good," he said and looked down into his wife's soft brown eyes. Elisha was a cute brown-skinned around the way girl who closely resembled Taraji P. Henson. She was short at 5'3, extra-thick and usually wore her hair in a simple bun or a ponytail. She was low maintenance but knew how to put herself together when necessary. Tino loved his wife's curvy, juicy body—she had an hour glass shape and kept her figure in order. But even more important to Tino than her looks was her calming vibe.

"What are you up to bad boy?" she said with a smirk.

"You know." He rubbed her nose with his softly and closed his eyes to take in her scent. She reached up and enveloped his lips with her own. They kissed, connected and got caught up in their own world for what seemed like an eternity in the middle of their living room.

Finally, Tino lifted her up by her bottom and carried her into the bedroom. He bumped into a few walls and nearly tripped on the way but made it there fast. He shut the door and locked it behind them. The kids could be very nosy sometimes.

He playfully dropped his wife down across the bed and switched off the light next to the bed. He stood over her and examined her shapely body under the moonlight coming in from the window. She had on a pair of leggings and a tank top that accentuated her every curve. She smiled up at him—her white teeth glimmered in the darkness.

"I'm blessed," he said as he started to slowly pull her pants down.

"Oh really?" she asked.

"Yea. I got a gorgeous wife and a beautiful life. What more can a man ask for?"

"You help make this life beautiful love," she told him with a giggle as he continued to strip her naked.

After stripping down himself, he gently rubbed between her lower lips waiting for her to react so that he knew exactly where her spot was.

"Oh!" she exclaimed suddenly and he knew he had found it. He immediately opened up her legs and dove in with his tongue. She writhed and tried to escape his clutches but he held her tight until she finally came just minutes later. She continued to moan and shake for a long while. Once he knew she was finished he sat up and slid deep into her wet warmth.

Elisha had to grab Tino's mouth tightly to stop his shouting from waking up the kids in the next room. He closed his eyes and went to another place just as he came deep inside of his wife. His body went stiff for a moment and then he dropped on top of her. They were both a sweaty mess.

"Uhh," he moaned when he finally caught his breath. "Elisha. I love you."

"I love you too baby."

Chapter 5
Turning Point

"SB!" the female voice called out.

Shawn already knew who it was before he looked up. He ran his hand down his hot, greasy face slowly. It was an unusually hot day in the early fall, made worse by the hot air in the subway tunnel where Shawn was waiting for his train down on 8th street. He didn't feel like being bothered with chicken heads.

"Hey SB," Tammy said as she finally came near and sat down next to him on the subway bench. He was heading out West to meet Cage. Tammy had followed him to the station.

Shawn didn't respond. He had about five groupie girls floating around the hood who were checking for him as if it were their job. He had messed with a couple of them in the past and a few others he had just used for money. They gave it in hopes of getting some attention from him in the future.

If there was one thing Shawn could do it was lie to get what he wanted from a woman. He would make the proposition sound so sweet and simple that even the most hardcore feminist couldn't resist.

"Shawn why won't you just talk to me?" Tammy wanted to know. "Let's just talk. We been knowing each other for years now and you don't even acknowledge me half the time. What's up?"

Tammy was one of the most relentless women he had ever dealt with in his lifetime. He slept with her twice years before at a desperate time in his life and she would never leave him alone after that. Shawn was starting to think the only way to get rid of her was to push her onto the subway tracks.

"Shawn, you ain't gonna keep ignorin' me like that," she continued when he didn't respond.

"You don't tell me what to do. Just because we fucked once don't mean I belong to you," he said, starting to snap.

"I never said you belonged to me," Tammy said as she settled back in her seat, happy that he had finally talked to her. "I just want to know why you won't talk to me anymore. Do you think I'm ugly or something?"

Shawn got up from his seat and walked to the edge of the platform to see if the Market Street El's lights were in view. They weren't.

Tammy stood up and followed him as if he was going to jump on an imaginary train. She grabbed his arm to hold him back and he snatched it away.

"Wow! You a bird brained broad ain't you?" he said with a look of disgust on his face. "What don't you get? I don't want you. Let a nigga breathe!"

Tammy looked a little hurt, but stayed persistent. There was hardly anyone around and this was her best chance to have a conversation with Shawn one-on-one. She had always been the type to cling to men. She became fixated on them and became very insecure when they ultimately stopped liking her.

"But what is it though Shawn? Just tell me why don't you want me?" she pleaded with him. "What's wrong with me?"

Shawn's jaw dropped.

"You really wanna know?" he asked.

When she nodded he went off on a merciless rant.

"Well for starters you a damn stalker! You stay stalking my ass!"

"I—" she started.

"Second, your pussy stinks! Yes, you need a douche, soap,

wipe down, vinegar bath, summer's eve, autumn's day, whatever you broads do when you wash ya ass! Third, I know you *know* I got a fiancée and you still trynna holla at me? Now that's what you call a trifling whore. What the fuck I want with that?"

Tammy looked at him for a few more moments and then dropped her head down in shame. "Well I'm sorry SB..."

Just then the El train started making its way down the tracks toward them.

"Don't be sorry, sorry is for suckas! Just get a life and get off my dick!" he told her as he waited for the doors of the train to open. When they did he went in and stood inside of the door opening so that she couldn't get on. He didn't have to because she never lifted her head back up.

* * *

It was 10:30 in the morning when Kay got up from bed for work. She had an afternoon shift at her hourly gig and was so tired that she could barely keep her eyes open.

Shawn had come in after a long night of drinking and partying, right around seven in the morning. He kept her up, rambling on about how he thought she was cheating on him.

"You seein' another nikka?" he wanted to know. "Who is it? I'll kill 'im!"

He grabbed her cellphone so that he could search her contacts but Kay had it on lock. She had learned her lesson from leaving the phone unlocked in the past—Shawn had called everyone with a male sounding name in her contact list, including her boss' work line. He hounded her for the password but she wouldn't budge. The argument lasted all morning.

"Who is it?" Shawn demanded to know.

Ironically, Shawn nodded off to sleep only a half hour before Kay had to wake up. It was getting to the point where she would have to go to bed right when she got home from work if she wanted to get a decent night of sleep.

When she finally walked out of the house to go to work, sunglasses covering her droopy eyes, Kay felt like crying. She felt like she was on a treadmill to nowhere, going through the motions every day. She was living the dream life of many women, engaged to be married with a house and a man in it....

But was this life all that it was held up to be? And who was she living her life for?

As she rode to work, gas dangerously close to E and bank account not far behind, Melanie Fiona's song came on. It took her a minute to realize that it was telling her life story.

...gotta be out my mind...to think it's gonna work this time
a part of me wants to leave...but the other half still believes...

She finally couldn't hold back her tears any longer and started to let it all out as she drove down the highway. Her vision was temporary clouded but somehow things were starting to get clearer at the same time.

When Kay dragged herself home from work seven hours later, Shawn was on the couch spread out, scratching his nuts as he watched TV.

"Hey, baby," he looked up and said with a smile as if he didn't have a care in the world. "You cooking sumthin' tonight?"

I know this fool doesn't think I'm going to cook him some food!!! she thought and a strong feeling of rage flashed through her body.

What Kay didn't know was that Shawn was dabbling again. It started off as a little here and there, but it grew to doing a few lines a few times a week. He had just had some right before she got back from work and was in trip-mode.

Kay rolled her eyes and started to go to the kitchen.

"Where you going? Hold up, you ain't still mad is you?" Shawn said as he got up and went over to grab her by the arm. She snatched it away, but he just grabbed her more tightly and started to drag her toward the couch to sit down to talk.

"Let me go Shawn!" Kay snapped. When she jerked her arm back she accidentally slapped Shawn in the mouth, hard.

"Ooo," she said as she covered her lips. She couldn't hold back a little smile when she saw the astonished look on his face. She had never hit him before, let alone in the face.

But to her even greater astonishment, Shawn slapped her right back, even harder, across the face.

Kay held her stinging cheek and her head to the side for a long while; dramatically like a scene from a soap opera.

"Baby, I'm sorry," Shawn said immediately. "It was a reflex."

Kay didn't say anything. She just ran up the stairs, slammed the bedroom door and locked it. Shawn followed and started banging on the door demanding that she let him in.

"Get away from the door Shawn! Just leave me alone!" she warned. She could tell that he wasn't in his right mind.

Kay paced back and forth in the room as the sounds of Shawn's banging on the door got louder and louder. She was at her breaking point. He had stepped way over the line now, just blatantly hitting her in the face.

Something was rising up in her—she had reached her boiling point. She decided there and then that she was going to have a good knock-down drag out fight with him, then leave him for good. She didn't care if she was bloody and bruised at the end; it was going down on that day.

Miss thing was about to get her rumble on with a grown ass man. It was time to take her power back. Yes, it was on.

"Let's do this," Kay said and slapped her hands together.

She quickly took off her shoes, tied up her hair and threw on a pair of sweatpants. She then got down on her knees to retrieve her handy pipe from under the bed. She kept it there just because. The pipe was made of a solid heavy steel material and had a good grip.

Meanwhile, Shawn was still banging on the door like he had no sense and at that moment he really didn't. Surely the neighbors could hear him but he didn't care. All he wanted was to get in there and hold Kay tight. Talk to her. Apologize to her face. He started banging his shoulder against the door to break it open. Kay knew it was just a matter of time before he was in.

Finally, with one hard push, the door gave way and Shawn lunged in head first. Kay was waiting right there gripping the pipe like a baseball bat. She swung it like she was hitting a home run and it landed right on the backside of his head.

Ping!

Shawn stumbled forward, then back and finally fell down on his ass. Kay looked at him for a moment, then got back into her stance and started to take another swing in case he tried to get up again.

Shawn mustered up enough strength to grab the pipe before she had a chance to connect again—if delivered wrong, another blow could have put him down for good.

Kay was huffing and puffing. She finally let go of the pipe and relaxed a little when she realized he wasn't really fighting back. He was just sitting there in a daze—she could almost see tweety birds flying around his head.

Kay didn't gloat—she decided to just let him sit there and recover on his own. She grabbed her purse off the table and kicked him aside when he tried to grab her leg as she left the room and then the house.

Chapter 6
One Lump or Two?

"Yo, where you get that extra-large lump on your head? That shit is huge!" Shawn's friend John commented as they all sat at the bar drinking shots of Henny and bottles of Heineken.

"I fell and bumped my head, why you lookin' at me so close, gay ass nigga," Shawn snapped back defensively.

"Man fuck you," John shot back and took a drink of his beer. "Try to show muthafuckas some concern and this is how they treat you."

"Wifey fucked 'im up," Cage answered for him and broke out in laughter. "She said hey Shawn, would you like one lump or two? He said 'just one please honey!!'"

Shawn looked at him sideways and was about to say something but when he thought about it some more he couldn't help but to smirk a little himself.

Deep down, he was actually kind of proud of Kay; maybe even a little bit afraid of her. He finally got her to stand up for herself and fight back. She was a warrior now, having fearlessly gone toe-to-toe with him.

"Bitch ass nigga. You ain't shit," Shawn said shaking his head. "Told you that in confidence."

Everyone started laughing when they realized it was true.

"You should go get that checked out, you looking like Forrest Whitaker up in this jawn!" John immediately started taking jabs.

"Look like a alien tryin' to come out that bitch!" Cage commented and laughed.

"Shut the fuck up, before I whip all ya'll ass!" Shawn threatened.

"You do that and Imma call Kay. Hol' up, hol' up what's her number," Cage said as he pulled out his cell phone and they all burst out laughing again. Shawn decided to just let them have at it—the more he protested the worse it would be. As he predicted, they took a few more jabs and then finally let it go.

"So you heard about that robbery down at the barber-shop?"

"Yup, I know who did that shit," Ron nodded. He was always lurking nearby, all in everybody's business. "That nigga Will from down South Philly. Joe cousin."

"And you telling?" Shawn snapped immediately. He stared at Ron with a look of confusion on his face.

The more and more Ron hung around Shawn, the more Ron irked the hell out of him. He just had a funny feeling about Ron. He had been there when Kidd got killed. He always seemed to be around when there was some bullshit going on.

As paranoid as Shawn was, he didn't need someone like Ron in his space. Now, word would get back around to Aaron, the owner of the barbershop and long story short Will's days could be numbered, whether he really did it or not. In the hood someone was always listening in or watching. For all he knew Ron could be wearing a wire when hanging around them, try-ing to get somebody locked up.

Ron didn't say anything in response, he just drank his beer. Everyone looked at him funny, but they were all thinking the same thing.

"Yo I'm out," Shawn said as he got up from his stool. His paranoia took over—he just felt like he had to get out of there and get some fresh air. Before he knew it, he was on a bus heading back home to Kay.

In fact, something about Kay was suddenly much more appealing now. If he was honest with himself, he only got with her at first, three years earlier, for a steady place away from the hood to rest his head and get regular sex.

But today something was different. Maybe now it was because she had "broken up" with him and was withholding sex. Maybe it was because she had seriously tried to kill him. Whatever the reason, Shawn felt compelled to go home early for a change.

* * *

After Kay attacked Shawn she knew that she couldn't be with him for much longer—at least not in a serious relationship. He had brought her to a point where she was about to murder him, and that was a very dangerous place to be. The relationship was toxic—she was going crazy just like him. She was changing, and she didn't know yet if it was for the better or the worse.

Kay took another long toke from her blunt and flipped the page of her book. She had taken two days off from work and was getting some much needed down time. The house was quiet and it felt good.

But then she heard someone pulling at the door.

Who the fuck is that? she thought to herself and immediately went into defense mode. Smoking trees and living around Shawn for three years had her paranoid. She grabbed a small switchblade from one of her hiding spots and flipped it open, just in case. Holding the knife close to her leg she inched up next to the window so as to be out of sight.

The door flew open and in came Shawn, bringing the cool fall air and the smell of cigarettes with him.

"Oh it's you. What are you doing back?" Kay said, finally letting out a breath. She closed the switchblade and put it back in its place.

"Oh okay gangsta," he said and laughed. "What I can't come home to my baby?"

"Whatever," Kay said nonchalantly as she took another pull from her blunt and sat back down on the couch with her book.

"Gimme that," Shawn said and took the blunt from her fingers. "What you doing?"

"What does it look like I'm doing?" Kay said, starting to get annoyed. "Minding my business."

"Well somebody got an attitude," Shawn said with a little chuckle as he started to take his coat off and walk back toward the kitchen. *At least he isn't drunk,* she thought.

"What are you doing here so early?" Kay called after him.

"Again, I can't come to my house?" he said as he came back in the room with a half of a leftover turkey hoagie and a beer in hand. He passed the blunt back to Kay's waiting fingers.

"Well damn!" she exclaimed. In that short time he had already smoked about half of what was left. "With your greedy ass, this is all I have left you know!"

"I'll get you some more, chill," Shawn assured her. He flopped down on the sofa a few inches from her hip and started tearing into his sandwich. There were two things for certain that Shawn could do exceptionally well besides fucking with people and fighting in the streets: sleep and eat. Kay tried to get back into her book.

"What you reading?" he asked as he finished up the last bite of his sandwich.

"This self-help book," she answered and let out a long steady puff of smoke.

"What you need that for?"

"Oh I need it for sure. Messing around with your crazy ass," she answered. Shawn switched on the television and got more comfortable.

"Man. Why must you come home and interrupt my peace?" Kay complained.

"Shut up. You can read with the television on!" he said as he flipped through the channels. He could tell she was still pretty annoyed with him so he reached into his pocket and pulled out a short stack of bills. He counted off $100 and handed it over to her. She looked at it and then him.

"Use this to pay a bill or buy you something nice," he said. Kay just tucked the money in her bra quietly.

"Shawn, you know I don't like you out there in those streets with that bullshit. You're too old for this nonsense," she started in again. "It's time you go back to school or go get a job. You need a new plan."

"I know, I know," he said. "I'm working on it Kay. Tino trying to hook me up with this gig at a moving company."

"Oh yea?"

"Yup. Going to meet the manager Thursday." This was one time Shawn actually wasn't completely lying. He had been seriously thinking about going legit for some time now. He had a number of work opportunities that were popping up and things were slowing down on the slanging side of things. Folks weren't about crack so much as in the past. Now it was pills and powder. Making money on the streets was high risk and low returns—it wasn't easy going anymore.

He also knew that if he was to get a job it would impress Kay and she would probably stop pulling away from him. When he saw her eyes light up he knew what he had to do...

* * *

"Tino," Shawn said as he walked into his house without even knocking. Tino was expecting him. "What's up my nigga?"

"Sup Beezy," Tino said and slapped hands with his friend.

"Shawn how are you doing?" Tino's wife Elisha said as she walked in the room smiling brightly. Elisha was a very mild-mannered woman but could be a real firecracker when she wanted to be.

"I'm doing alright, you're looking good sis," Shawn told her and gave her a hug.

"Are you hungry? Let me make ya'll something to eat," she offered.

"Hell yea! Thanks Lish." Shawn was never one to turn down a home-cooked plate.

"Thanks baby," Tino said as he settled down in his arm chair and turned on the television. It was his day off and he wanted to enjoy it to the fullest. "You see that Mayweather fight last night?"

"I ain't catch it. Was in the house being a good boy last night just like you my nigga," Shawn said as he settled back in his chair.

"Shit, I went out. But brought my ass into the house right after it was over. I'd rather hang with my wife than a bunch of sweaty drunk niggas in the bar."

"I hear you. Me? I can't help but get caught up into the bullshit."

"That's cause you love the drama," Tino said, reading him.

"Yea," Shawn agreed. "I'm working on it."

"What you gettin' into this weekend?"

"Actually I'm trynna see what's up with that gig you was telling me about. The moving gig."

"Ole SB trynna go legit huh? Well I'll be dammed!" Tino teased.

"Yea, wifey ain't playing that dumb shit no more. I need to go get me a job, at least part-time."

Tino pulled his cellphone out of his pocket and looked through the address book for a number. He called when he found what he was looking for.

"Ay Joe, what's the deal with that moving gig, they still looking for people?... okay I got someone for you, real hard working brother... aiight then, what's the address?"

Tino leaned over and wrote down some details on a pad sitting on the coffee table.

"Aiight, thanks, one," Tino said and then ended the call abruptly. "He said go into the office mad early, like eight in the morning and talk to Bill."

"Damn just like that? Okay boss," Shawn said with a nod as he grabbed the paper. "That's what's up."

* * *

"Babe, I got it!" Shawn said as he burst through the bedroom door.

"Got what?" Kay asked groggily, just waking up from her sleep.

"The moving gig," he answered. "I start next Thursday, they pay $11 an hour plus tips."

"Worddd?" Kay said, waking up all the way. "That's great Shawn!"

She reached up from her place on the bed and gave him a big hug. He felt amazing.

For once, he had come in the house early the night before, got a good night's sleep at home and woke up at seven in the morning to make his walk-in interview at 8. Kay let him take the car because she was exhausted after doing a late shift.

"I feel good baby!" Shawn said and puffed out his chest. "Bout to start this job babe."

"I'm so happy! And proud of you!"

As the thoughts started flooding Kay's mind of what this meant for him and also for their relationship she became overwhelmed with a feeling of joy. This might mean the end of their drama; finally the end of Shawn's block-hugging days.

Chapter 7
Clutch

Shawn was power-puffing a cigarette outside of the court-house. It was nine in the morning, a few days after he got his new job, and he was due in to child support court at 9:30 for a hearing. He hated going to these hearings because there was always a chance of going straight to jail and he couldn't afford a lawyer.

He had missed a court date earlier that year so he knew he couldn't afford to miss another one—especially not when he was starting a new job. As he finished off the last of his second cigarette he sent a quick text to Kay, letting her know that he was about to go in.

>*baby down the courthouse, call you when I get out*
>>*ok. is everything okay? you're not in trouble are you*
>*naw, everything's good. see you later*

* * *

"Baby I'm booked!" Shawn said into the receiver.

"What?" Kay asked in confusion. She was at work and got up from her desk to take the call.

"I'm in the clink. They locked me up over this fucking child support shit!"

"They locked you up?" Kay repeated. "Oh no Shawn. Why??"

"They said they need $2,500 or I gotta stay in here for 30 days baby," he explained. He sounded calm but distressed. As

61

if there was no point in fighting it.

"Who has $2,500??" Kay started screaming as the situation sunk in. "What do they think we're rich over here??"

"It's fucked up because I'm supposed to start this new job Thursday. And that asshole judge still locked me up!"

Kay was quiet as a number of scenarios ran through her mind. It was Tuesday. She was trying to figure out how she could get that kind of money together in a day so that he wouldn't lose his new job before it started.

"Shawn I'm going to do what I can. I love you okay," Kay said, fighting back tears. She knew she had to be strong at this moment.

30 days, Kay thought as she slowly walked up to the ATM to make a cash advance withdrawal from her card early in the morning. $600 was the maximum. *After 30 days he will be right back out there in those streets. Back to the same bullshit.*

She pulled out her next card and did the same, praying that it would be approved even if it went over limit.

Lastly, she went to her own bank to withdraw the balance of what was left in those accounts. It was all she had available to pay her bills. When she was done she had $1.02 to her name.

She had found a guy on Craigslist willing to buy a set of electronic devices, including used cellphones, modems and routers in good condition for $100. It was the last bit she needed to make the $2,500 she needed for Shawn's bail and still have enough to get home.

She pulled up to the Starbucks on City Line at around noon with the electronics packed in a box in her back seat. The guy told her he would be driving a black Camaro.

When she finally saw a car pull up that fit the description, she got out with the box and stood by the driver's side. The driver, a lanky white guy, got out and walked over. He didn't say anything, just started inspecting the goods.

"Okay, well I'll give you 75 bucks for it all."

"We agreed $100," Kay said sounding exhausted. If she sold everything separately she could easily get over $200.

"Well this isn't exactly what I expected. $75 take it or leave it."

It took everything in Kay not to tell the rat-faced bastard to shove it where the sun don't shine, but she needed that $75 in order to make it. She wouldn't be able to put anymore gas in her car but at least she would have enough to make it to the courthouse to pay the bond. If Shawn didn't have any cash they would be starving for a while.

Would he do this for me? she thought for a moment....

Yea, he would.

She took the cash. She now had exactly $2,506.75. She took her time counting it all out on the car seat.

Kay sat at the gas station down on State Road waiting. She had given the clerk at the courthouse every dime of the money she had except for $6.75, which she put in her gas tank and the parking meter. She wasn't even sure she had enough to get all the way home, but at least Shawn was a free man. In a worst case scenario she would just have to call her road side service for a tow or more gas.

Suddenly she saw a figure walking down the road with a walk similar to Shawn's unforgettable George Jefferson stroll. No matter how fucked up he was he always had a little hop in his step.

As the figure got closer she knew it was him. He was carrying a clear plastic bag containing his belongings and struggling to keep his pants up on his ass. He seemed a bit disoriented and tired.

When he was finally just yards away from her car, she could see that signature smile spread across his face. He looked so relieved. That smile alone made every penny of that $2,500 she had just hustled around town for worth it.

"Baby," is all he said when he got into the car. They embraced for what seemed like hours. Shawn couldn't get the smile off his face.

"You wouldn't believe that shitty ass food they had in there!" he started with his stories. "And you know I like to eat!"

Chapter 8
Seventy-Sev

Shawn had been working at his new job at R&R Moving for over 10 weeks. It was back breaking work, sometimes in high heat, but he enjoyed it. As usual he made friends right off the bat.

"Yo Shawn, boss said go in and get your check," his co-worker Terrence said as he came back to the truck. Terrance was annoying and talked a lot, but he was a reliable driver and worker. He was one of the few black workers who had his license.

"Bet."

Shawn was only making about $11 an hour plus tips at his job, but since he was working 80 to 100 hours regularly every two weeks his check had been pretty nice so far. He was able to take more of the burden off of Kay by paying a few bills and still having enough left over to play with. He was so tired at the end of the day he didn't have any time to go hang out in the hood. Kay was in heaven.

Shawn was starting to wonder why he hadn't gotten a legal gig years ago. After spending just a couple of days in the slammer over his child support matter he knew that was one place he wasn't trying to visit again anytime soon.

Shawn went into the office and saw his boss Bill, a red-headed working class Irish guy from Delaware, staring down at something intently. He glanced up when he saw one of his hardest working employees standing in front of his desk patiently. Shawn was not only efficient and prompt—he also diffused a lot of situations with their moving clients with his charm and quick wit. He and Shawn got along nicely.

"Hey Shawn," Bill said with a weird, tight smile as he stood up. "Good job today."

"Thanks," Shawn nodded. He stood with his hands clasped in front of him, military-style as if he were reporting for duty. "Terrance told me you got my check."

"Yea, bout that..." Bill started. "I called you in because I needed to let you know in advance that payroll got an order from the Philly child support court to garnish your wages."

Shawn's face started to twist up like Scooby Doo's. He assumed he could start paying them himself through the mail. "What? Garnishing for what?"

"For child support arrears. I wanted to let you know now so you ain't surprised."

"Arrears?"

Shawn's heart started beating rapidly as Bill handed him his check in an envelope. He slid out of the office without another word and started walking outside. He finally just ripped open the envelope and his heart almost stopped when he saw the figure.

$92.59.

"Oh hell no," Shawn exclaimed. "Uh uh, hell no! They musta fell and bumped they heads!"

Shawn looked up at the logo on the R&R truck that he was about to get into for a ride home and shook his head in disgust. He thought about how over the past two weeks he had done over 90 hours of back-breaking labor lifting boxes, organizing truck loads, managing nit-picking customers who didn't even tip right and driving in a hot ass truck cab without air conditioning listening to his riding partner complain about his girlfriend all day so that they could pay him $92?

And he had already spent the money he thought he would

get—over $600—in his head. Devastated and pissed, he did an about face and stormed right back to the office. Bill looked like he had been waiting.

"Shawn, I'm sorry man but—"

"Man I quit! Fuck this shit!"

* * *

"But why'd you have to just up and quit though?" Kay asked as she drove Shawn home.

He had left the R&R office after cursing Bill out and started David Bannering down the highway instead of riding home with Terrance as usual. Kay happened to call him just as she was getting off of work herself. She picked him up walking near a wooded area off of Route 95.

Shawn looked at her like she was dumb. "Do I look like Kunte Kente to you Kay? We niggas free now! I ain't nobody's fuckin' slave!"

Kay shook her head in distress. She was torn between feeling bad for him and being angry with him for losing what had been a good job for some time. It kept him happy and out of trouble for weeks.

"So what are you going to do now?" she asked, not really knowing what to say.

"What I'm gonna do? I'm gonna go buy a $90 pair of Nikes and a pack of gum!" Shawn answered obnoxiously.

"Stop being an asshole, this affects me too you know!" Kay tried to say calmly.

"This don't affect you! Did they rob your check too?" Shawn asked.

"I don't give a fuck what you're going through Shawn don't take it out on me. You know I was counting on part of that check to pay the light bill and some of the mortgage!"

"Well you should have known better, cuz it's lights out now nigga!" Shawn ranted. "That'll teach you to count my money!"

What started as a fairly calm conversation turned into an all-out screaming match in Kay's tiny car. She swerved a few times because she was so distracted by the argument.

"Pull over!" Shawn finally screamed. His spit launched onto the dashboard as he pointed. "Pull the fuck over!"

"Pull over!?"

Kay pulled the car over so fast that the tires screeched. She was mad too and so fed up with his smart mouth. They were on a busy street about 10 minutes away from their house but Shawn didn't care. He slammed the car door shut so hard that the window nearly broke.

He started to storm away across the street, but then realized that he had dropped his $92.59 check in the car.

"Hol' up!" he yelled and stepped right in front of her car with his palm out like the Iron Man. Kay nearly ran him down.

"What the fuck do you want!?" Kay screamed.

Shawn came back around the passenger side and snatched open the door. He reached down and grabbed his check.

"Gimme my seventy-sev!"

* * *

"You got a good woman man, you better stop trippin' before she leave your ass," Cage warned as they sat drinking Heinekens at a small gathering in the projects. "Not every woman gonna go bail your ass out of jail like that."

"Yea I know. I was drawlin' but on the other hand she got to learn how to stop pushin' my buttons," Shawn answered. "She knows how I get!"

It was less than four hours after their argument in the car and Shawn was already out of loot. He had bought a new pair of

Nike kicks on sale down at the Gallery, spent $15 on a small bottle of Henny, $3 on a 40 ounce of 211 and gambled the rest away in a card game. Shawn couldn't keep cash in his pocket if it was sewn into the seams. He was back at square one and feeling guilty now that he didn't at least break Kay off with a $20 bill.

"Well you ain't no walk in the park," Cage told him with a nod. Only he and Tino could get away with telling Shawn about himself. "You better go apologize, if she even there anymore."

"Don't say that."

"Hey SB!" a high-pitched voice said from behind him, shaking him from his paranoid thoughts. By the look on Cage's face he could tell it was someone he probably didn't want to see at the moment. He didn't even bother turning around, but he didn't have to because Shelly came right around and sat at the kitchen table with them. She stood about 5'6 150 pounds with a caramel complexion, slim waist and a pretty face. But she wasn't Shawn's type because she was too slutty and easy. He liked a challenge.

"What you been up to?" she said with her crooked smile. Shelly was one of those chicks who got passed around the hood often. She usually did it for money, but when it came to Shawn she would gladly go a round for free. Shelly had a big crush on Shawn since they were in high school and was constantly trying to close the deal with him.

"Sup," Shawn said nonchalantly.

"I been asking Cage about chu," she admitted. "Where you be hidin' your cute self at?"

Shelly could tell by the look on his face alone that he was broke and hurting for money. He had that "yea, I'm fucked up" face on. He was the perfect prey. She leaned over close to his ear to say something.

"Yo, you trynna get high?" she whispered just loud enough for Cage to hear.

Shawn thought about that for a moment. Over the past few months he was too busy working to even think about doing that. Plus his job did surprise drug tests. But now that he had quit the job it didn't even matter anymore.

"Where you get it from? It bet not be that bullshit," Shawn answered.

"Nope. You know I don't get down like that," Shelly assured him. "Come on, I got a nice little stash back at the crib."

Cage looked at Shawn and tried to say "no" with his eyes. When Shelly's eyes were averted he quickly shook his head no. But Shawn was too faded at that point to really think straight.

"Come on in," Shelly said as she walked in and left the door open. Shawn slowly shuffled his way inside. Every bit of his being was telling him to turn around and make a beeline down the street until he reached the Market El train.

"Go head, have a seat," she said as she pointed to the couch. "I'll be right back."

Shawn pulled out his phone and checked it for messages. Surely Kay had called him by then to see when he was coming home.

She hadn't. Zero messages.

"Fuck her then," he said defiantly as he tossed the phone on Shelly's coffee table, but he was disappointed. A few moments later Shelly came back into the room dressed in a small pink nightie and carrying a small decorative box. She sat down right next to his leg and started pulling out her supplies.

"I'm glad you here SB, I hate doing this by myself," she said as she set things up. All she could think about was getting Shawn back into her bedroom and getting it on.

When she finally had everything prepared she handed him the plate first. He tasted it a little first and then snorted two lines quickly.

70

"Good ain't it?" she chuckled and then took a few hits herself.

"Yea, that's aiight," he said with a few nods. Shelly switched on the television and then got up to go get a couple of beers from her refrigerator.

When she came back she couldn't help but eye the slight bulge in his pants as he lay back trying to relax. He still had his fitted cap on, turned to the side and his Nikes were white like they just came out of the box.

"Won't you get comfortable?" Shelly said and came over to take his shoes off. Shawn let her—he was slowly starting to feel it.

"Lemme go to the bathroom," he said as he started to feel a little queasy. As soon as he shut the bathroom door behind him Shelly pounced on his cellphone, which he left on the table. He hadn't locked the phone after checking it just a few minutes before.

When he returned, Shelly was lying back, spread-eagled on the couch with her landing strip full exposed. She was playing with herself.

Shawn just sat down on the other end of the couch, trying to ignore her.

"Come on SB," she whined in her high-pitched voice. "Come play with me!"

Shawn was getting horny, but couldn't shake the thought of how fast and easy she was. He thought of how many dozens of men had run up in her that week alone. Before he had a chance to protest, she dropped down on her knees in front of him and started to unzip his pants.

"Naw naw," he protested weakly, thinking about how fast Kay would probably leave him if she found out, but Shelly was quick. Her wet mouth was devouring Shawn's manhood within a moment. He moaned and threw his head back.

She was a pro. He enjoyed the sensation for a few minutes, but when Shelly got up and tried to straddle him on the couch, he snapped out of it. *This bitch should probably have a yellow "hazardous" banner plastered across her pussy*, he thought.

"Naw, naw I gotta go," he said and pushed her roughly off of his lap. He got up and snatched his cellphone off of the table to check the time. It was 11pm. When he noticed that the phone was still unlocked, he looked over at Shelly peculiarly.

"Why you always tryin' to play me like that? I want you nigga!" Shelly shouted. She was high now and even hornier than she was at the party. "Fuck me!"

Shawn didn't say anything—he just slipped back into his sneakers. He then reached down to do another line and headed straight for the door.

"You goin' home to that bitch huh?"

Shawn turned and shot her a look that could kill. Her facial expression softened. He turned back toward the door.

"SB, how you gonna just use up my shit then just bounce like that!" was the last thing he heard as he slammed the door behind him.

The whole ride home from the city Shawn had a boner. He was jittery and hyped up—all he could think about was getting home to Kay as early as possible to increase his chances of getting some. He would apologize to her immediately and be nice.

When he walked into the door, he was happy to see Kay sitting on the couch working on her laptop.

"Heyyy baby," he said with a smile, trying so hard to be good despite his altered mind state.

Kay just looked up at him with her mouth twisted up. She had been hoping he would stay out all night. "Hey. Ran out of money huh?"

"Yup!" She knew him like the back of her hand. Shawn kicked off his sneakers, which he never bothered to lace up again. He kneeled down on the floor in front of her. "And I wanted to see my baby."

"Yea right!"

"Look Kayby. I'm sorry for ramming on you like that earlier. I was just mad at that job," he said calmly. "You know."

"Right," Kay said again.

"Come on now baby, you ain't gonna hold that against me?" Shawn asked just as Kay's cellphone started to ring.

"Wait, who the fuck is that calling you at one in the morning?" Shawn said immediately switching into "crazy nigga" mode. He stood up and looked down at her phone to see the name, but only a phone number displayed on the screen.

Kay picked the phone up but didn't recognize the 215 number. She was a little nervous about who it could be, but the look in Shawn's eyes said she had better answer it or he would.

Shawn's eyes were glimmering with jealousy as she said "hello" into the receiver. He was already fantasizing about cursing out the dude on the other line and then stomping on her cell phone until all of the wires and chips came out.

"Hello, can I please speak to... Kay?" the high-pitched female voice said on the other line.

"Um, yea, this is she. May I ask who this is?" Kay said politely.

"Oh okay! This is Shelly," the voice answered. "The girl that's fucking Shawn now."

"Oh really?" Kay said nonchalantly and folded her free hand under her arm.

"Yes, we been seeing each other for months now," Shelly lied. "I just sucked his dick tonight in fact, right before he went back to you. I got him all warmed up for you!"

"Well didn't he like it? Why didn't you finish the job?" Kay asked. Shelly was surprised and didn't really know what to say in response. Shawn calmed down, assuming that Kay was talking to one of her friends about work—that was until she said Shelly's name.

"Cat got your tongue Shelly?" Kay asked. "Girl truth is, I really don't give a damn who Shawn is dating or fucking, you can have him. But don't call my phone again, call him. Don't you have his number?"

"Who the fuck is that?" Shawn said and snatched the phone out of her hand.

All Kay heard was Shawn's side of the conversation—a whole lot of denying, accusing and cursing. Sure, Kay and Shawn had slept together a few times in the past few months, but she just wasn't really into it anymore—especially after this. He had thoroughly drained her dry.

"Bitch I 'oun want yo ass, wit ya construction zone pussy, hard at work! ... What you say? ... Nah nah nah fuck that! You ever call my fiancée's phone again I swear I'll choke the shit out you....in broad daylight right in front of your mama and 'nem! .... Oh yea? Well try me then bitch!" Shawn yelled ignorantly into the phone and then clicked it off.

"That ho lyin'," he said, immediately starting to make his case. Kay just tuned back into her computer screen and sucked her teeth, knowing he was lying.

"She sounds like a fucking chickenhead Shawn," she said as she shook her head in disappointment. "Come on now, you can do better than that."

Shawn just stood there looking confused. *What just happened?*

Chapter 9
Sliding Doors

"Lemme get a dub," Ursula demanded as she walked up to Shawn and his friends politicking near the store. She was a skinny old school crackhead from around the way who everybody knew because she had a biting tongue and was fast on her feet. You couldn't leave anything of value around Ole Urs and turn your back—it and she would be gone in a flash. Shawn gave her a cold glance and then continued with his conversation.

"SB? Nigga you hear me? I had asked you for something!" she said, talking over their conversation.

"Why don't you stop being disrespectful Urs? I know you see me talking," Shawn said, finally giving her the attention she wanted. "Shit! You ain't got no manners whatsoever."

"I need it now nigga ain't got time to be waiting on yo bitch ass!" she snapped.

"You and all your other roach friends been waiting around since the beginning of time, you can afford to wait a few more minutes!" Shawn told her, losing his patience. Tino snorted, trying to hold back a laugh.

"Now I know you ain't talking 'bout somebody wit ya big ass head shaped like a peanut. Head hooked so sharp you can hang a coat on it!"

Everyone started laughing.

"Why you lil monkey ass bitch! Breath smelling like you was snacking on chocolate shit cookies!"

"Better than smelling like a musty bag of balls!"

"Ya pussy smell like musty balls! And ya ass so flat you can roll a nickel through the crack!"

"Huh? My ass might be flat, but at least my beard don't look like a thousand spiders having a meeting!"

"Well I'll give you that, you do keep ya beard shaped up better than mines!" Shawn quipped back as he scratched his own chin. By then everyone was having a laugh at both of their expense. Ursula snapped once she realized what she had said.

"Why you greasy-faceded son of a bitch!"

"Roach aunt!"

Ursula went blank and started screaming curse words at him. Shawn just laughed maniacally when he knew she was through—that laugh was like getting punched in the gut repeatedly.

One of the other more peaceful brothers calmed her down and started to lead her away from the group. She snatched her arm away and stormed back over to Shawn.

"Give me that dub nigga!"

He finally obliged. She paid him promptly in two wrinkled, sweaty $10 bills and then disappeared as quickly as she came.

* * *

"Who do you think I'm cheating with Shawn??"

"You tell me!" he wanted to know.

It was one of those bad nights. Shawn had come in pretty early compared to his usual routine, around 12 midnight, but he was still very drunk and high.

Shawn was fed up with Kay acting like she wasn't interested in him anymore; like she didn't love him anymore. He seriously suspected that she might be dating someone new, while they were still living in the same house. Even though in truth, she wasn't.

Kay's job allowed her to work from home from time to time. She had a deadline to meet the following morning and assumed that she would have some peace until then since it was the weekend.

Shawn came in the house early, brought a chair into her office, sat it right across from her desk, and immediately started in.

"Why didn't you call me all day?" he asked.

"I was busy."

"You fuckin' with somebody from your job, ain't you?" he asked. "Who is it, a nigga or a bitch? And you bet not be fucking with no white boy over there in *Jersey*! I will come after both ya'll ass like Jason in those woods!"

Kay looked at him like he was crazy. "You're out of your mind Shawn, you need help."

"I need help? I need help?" he drawled. "You the one wit ya head in a computer all day! Why don't you go outside and live your life?"

"So now I should go live my life?" she repeated. "Just a second ago you said I was out there cheating on you with guys and girls and white boys. Whatever Shawn."

Shawn just got angrier and angrier with each calm response. Kay didn't realize it, but her nonchalance only made things worse. He didn't like that she wouldn't fight with him anymore.

"You probably cheating on me with this damn computer!" Shawn accused. "Kay I was born at night, not last night! Who you talking to on there?"

Shawn got up and tried to look at her screen, but Kay pulled it away from his view. That made him even madder.

Suddenly he slammed the laptop closed with one slap and

then snatched it up from her desk, ripping the power cord out of the wall.

"Shawn, no!" Kay screamed. It seemed like everything started to move in slow motion.

Before she knew it, Shawn had lifted the laptop over his head and then slammed it down on the ground. It broke into several pieces. He looked down at the mess as if it had just appeared there magically.

"Oh my God! My work!" Kay exclaimed as she grabbed the sides of her head and tried to make sense of what had just happened. He had ruined her laptop, which had hundreds of files and software programs she needed in order to make her living. All in a matter of seconds. She was speechless.

Shawn immediately knew he had taken it too far by the look on her face. The silence in the room was deafening.

Finally he left the room in a huff and made his way outside. He dialed Cage as he walked to the corner.

"Yo what you up to tonight?"

"Thought you was in for the night," Cage replied. "Yo the bul Wayne having a lil party down the way. That new sports bar on Broad Street."

"Aiight, come scoop me from the crib."

* * *

Kay loaded her last bag into her car and then went back inside of the house to do one more quick look over.

A tear fell down her cheek as she thought of all the memories she had of that house but she wiped it away quickly. She liked the house but hated the negative energy flowing through it. Her mind was made up.

When she came back out the tow driver was waiting patiently with her back up van hooked up. She gave him the signal for five minutes and they could go ahead and get on the road. She had made arrangements with her friend Tisha who lived in Jersey to keep the van in her driveway until she either sold it or gave it away. Tisha was her confidant and helped her figure out what she needed to do.

Kay had finally decided it was time to move on. She had her time with Shawn, it didn't work out, and that was that. When he destroyed her laptop, which was her livelihood, that was the last straw. She left her ring, which she barely even wore in the past year, on the living room table along with a note when her phone rang.

"Hey girl," Kay said. It was Tisha.

"What's up, you on your way?"

"Yup," she replied with a nod. Just then she saw that Shawn was trying to call her on the other line. She promptly pressed the reject button and knew she had to be on her way. She checked the time—it read 5:35pm. "I'll be there in about 15 minutes okay?"

"Alright, see you in a little while."

"Thank you again Tish, you know I love you for this," Kay said for the thousandth time.

"Anything Kay, you gotta do what you gotta do love and I'm happy to help out."

Kay came out of the house and pulled in front of the tow truck driver. She signaled him to follow and pulled off, starting a new chapter of her life.

* * *

Shawn stirred and his eyes slowly adjusted to the light coming into the window. He didn't recognize the place where he was laying.

He was sleeping on his stomach with one leg hanging off

of the side of the bed. Sweat was beaded across his forehead and down his back. He slowly turned his head to the other side and saw a random girl laying there with her ass out.

"Ugh, shit," he moaned.

Slowly the events from the previous night started to come together. Him breaking Kay's computer... storming out... meeting some girl at the bar on Broad Street... coming back to her crib. After that it was a blackout...

A voice within told him that he had to get back to his house and fast. Actually, it shouted.

GET YOUR ASS BACK HOME!

The voice in his head was so strong it made Shawn jump out of the bed and immediately start scrambling for his clothes, even though his head was pounding. After a few frantic moments he had found everything but one of his brown Timberland boots.

"Where the fuck is my other boot??" he finally yelled out, waking up the girl whose name he couldn't remember to save his life.

"Where you goin'?" she asked groggily as she realized what was going on.

Shawn dove to the ground and searched under the bed. It was nowhere to be found.

"Where's my shoe at?" he leaned back up and asked her. She didn't respond.

Shawn wiped his hand down his face and weighed the pros and cons of walking out the door with just his socks on. He scratched the side of his face nervously.

"Why you leavin' so soon? We gotta finish what we started last night," the girl said as she got up on her knees and scooted over to where he was standing. He was suspended in thought. Wearing just a clingy t-shirt with no bra or panties, the girl started to unbuckle his jeans. Her weave looked about two months past its expiration date.

"Naw, naw," he said reluctantly and walked away from her. She had a nice pair of lips on her, but he was too jittery to even think about getting head from this stranger.

"Fuck it," he finally said and took off his other boot. "I gotta get home."

"Uh uh, nigga you bet not just leave out like that!" The girl became irate and threw herself in front of the door to stop him from leaving. She wasn't used to being rejected by men, especially not twice in one night. It made her want him even more and she was horny.

"Girl get out the way, I don't know you," he said with his face twisted up in disgust and pushed her out of the way with ease.

"Fuck you den nigga you ain't all dat anyways!" she yelled after him. Shawn just calmly found his way down the stairs to her front door.

The girl went into the closet to find the boot she hid from him, hoping it would stop him from leaving her before she woke up. She ran down the steps after him and snatched open the door.

"Here's your raggedy ass boot!" she said and threw it at the back of his head. It was a clean hit. "Big head muthafucka!"

Shawn turned his head slowly and gave her what Kay called his "Manson Glare." It took everything in him to not to rush her at that moment and choke the shit out of her. Instead, he put his boots on.

"Fuck you slut," he said dismissively and took off down the road. He had more important business to take care of at the moment.

"Ay yo Shawn!" he heard someone call out to him from

behind. It was his boy Les, who was always on his hustle whether it was legit or not.

"Les, my nigga," he said as he turned back around to go give him a pound. He pulled out his phone and looked at the time. It was 3:16pm. He knew he really shouldn't stop, but Les was telling him about a new money-making opportunity. Shawn would have to get in on it.

When Shawn finally made it to the El station he could hear the train rumbling downstairs. He took off down the steps, three at a time, trying to make it. He turned the corner and saw the doors just as they were closing. He sprinted toward them but it was too late. The El pulled off—he'd have to wait for the next one.

By the time Shawn arrived back at his house it was 5:42pm and he had smoked all of the rest of the cigarettes he had left in the box. His walk quickened when he saw that Kay's car wasn't in its usual spot.

He'd never know that if he had just been a few minutes earlier, had he been there to catch that El, had he not stopped to talk business with Les, he would have made it home just in time to see Kay before she left the house...

As soon as he walked through the door he felt a vibe that didn't feel right. The house was too quiet and he noticed a few things missing.

"Kay!" he yelled out even though it was obvious she wasn't home. He ran upstairs to the bedroom and looked around. "Kay!"

By the time he found the letter with Kay's engagement ring sitting on top his heart was thumping hard, trying to make its way through his chest...

I'm out. Can't do it anymore Shawn! I'm giving you three months alone to get your situation together here and find a place to stay then you have to leave.

Please stay out of those streets and work on your life—an idle mind is the devil's workshop!

You know I love you and I wish you the best. But we can't be together anymore.

P.S. I got myself a gun. If you try to come find me or start drama with my peeps I will shoot your ass, with no hesitation. I mean it, no cops anymore, just me you and this nine! If you think I'm playing, just try me!

Take care, be smart and responsible,

K

Damn, he thought as he put the letter back down on the table and sat down, shaking his head. *Shit, she crazy! I created a monster…*

Part II – The Transition

Chapter 10
So, When You Coming Back?

Dear Jerome
It's me, your son Shawn, remember me?
I remember you lying there on your death bed. You opened your
eyes, trying your best to see your son.
As I watched you I knew that you weren't ready to acknowledge me
yet. All the pain I experienced as a youth,
all the promises that were broken.
If only you knew that I wasn't mad at the broken promises, it was
that straight jab to the sternum!
Damn man! I was only six years old…
I still remember that punch Dad—that punch caught me off guard.
I lost my breath then start shittin' and pissin' my pants
all at the same time.
I was wearing pampers for 14 months since that happen!
Remember that? Dad, why don't you answer me!
Damn you're rude!
You ain't gone never change is you. Stubborn ass…

Shawn dialed Kay's number for the third time that day. For whatever reason it was going straight to voicemail and he was getting more and more pissed as the hours ticked along.

"Yo Kay, call me back," Shawn said briefly and clicked off the phone. He went back into the sports bar where Tino and Cage were watching the Sixers play. The team had just barely made the playoffs for the first time in several years post-Iverson and that meant a lot of Philly sports fans were in heaven—at least for the time being.

It had been over a month since Kay left Shawn all alone at the house. He was spending less and less time there because the silence and loneliness was too much to bear. To date he had made no plans to move anywhere else because he was counting on getting Kay to come back. He didn't even know where she was exactly—she just disappeared.

"Oh, oh, oh..." his boy Tino said as he watched the television anxiously.

"Damn!" Tino exclaimed in disappointment as Miller's wild shot ended up bricking. The Pistons were up, but not by much.

"If this motherfucker don't pass the fucking ball!" Cage yelled at the screen. "You see this?"

Cage directed his question to Shawn, but he was busy typing something into his phone.

"You serious? Checking your phone, it's the fourth quarter man!" Cage said and tapped Shawn with his beer. Shawn looked up with tired eyes.

"They back up yet?" Shawn asked.

"This is the playoffs and you tapping away at your phone like some little teenager," Cage teased. "Sup with you dawg?"

Shawn didn't answer—he just took a long drink from his beer and looked back at his phone for a reply.

"Oh never mind, I know," Cage said and waved his hand.

"Nigga, you don't know shit," Shawn said as he scratched at his beard, which was looking pretty rough those days.

"I know I told your ass to chill before she up and leave your ass," Cage shot back.

If looks could kill Cage would have been dead on the floor still holding his beer.

"You should talk, ho ass nigga."

"Don't get mad at me for telling you the truth, you know I don't tell you no lies," Cage said reading his expression like a book. Shawn was in fight-mode.

"One thing I do know if you don't shut the fuck up about my girl we gonna rumble," Shawn threatened.

"Nigga I ain't scared of you, we can take this outside if you want," Cage shot back as he pointed toward the door. "I'll drag your ass all up and down this block!"

Shawn stood up and put his finger in Cage's face but Tino held him back.

"Yo, yo, yo chill!" Tino was amused by their antics as usual, but tried to calm Shawn as he eyed the security guard. "Ya'll ain't gonna fight up in here. You know I know the people who own this spot."

Shawn shook Tino off of him and stormed off out of the bar.

"Yo nigga, you ain't paid your tab!" Cage yelled after him.

"Fuck you and the tab!" Shawn shouted back and then was in the wind.

He walked out the door and right into Huey, one of the biggest trouble makers in the projects. Huey's father was a cold killer who had been locked up since he was little and his mother was a crackhead. He hated his mother so much that he sold her the crack and didn't even think twice about it. He didn't give her any breaks either.

"Ay sup partner," Huey said to Shawn with a sly smile on his lips. He and Shawn had a love-hate relationship—sometimes they would beef, other times they got along and could spend all night in the club together drinking.

This wasn't one of those times. Shawn was in a shitty mood and felt like ramming on the first person he saw. Shawn thought about head-butting Huey after he called him "part-ner." He hated that, he only had a few "partners" as in people he rolled with on the regular—Tino, Cage, his cousins, his sisters and Kay. He was beefing with half of them at the moment.

Shawn nodded in Huey's direction and kept it moving. Huey immediately felt slighted.

"What, you can't speak?" he called after Shawn. "Let me buy you a drink."

"Now ain't the time Huey," Shawn said as he turned his head back with his hand up and a cigarette clenched tightly between his fingers.

"Oh ok nigga I see how you is," Huey said with a frown as he went ahead and opened the door to the bar.

Niggas all in their feelings, just like bitches, Shawn thought as he kept walking down toward the El. He pulled out his cell phone and tried to call Kay's number yet again. After one ring it went straight to voicemail.

He stopped in the middle of the street and shouted off a nasty voicemail message calling her every name in the book from an Asshole to a Zoo animal. He kept rambling until the operator turned him off and asked if he wanted to save the message. He clicked off the phone and called her back again, continuing his thoughts.

When he was done leaving voicemail messages, he typed off a few text messages along the same lines. He didn't stop texting until his fingers got tired and his cigarette burned down to the filter.

Finally, he shoved his cellphone back into his pocket and kept walked down the road. He heard his phone buzzing in his pocket and hurried to pick it up.

But it was just Les, the same person who had kept him from catching the El the day Kay left him. He was probably calling to update him on what was going on with his little investment, but Shawn wasn't in the mood to deal with him at the moment.

"Leave a message nigga," he mumbled under his breath and lit up another cigarette. He wanted to go home and rest his head so bad, but couldn't stand the thought of sitting up in that empty house alone.

* * *

Kay had to quit her job in order to leave town since they wouldn't let her work from home full-time.

She had family Down South and in New York, so that's where she headed. First she went south to see her people, get her mind right and get away from the hustle and bustle of the city, then back up north.

As soon as she came back to New York she wondered why she had ever left. It was as if she had never gone away—she settled right back into the New York life.

But it had been a month and she still hadn't found a job yet—she was starting to get nervous about her decision to leave. She needed work and fast.

She decided to put on something professional and hit the streets of Manhattan to try to find a job as a waitress, hostess or bartender. She could no longer hang onto her pride—she needed cash to cover her bills and expenses.

"Hi," she smiled as she walked into the first restaurant she saw in the busy restaurant row area of the city. "Could I speak to the hiring manager?"

"Sure, what is this in regards to?" the young blonde hostess asked.

"Job openings?" she answered, while thinking, *shouldn't*

that be obvious since I asked for a hiring manager?

"Well I don't know if we're hiring right now, but give me a moment," she answered curtly and went to the back.

A few minutes later she came back out with an application in hand.

"I'm sorry but the manager isn't available at the moment. He asked if you could fill out this application? There's also a short test of serving skills."

"Okay, thank you," Kay said as she took the papers and settled into a booth near the door.

What is foie gras?

Name four types of red, white, dessert and sparkling wines…

The questions only got more and more difficult as she moved her pencil down the page. She knew some of them, but not enough of them for her to be a serious contender for this job.

When she finally handed the application and test to the hostess, half of the answers were blank and the other half were mostly wrong or incomplete. She just smiled, nodded and left.

Time after time, Kay walked into each restaurant and ended up either taking a difficult test about foods and wines or just handing an employee her resume, who probably ended up throwing it right into the trash.

"I don't know what I'm gonna do," Kay said to Tisha as they chatted over happy hour drinks. Tisha and her cousin Joy had taken the Patco train into Manhattan after work to meet her for drinks. Kay was immediately disappointed when she saw that Joy came along. Joy was recently married and thought that made her the authority on all things—all she wanted to do was flaunt her ring, sit around and judge other people.

"I'm flat broke Tish, I need a job!"

"Don't worry girl, it'll work out. Just give it some time," Tisha tried to reassure her. "Why don't you try to go back to your art in the meantime? Or start your own business?"

"That would take months or even years to start making money. I need cash flow now to pay the mortgage on the house," Kay explained.

"Just rent it out then," Joy said. Her name was a contradiction of who she was, because she was one of the most joyless people Kay had ever met. Kay only hung out with her because of Tisha.

"I can't do that 'til Shawn moves out," Kay said flatly.

"Well then tell him to leave then!" Joy told her.

"It's not that easy. It's more complicated than that," Kay said and rubbed her forehead in frustration.

"Whatever, you shouldn't be the only one paying the bills for the house if he's living there Kay, wake up," Joy said and rolled her eyes. "That's what you get when you mess around with those unemployed hoodlums!"

"Cool it Joy," Tisha snapped. She could tell Kay was starting to get annoyed and regretted even bringing it up. There was no way Joy or anybody else could ever understand the situation looking at it from the outside.

"Shawn is working on some things. He is working on getting his life together and he isn't a 'hoodlum.' When he gets a new job he will come through for me and take care of things," Kay defended him, trying to stay calm, but thought about why she was even explaining herself. "In the meantime I told him he could stay there, period."

"Okay, fine. Well, don't go around complaining about your little thug business if you don't want advice then," Joy said sarcastically and rolled her eyes again.

Kay slammed her drink glass down on the counter and

stood up. "Excuse me, but did I ever ask you for your raggedy ass opinion Joy?"

"Calm down Kay," Tisha put her hand on her wrist. Kay was normally mild-mannered, but her best friend knew how she could get when she had a few too many to drink, and it had gotten worse under the pressure of what she was going through with Shawn. Kay was unemployed, running out of savings, buried under past-due bills and single for the first time in over four years. She also had just demolished three martinis. Joy had picked the wrong time to get self-righteous.

"Hello! When you say you don't know what you're going to do obviously you're looking for a solution!" Joy shot back.

"So did I say 'I don't know what I'm gonna do JOY?'" Kay asked her seriously. "Did I ask YOU anything? That was my question."

"No, but I'm sitting right here listening to you go on and on," Joy responded, starting to get uneasy. "And I'm just trying to help."

"I don't need your type of help and I don't need your judgments, okay?" Kay said through clenched teeth. "So just mind your own fucking business, drink your drink and keep Shawn's name out your mouth!"

"Kay!" Tisha said. She grabbed her friend's arm to drag her away from the bar.

"Don't talk to me. Get your cousin!" Kay told her.

"You need to calm down! You're coming out of your character."

"Why do you always have to bring her when we hang out?" Kay asked her and pointed. "Ever since she got married she thinks she's fucking Iyanla Oprah Vanzant!"

Tisha couldn't help but chuckle, blowing a little snot out of her nose. Kay shook her head.

"You don't get it Tisha, I'm under a lot of pressure."

"No I do get it Kay. I've been there before. But come on, you know that's my cousin. Chill out and let's have another drink."

"Tish, I know you don't think I'm gonna sit here with her ass. I'm heading home," Kay said as she cut her eyes at Joy. Joy looked away and took a dainty sip of her drink, ensuring that her diamond wedding ring was in clear view.

"I'm gonna walk with you," Tisha said.

"No, you stay here," Kay said with a sigh, calming down. "I need to get back anyway and look for more job leads. I shouldn't even be here right now spending money I don't really have."

Tisha looked at Kay closely. She could see the pain and insecurity in her friend's eyes. "Okay Kay but I got your tab. Go home and get some rest."

Kay looked at Tisha for a long while and even in her drunken haze wondered how she was blessed with such a good friend. They hugged and then Kay went over to grab her bag before leaving the bar. She held her head high even though inside she felt as if she was way down in the pits.

* * *

Shawn was in the wrong state of mind, especially after he had tried time and time again to get Kay to come back home. It was now two months since she left and he was really going through it. He was starting to feel depressed and thinking bad thoughts. He was irrational and at the point where he might go out and do something really stupid, just because.

One object of his anger was a guy from around the way who everyone knew as George. He had always suspected that George had something to do with his father's death. Because of that he never really liked him.

Shawn was sitting at the bar entranced in thought. He was already five Hennesseys in and ready to go off on anyone who said something wrong to him at that moment.

"Yo SB!" a voice said and slapped him on the back. Shawn, eyes glassy, turned around ready to throw a punch.

"What the fuck you want!" he yelled.

"Yo SB! Chill out muthafucka, it's me!"

Shawn's expression relaxed a little when he recognized his best friend Cage's face.

"Don't be sneakin' up on a nigga like that!" Shawn chastised him.

"What's wrong with you?"

"That nigga George's face. That's what's wrong!"

"Oh, you on that again huh."

"I think Imma go holla at Lift."

Cage cringed a little when he heard him say that. They called him Lift because he had lifted a whole lot of corner boys from their bodies. He was officially an old head at 48 years old who was always on the run and rarely hung out down the way unless there was something major going down. Though he kept to himself, he was one of those dudes who didn't have any value for human life whatsoever if it came down to his money.

"Lift? You sure?" Cage said, scratching his beard. "You know that mufucka thinks gettin' locked up is a vacation!"

"Lift's a thorough ass old head. I fuck with him, and he know everybody who knew my Dad. I know you got my back if I move on that nigga."

Everything in Cage was screaming *hell naw*! People tended to get killed messing around with Lift. But he knew that if he fronted on Shawn, especially about something related to his father, he would never live it down. They were already on thin ice after beefing over Kay leaving. For the next few months, every time Shawn got drunk he would probably pick Cage as a target. They would eventually come to blows and their decades-old friendship would be over.

"Yea, you know I got you nigga," Cage said reluctantly and slapped Shawn's palm. He hoped that like all the other times he would just let those angry thoughts go.

"Aiight, deuces nigga," Shawn said as he pushed the stool aside and walked out of the bar with his *I will fuck a nigga up* face on.

Chapter 11
No Good Deed Goes Unpunished

A week had gone by and Shawn was still restless. He was letting his anger consume him. So when Tanisha, a friend of his from around the way, invited him to a birthday party at her house Shawn accepted—he needed the positive distraction. Shawn was always invited to family parties—even though he had a reputation for breaking up a party now and again, everybody still wanted him around because he made the atmosphere lively. Also, Shawn had dated Tanisha's sister Camilla for a little while way back in the day, so he was a close friend of the family.

Right before Tanisha was about to see her cake and blow out the candles, there was a knock at the door. Her aunt Deidre, annoyed at the interruption, went to find out who it was.

"This a private party," Shawn could hear Deidre saying. Her voice got progressively louder as she kept talking to whoever was at the door.

"I don't care, this party for *family only!*" Deidre stressed as if she was about to go off. Shawn walked to the door to find out what was the commotion.

"What's up Deidre?" he said, but didn't really need an answer when he saw Huey and his cousin standing there. They were both known trouble makers in the neighborhood.

"That nigga SB ain't your family, but you let him in?" Huey protested with a hurt look on his face as he pointed like a little child.

"Shawn is our family! We don't know you!" Deidre shouted back at him.

"Deidre, Deidre, let me handle this," Shawn said pushing her aside from the doorway. Shawn was very protective of women he cared about and knew Huey wasn't beyond punching an older lady in the face. He stepped out on the porch and closed the door behind him.

"Ya'll this a private gathering, they only want close family and friends here," Shawn tried to explain calmly.

"But Leon told me to come on by, why ya'll trippin'?" Huey was lying. He had only heard about the party from a few people talking around the hood but he wasn't specifically invited. He didn't think it would be a problem to come by— Tanisha and her sisters were some of the prettiest girls on the block. One of Huey's biggest pet peeves and insecurities was feeling as if he was being slighted or disrespected, especially by women.

"Ain't nobody trippin' for real, we just keepin it a private party my man," Shawn explained.

"But you can be up in there though?" Huey kept at it.

"Come on cuz," Huey's cousin Bennie tried to diffuse the situation and pull him away. He knew both his cousin and Shawn had hot heads and he couldn't afford to be mixed up in any drama at the moment. He was on probation for just a few more months.

"You know what, that's the second time you fucking tried to play me SB," Huey said and pointed at Shawn in a threatening manner as he started walking away. "There ain't gonna be a third."

"Is that a threat?" Shawn asked. His entire demeanor and facial expression changed. That anger he was trying to escape flowed back into his veins.

"That's a promise nigga," Huey said back. Then he made a gesture with his hand like he was pulling a trigger in Shawn's direction.

"Try it pussy! I dare you," Shawn spat with his hand up and started walking toward them, wondering if he should just lay him out there and then.

"Shawn no! Come back inside the house!" Miss Deidre said and ran out onto the porch to grab Shawn's arm before things got out of hand. She continued to hold him back as Huey walked all the way down the street. The last thing Miss Deidre wanted was for Shawn to get in trouble and go to jail on her niece's birthday.

Shawn mumbled something under his breath and shrugged it off. He turned back around to follow Miss Deidre inside. Everyone from the party was crowded around the door and windows looking.

"Thank you Shawn!" Tanisha said gratefully. "That nigga always coming by here tryin' to talk to me and my sister. With his ugly ass!"

"No problem," he said and grabbed Tanisha around her neck playfully to lead her back into the dining room. "You better come in here and make a wish before it expires."

On the outside Shawn was the picture of cool calm collectedness the rest of the party. But inside he knew that Huey and his fragile ego would probably be a new problem for him to deal with.

* * *

"Ay boss!" Shawn called for the bartender with his finger up. He came right over.

"What you want?" he asked Kay.

Kay had finally made her way back to Philly months after

she left. Shawn was so happy to see her that he asked her out on a "date." She agreed to go out, but refused to call it a a date.

"Uh, let me just get a vodka cranberry," Kay said as she scanned the liquors.

"Any kind in particular?" the bartender asked.

"Naw, just the house vodka's fine," Kay answered, always cost-conscious.

"No, give her Grey Goose. And make that two," Shawn said, motioning with his hand to the bartender. "We drink The Goose down here baby, none of that cheap ass shit."

"Well excuse me," Kay said and held up her palm in sur-render.

"You excused," Shawn said with a wink and a smile as he grabbed his pack of Newports from his shirt pocket. He asked the bartender for an ashtray when he came over with their drinks. They were at one of the rare bars where smoking was still allowed.

"When you gonna quit smoking?" Kay asked him as she took a sip of her drink.

"When you gonna quit asking me that?" Shawn snapped back. "If you knew what I got goin' on you'd probably start smoking cigarettes too."

"What's going on?" she immediately wanted to know. "You know I hate it when you keep me in the dark."

Shawn took a long puff of his Newport and tapped it down unnecessarily on the ashtray.

"This lil nigga..." he started. He told her the whole story of what happened at Tanisha's birthday party. He told her how Huey was out there telling everybody he was gonna shoot his head off.

"They say no good deed goes unpunished," he said.

"You think he's serious?"

"He retarded, so yea probably," Shawn admitted. When he looked up at Kay's face he could see the concern. "But I ain't worried Kay and don't you worry 'bout it either. I'm God's son."

Kay was quiet.

"You know you can still stay up at the house for a while Shawn," she said. "Stay away from the bullshit."

Shawn smiled a little, enjoying the attention he was getting from her. "Kay I ain't run a day in my life. I be damned if I live in fear and let some lil nigga have me running away with my tail between my legs. You run from your problems you'll be running all ya life."

"It ain't about that Shawn," she told him. "You shouldn't be down there in the first place!"

Shawn didn't answer, just drank the rest of his vodka and put up his finger to order another one.

"And a Heiny."

Kay knew it was useless pressing the issue with him, he was stubborn and hardheaded. But at the same time she was glad he said something to her about it. All she could really do at that point was pray.

* * *

Since she was in town, Shawn reluctantly decided to bring Kay down to the neighborhood for a fourth of July barbecue at his cousin's house. It was one of those rare occasions when he let her mix in with his friends down the way. Shawn looked at everyone who hugged his girl too long sideways, no matter how long he knew them. He didn't trust anybody.

"Hey Kay," Cage said and gave her a long hug. He quickly caught one of Shawn's sideways looks.

"Okay, okay, that's enough," Shawn said and pulled Kay away.

"Calm down nigga," Cage laughed him off.

Shawn was starting to get annoyed as the day wore on and started drinking more. He couldn't really relax because he was constantly watching Kay to see if she was looking at anyone, or if anyone was looking at her. His insecurities and paranoia started to take over. His mood started to take a bad turn.

When George came near them, the same guy who he was suspicious of being involved in his father's death, his whole mood went south. Shawn was over at the grill filling up his plate and getting a new beer when he glanced over and saw George sitting at the table talking to Kay.

"You SB's girl?" George asked out of nowhere. "The one that do the arts and stuff?"

"I'm his good friend, and yea I paint sometimes. How you doing?" Kay said, trying to be polite.

"Oh that's good, I gotta get one of your paintings one of these days…"

"Nigga you know you ain't buyin' shit!" Shawn snapped on George as soon as he heard what they were talking about. He stood there holding his plate of food in one hand and a fresh cold beer in the other. "Don't be coming up to my girl on some jo shit!"

"SB what…"

"Man, get the fuck outta here!" Shawn yelled and pointed out toward the sky somewhere. He looked like he was about to throw his plate at George's face and pounce on him.

"Shawn, calm down," Kay said.

George shook his head, got up and walked away anyway, not wanting to get into a thing at the moment.

"Fuck that nigga," Shawn said as he sat down with his plate and watched George leave. He took a bite from his burger but then threw it down when he realized that he wasn't even hungry anymore.

"Shawn people say things like that to me all the time, I don't care if they don't really buy my stuff, it's just talk," Kay reasoned. "Calm down.

But Kay had no idea of the deeper issues Shawn had with George; that he might be involved in his father's death. He had already questioned Lift about it and was still waiting for information about whether George was involved.

"Kay, don't tell me what to do. All that nigga wanna do is get up in my business," Shawn shot back loudly. "Fuck that nigga."

"Shawn if you're gonna start tripping I'm gonna leave," Kay said, shaking her head. She sensed that he was in one of his moods. "I don't need any of this bullshit."

"Well do what you gotta do," Shawn said defiantly. "You gonna choose some random nigga you don't know's feelings over mine? Then I don't want you here anyway!"

It was then that Shawn realized, in his drunken state, that everyone in the vicinity seemed to move in closer to them, listening into their heated conversation. Some were brazenly staring as if they were watching television.

"The fuck ya'll bitches looking at? Sitting around here looking for damn some drama! Get a fucking life!" he growled at them.

Kay shook her head and decided to just stay quiet to keep the peace. About 20 minutes later she got up and gave Shawn a hug and a kiss on the cheek.

"Where you going?" he asked.

"I'm just gonna go home and do some work," Kay said, trying to stay cool.

"Well I'm coming with you then," Shawn said as he grabbed his beer and clear plastic cup of vodka with cranberry off of the table. Kay rolled her eyes and he followed her to the car. He got in the passenger side and slammed the door. She just looked at him.

"Okay, let's go," he directed, pointing at the street with the hand holding his vodka cup.

"Shawn I'm not trying to go home and fight with you!" Kay said. "Go hang out with your friends."

"I see those niggas every day. I ain't seen you in months, and now you trying to chase me away?" he asked. "What you got a hot date or something?"

Kay rolled her eyes and looked out the front window of the car. *Same old shit,* she thought.

"Shawn you aren't in the right state of mind. I came out here to be peaceful, see you for a little bit, handle some business and leave out."

Shawn gave her the 'Manson Glare.' He looked mean and crazy, but Kay could sense that he was a really just a little hurt underneath.

"We can hang out tomorrow in the city before I go. But stop drinking so much," Kay pleaded with him.

"Whatever. Fuck you Kay," Shawn said and snatched the car door back open. He stepped out so fast that his beer bottle crashed to the street but he didn't care.

"Hope you enjoy your little date!" he yelled and then slammed the door as hard as he could.

"Shawn you're gonna stop slamming my fucking car door like that!" Kay yelled out of the window at him as she started up the car. Shawn just kept George Jefferson-strolling down the sidewalk back to his friend's party.

* * *

Kay fully expected to spend that July 4th evening in the

house by herself relaxing, smoking, sipping on a drink, working on her life plan and listening to the fireworks outside. She left Shawn down in the projects with his friends and didn't care either way if he stayed out all night—she didn't have any claims on him anymore.

But she was a little startled when she heard the familiar sound of keys jingling in the door and in popped Shawn. He had a serious expression on his face but at the same time looked relieved when he saw her sitting right there on her laptop with raw drawings and papers sprawled all over the table.

Kay could already read his thoughts—she had come to know him like the back of her hand over the years they were together. He came home thinking he would either find her there with another man or that she had left him again.

Shawn didn't say anything—he just trudged upstairs to the bathroom after he confirmed that she was alone. Minutes later Kay's nose turned up at the smell of him blowing up the spot.

"Shawn, why don't you close the fucking bathroom door!" she shouted upstairs.

"I don't have to close the door in my own house!" he shouted back.

"This ain't your house Shawn," Kay immediately responded. "You don't pay any bills here!"

Kay heard the toilet flush and knew she had started something, but it was something that had to be addressed. It was over three months after she left and Shawn didn't seem to have any intentions of getting a job and moving to another place anytime soon. Or paying any bills for that matter.

He came barreling down the stairs ready to pop off—all he had needed was a reason at that point. Kay closed her new laptop and put it in the bag quickly, not wanting a repeat of the last time they were together. When he made it into the room she was already sitting there staring right up at him with her arms crossed, ready for war.

"What you mean this ain't my house? I helped make it what it is today! This my house just as much as yours!"

"Shawn you might have spent some time and a little money on fixing up the house, but you haven't helped pay the mortgage in months! Not a utility bill, not a cable bill, nothing," Kay ran down on her fingers. "This shit here ain't free you know!"

"Well maybe you wouldn't be so worried about money if you just used your brain!" Shawn said snidely.

"What the fuck's that supposed to mean?" Kay asked and looked up at him with her eyes squinted.

"It means you got a degree from college and workin' for peanuts! Why can't you go get a job at one of those corporate jawns downtown? Or a bank?" he asked. "Girl, you so smart til you're stupid!"

Kay stood up, put one of her hands on her hip and looked him directly in the eyes. "Look who's talking Shawn! You got access to military money, school grants, a brain in your head, cook your ass off and can sell an icicle to an Eskimo but you still wanna run the streets all day long! Coming up in here with that 'SB' shit, you ain't supposed to bring that bullshit home!"

"You *love* SB. That's who you fell in love with," he said confidently with his chin up in a taunting manner. "You love drama baby!"

"No, it's you who love the drama. I just had to tolerate it, up 'til now!"

"Yea I love the drama, but yo ass the one who picked up and left without telling nobody! You couldn't send a nigga a text message? And where my van at!"

"It ain't your van Shawn! You didn't pay the dealership and you damn sure don't pay the insurance and registration. You gotta pay to play my brother!"

"That's my van though. I slept in that van some nights! I kept that shit tuned up. I'm the one who kept it running. Why you think that old ass van still running Kay!"

"Shawn you don't even have your license though! Last time you got pulled over I had to go in front of the judge and pay the costs! Your list of traffic offenses was so long it rolled to the fucking floor," Kay said with an exaggerated gesture. "The judge almost locked my ass up for letting you drive!"

"I told you I won't get pulled over no more. If I could use the van I could go handle some business. You supposed to be my girl—we supposed to work this shit out!"

Kay shook her head no. "It's only so much a woman can take Shawn!"

"What you mean?"

"You used to take the van to go hang out in the hood, not to get a job! You can't leave those streets alone Shawn, you just wanna thug it out day and night!"

"Girl you LOVED the thug in me. You knew I'm a bad boy when you met me!"

Kay shook her head and bit her lip. She couldn't contest him on that because she knew he was right.

"Well, I was young and dumb," she said after a few moments. "I'm older now!"

Shawn flopped down on the couch and rubbed his face with his hands. Then he started rambling.

"All this bullshit don't make no fuckin' sense to me Kay. All this hatred that's in the air it may be a little bit my fault. But you could have told me you was so cold years ago! Damn! I already knew you was mad but damn it's just over like that?

All I tried to do is be thoughtful sometimes more than needed, but this time it wasn't my fault!"

"You just said it *was* though. See you don't make any sense Shawn," Kay responded and threw up her hands. He ignored her and kept talking.

"When you met me you told me you was gonna Febreze me. Clean me up and spray away all my pain," Shawn continued talking. Kay just flopped down and decided to let him ramble on. Even though she didn't really understand what he was trying to say half the time she could tell that he was hurting. "Now you out there fucking with other niggas. Yea you think I don't know; I was born *at* night, not last night!"

"Shawn when we were together you treated me like I was just some chick from the street, not your fiancé. Look at how you talk to me! I tried to help you and you just never appreciated it!" Kay said and started to get emotional. "Four years of this shit!"

"Oh quit cryin' Kay. I ain't trying to hear all that bullshit," Shawn dismissed her when he saw a tear drop—he hated when anyone showed signs of weakness, including women. "If you stayed here at OUR house we could figure it out. Just stop acting like a scared ass broad!"

"Fuck you Shawn! It don't matter anyway, I can't stay here with you. You don't know how to act," Kay said, getting angry again. "You brought the streets into my house. I didn't do shit to you Shawn, you do it to yourself!"

"All you know how to do is run!" Shawn yelled.

"All you know how to do is ram on people! And you'll lie about whether the sun is shining outside. And I don't even know what the fuck you're talking about half the time!" Kay shouted back.

"Well maybe if you just *listened* to me! Maybe if you really *heard* me you would know what I'm talking about!"

Kay shook her head and tried to calm down but her chest was heavy with anger. "Shawn if I stay here either you're gonna hurt me or I'll hurt you. Either way I don't want to mess up my life!"

"Well fuck it, just leave then! Bitch please! I don't need you," Shawn dismissed her with a wave of his hand.

"I'll show you a bitch! This is my house motherfucker, YOU leave!" Kay yelled. "I'm not fucking around with you anymore Shawn. I put up with your shit for years and I never once sent you to jail. But if you decide you want to start tripping now I'll do what I gotta do!"

Shawn gave her another one of his crazy stares as his nostrils flared. Finally, he got up from the couch and stormed to the door.

"You know what I'm not even going to go there. I ain't gonna give you the satisfaction Kay! Am out! You ain't no bitch, youse a monkey and I ain't gonna turn gorilla in this jungle. Am out, deuces!!"

Chapter 12
Chuuuurch

Shawn went up to his mom's house late after his fight with Kay and fell right asleep on the couch. After that fight he decided that he needed some church in his life—he could tell that Kay was at the end of her rope with him, hanging on by a string.

It was a known fact that if you stayed at Momma Rhonda's house on a Saturday night, you were going to church in the morning on Sunday. The sounds of gospel music early in the morning shook him right out of his sleep, just like when he was a child.

"Hey brother," Shawn's sister Rose sauntered in the kitchen as he stood with his head stuck in the fridge, looking for something to eat. He knew his mom had to have cooked something good the night before. He didn't care if it was the morning; he would eat anything his mom made.

Shawn's sisters were knockouts, so that meant he had to spend a lot of his time knocking out brothers who messed with them over the years. It wasn't long ago that he got into a fight with one of his sister's exes, who was stalking her at her job. He was also very protective of his young nieces.

"You goin' to church?" he asked Rose.

"Naw, gotta work. What you doing up here anyway?"

"Tryin' to get the Lord in my life!" he said with a wink.

"Right!" she said with a laugh.

"Get out my fridge boy!" Ms. Rhonda said as she walked

into her kitchen and smacked him on the back of the head play-fully. She had been trying to get him to church and was happy to see him at the house on a Sunday morning.

"Hey Ma!"

"You know you goin' to church with us right?"

"Nope. I'm just goin' to eat and roll out," he said as he pulled out a tray covered in foil wrap. "What's this?"

Ms. Rhonda slapped his hand. "Boy put that back if you ain't coming to church with us!"

"Ow! Calm down ma! I'm going, I'm going," he said with a smile and kissed her roughly on the cheek before heating up a plate of her leftovers.

"Well you'd better be!"

The church was packed and hot. It was a traditional black church filled with sounds and buzzing with people.

Shawn guided his sister Shondra and mother into the aisle ahead of him. He really wanted to sit more toward the back since he wasn't properly dressed for church, but his mother was having none of that. She sat up near the front row and so did her kids.

"Good to have you here brother!" Shondra said with a big smile. She and her brother had the identical perfect smile that could brighten up a room.

"Glad to be here sister," Shawn said and gave her a hug.

When the choir started humming it was a warning that some praise and worship music was on the way. They started clapping and the drum beat dropped soon after. Almost imme-diately Shawn's mother and sister jumped up from their seats and started clapping to the music. Shawn could feel the floor of the church shaking under his feet.

Shawn started nodding his head to the beat and smiling.

He started to feel good. Soon enough he was feeling the Spirit and got up to dance as well.

He hopped around and did his little Charlie Brown dance, making a few of the folks nearby laugh and get even more fired up themselves.

The pastor's sermon was about friendship. The ultimate message was that you have a true friend in the Lord. But what the pastor said in the middle of the sermon was what caught Shawn's attention the most.

He said that true friends lead you to your path and, at least for a time, walk besides you on that path. It got him to thinking about who were his real friends—who would guide him to the right path?

His friends?

His family?

Kay?

Was anybody in his life a true friend? Did he really have anybody?

His paranoia set in but the sound of the pastor's voice signaling the end of the service settled him back down.

"Before I go, remember this," the pastor said in closing. "Your true friends on earth can guide you to the right path, but it's up to YOU to decide whether or not to stay on it."

Shawn suddenly got the strong urge to talk to Kay as the choir started singing a song. He pulled his cellphone out and sent her a text message right in church.

> *I'm sorry for ramming on you baby. I love u n I need u*

One of the deacons shot him a mean look for texting while the service was still in session. A few seconds later he was surprised to get a quick reply from her.

>> *love you too. we'll talk*

* * *

Cage had a girlfriend down in North Philly as well as in West Philly where he had his own rowhome, which he inherited from an uncle. Neither of his girlfriends knew about each other, which made the situation all the sweeter for him. Traveling from West to North was like going from Baltimore to New York City for some folks in Philly—it was a completely different world.

As far as Cage was concerned he was never getting married. What for? He had everything he needed—a good woman at home who cooked, cleaned and took care of him and a young side chick who satisfied his every sexual desire on command. He had a baby's mother from when he was 16 who ended up moving to Pittsburgh with her family just a year after his son was born. His son was now 14 and Cage had barely seen him twice in over a decade.

His young girl Tanya, who lived in West Philly, had just turned 19. She was a "round the way" girl with a big behind and a caramel complexion. She was attracted to older men because she never had a father in her life. Wilhemina, who everyone called Willie, was a tall 25-year-old beauty with a flawless chocolate brown complexion who could have been a model. She was ghettofabulous and proud, but she was also a good hard-working woman with children and she loved on Cage hard—to a fault.

Cage on the other hand was a loyal partner when it came to his boys, but thought of himself as something like a pimp when it came to women.

"Willie where you put my Phillies jersey?" Cage asked, standing in the doorway of the kitchen.

"Boy when you gonna retire that old raggedy ass jersey? That joint from 2003, let it be," Wilhemina said as she stood in front of the stove frying up a pair of T-bone steaks for dinner. She was still dressed in her scrubs after coming in from work. It had only been two hours that she was home and already she'd fed her two kids, made sure they were upstairs doing their homework and was now cooking a very special dinner for Cage.

"I already hear that shit enough from the boys, don't need to hear it from you too," Cage said. "That's my lucky jersey. When it falls apart Imma turn it into a belt to keep my pants up!"

"Why don't you just wear one of those button-downs I bought you, that jersey shit is just weird," Wilhemina said shaking her head, but finally she relented. "It's tucked in the bottom drawer."

"Thank you! Stop moving my shit please."

"Why you looking for it anyway, you ain't goin' out is you? You see me in here cooking," she yelled.

"Imma eat," he yelled back as he went to their back bedroom. "But then I gotta go out for a few hours."

"Out where?" she said and stopped in her tracks. She didn't hear anything in response, so she turned off the stove and followed him back into the room.

"Where the fuck are you going?" she asked again as she watched him pull on his jersey and start picking through his sneaker collection.

"Just out to the crib, gotta check on some things."

"Out West? Cage you always going down there why don't you just sell that house and come live with me?"

"This you and your kids' house Willie, I ain't gonna be like one of these mooching ass niggas living off his woman. I got my own. That's why you respect me so much remember?"

"Who said I respected you?"

"Quit playing before I throw your ass out this window," he said, pointing in that direction.

Wilhemina watched him quietly as he slipped on a pair of his best sneakers and went into the bathroom to examine himself in the mirror. She saw the hair clippings in the sink, which he didn't even bother to clean up.

"You just gave yourself a shape-up? What the fuck for if all you goin' to do is visit the crib and come back?"

"I ain't goin' through this with your ass tonight Willie, I'll be back later. Wait up for me."

Wilhemina slammed her fist hard into the wall and stomped back down the hallway. She had had a whole night planned for Cage to celebrate their three-year anniversary, but it was clear now that he had completely forgotten.

"Willie, stop being that like that. I'll be back later."

"Fuck you Cage! Stay out all night I don't care! And you ain't getting none of this food right now so be out!"

Cage did just as she told him—five minutes later he passed right by the kitchen and left the house. When she saw him do that all rationality left her brain. She grabbed the pot full of steaks and ran with it to the door. She threw the entire contents, $20 worth of prime steaks she had picked up from Reading Terminal, out at Cage's truck like she was pitching for the Mets. It missed his back window by inches and landed on the street. Apparently Cage didn't see anything because he just pulled off.

That was one thing about Cage that Wilhemina couldn't stand—he never wanted to fight. If she told him to do something he took it literally without ever wanting to challenge her. She wanted a good fight every now and then, just to show that he cared.

She went back into the house and slammed the door shut angrily. She stomped into the kitchen, sat down at the table and huffed loudly, trying to catch her breath. Soon she broke down in tears.

She had been riding with Cage for years now and still felt like she was just his on-again off-again mistress.

Wilhemina had been raised by a single mother who rode her hard. She raised her to work hard and always sacrifice for others. She was beaten on the regular like a slave. On the other hand her mother spoiled and coddled her two brothers, which eventually caused them to become two lazy hoodlums. Besides her hard-work ethic, the one lesson Willie learned from her mother was that she didn't want to become a lonely old bitter angry woman. So she clung onto men and tried to whatever she could to please them and keep them around.

She cooked, cleaned and took care of Cage, even though he didn't even want to live with her, let alone marry her. Sometimes he would ride up to her house, drop off a bag of laundry, and then leave right back out of the house. She put up with it because at 25 she was terrified of being alone again with two young kids.

She had dreams of becoming a model as a young girl and was even chosen on a few model searches for local runway shows, but when she got pregnant with her first child at 18 all those dreams crashed and burned. Soon she found herself right on the path to doing what her mother had done and she hated herself for being so stupid.

Now she worked at a nursing home in the suburbs and every day she wanted more for her life, but every day it seemed like she took one step forward then two steps back.

It was as if something was blocking her blessings at every turn.

"Mommy are you okay?" she heard a tiny voice say from the doorway. It was her seven-year-old son, who was like her little protector. Her kids were her strength in many ways and they always seemed to know when their mommy needed love.

"Yes bookie," she said and wiped away the tears. "Come here."

"So what you crying for?" he asked as he walked up and sat on her lap. Her five-year-old daughter appeared closed behind him.

"Cause I'm so happy I got my two babies," she said with a smile. "Mommy loves you so much."

* * *

"Hey bitch, what you up to?" Tanya cackled into the phone as she walked down her West Philly block. She was wearing a pair of short-shorts, a shirt that showed off her belly ring and a pair of fake red-bottom heels Cage bought her. Tanya swore up and down that everything he bought her was the real deal.

"Ain't nothin'. What you want," her friend Shamika said.

"'Bout to go see my nigga," Tanya told her nonchalantly. "He takin' me out to Red Lobster tonight."

"Ohhh I'm so jealous! Bring a cheesy biscuit home for me! And some shrimps. Man I need me a nigga like that. Take me out and shit."

"Girl and this nigga so sprung! He buy me all kinds of shit," she bragged. "He got me a Prada bag last week and I ain't even have to ask. I got that nose wide open!"

"Prolly from down 52nd street," Shamika said with a little ki-ki.

"Ho don't try to play me. That shit the real deal, I checked."

"Okay, whatever you say," Shamika said and rolled her eyes. *Stupid bitch*, she thought.

Tanya was an attention-seeker. She would do just about anything for attention from men. She thought that getting money and things from them was a sign that she was doing something right in life. She happily traded sexual favors for trinkets. Her mother gave up on her when she was just 13 and brought her in to get an abortion. Her mother had given her absolutely no advice about men and life but somehow expected her to figure it all out on her own.

"All I gotta do is suck his dick, fuck 'em, put him to sleep and I get whatever I wanttttt," Tanya continued bragging as she crossed the street toward Cage's house.

"Shit, take 'im for everything he got then bitch," Shamika advised her. "I gotta go though."

"Me too, I think I see his truck pulling up."

Tanya clicked off the phone and sashayed up to Cage's truck just as he pulled into an open parking space. She smiled and licked her thick lips seductively right before she climbed in. Cage grabbed her ass before she had a chance to sit down.

"Stop!" she pretend-protested and slapped at his hand. He was wearing a red Phillies fitted baseball cap to the side along with his matching jersey and a pair of dark jeans. He smelled like fragrant oils. Tanya reached over, closed her eyes and tongue-kissed him deeply for several minutes. Cage was loving every moment.

"Keep it up Imma take your ass right in the house instead of this restaurant," he said as he put the car into gear.

"Naw, I'm hungry!" she said with a smirk. "You can get some of this later. Maybe!"

* * *

"Take this down to the registration office. They'll give you a form to sign and confirm your enrollment within a couple of weeks. Maybe sooner," the lady told Shawn after he finished signing off on his financial aid for the fall semester. He had finally decided to go back to school at a community college nearby. He had transferrable credits from his time at college before he joined the Army and also a semester's worth of credits for time he spent at another community college years ago.

"Thank you," he said and nodded. He set off on his way to the registration office, which was located on the other side of the building.

When he finally looked up from his paper, he saw a young dirty blonde white girl eyeing him down like she was a tiger and he was a big piece of steak carrying a bottle of A1 sauce. He nodded and smiled her way but kept his stride.

By the time he reached the registration office it was closed.

"Dammit!" he cursed. He had hoped to get everything settled before the end of day that day so that he could call Kay with his class schedule. But he would have to wait until Monday.

"What's wrong?" Shawn heard a voice behind him ask. He turned around and there was the smiling white girl from earlier.

"Uhh… need to register for these classes," he said.

"You know you can do that online right? You don't have to go to the office," she explained. "I can show you."

"Oh yea? Can you do it now?"

"Sure! Let's go to the library," she answered enthusiastically and gestured for him to follow her.

* * *

Later that same evening Shawn was down the way hanging in front of Cage's girlfriend's house with Tino, Cage and a few more of his regular running partners.

"Nigga please!" Cage said when he heard that Shawn had

enrolled in school.

"Don't hate the playa hate the game!" Shawn said with one of his trademark laughs. In truth, he didn't give a damn what anybody thought about his plans. He was doing it for one reason—to convince Kay to come back.

"You wanna be a teacher when you grow up?" Cage teased.

"Nigga I am already; I teach Ass Whippings 101. Want me to give you a lesson?" Shawn threatened playfully with his fists up in a boxing stance and started sizing Cage up.

"Well I'm proud of ya bro," Tino chimed in. "Even though you made me look bad over quitting that moving gig. I vouched for you nigga!"

"You know I had to quit that job T, I'm a lot of things but I ain't nobody's slave. 80 hours for $100? I don't think so. Imma try this school thing out though."

"Nigga you ain't finna stay in school. I give it two weeks," Ron said, trying to join in on the conversation. Shawn's expression changed into an angry sneer.

"Was I even talking to you?" Shawn snapped at him. "Was anybody fucking talking to you Ron? And by the way, where was you again when Kidd got shot?"

Just then Shawn's cellphone rang—Ron was saved by the bell because Shawn was about to really go off. He never seemed to get a straight answer from Ron about his whereabouts when Kidd was killed. As Shawn glanced at his phone he saw that it was the white girl Meghan from earlier who had helped him register for school calling. He gave her his number because she said she wanted to be in his study group.

"What she want..." he mumbled to himself and walked away from his friends. "Hello?"

"Hey Shawn! It's Meghan," she said. "What are you

doing?"

"Ummm, hanging with my boys, what's up?"

"Oh okay. I was wondering if you were busy tonight? My friends and I are going to this bar out in Manayunk."

"Manayunk huh?" Shawn thought as he puffed his cigarette and put two and two together. This girl was trying to holla at him for real. "I can't make it up there tonight, maybe another time."

"Awww come on. I'll pay for all your drinks, all you have to do is make it up to Main Street somehow," Meghan pleaded. "You can bring a friend too."

The offer of free drinks was tough to pass up. He asked Meghan to hold on a moment.

"Yo Cage, you got your truck?" he asked his friend. He knew Tino was going in the house but Cage was always down for late night shenanigans. When he glanced around he noticed that Ron had disappeared.

"Yea, what's up?" Cage asked.

"We ridin'. Down Manayunk."

When Shawn and Cage arrived at the mostly white bar in Manayunk they had to deal with all kinds of stares and glares from the patrons and waitresses. Two thug ass black brothers showing up would always raise a few eyebrows in that type of place.

"Shawn!" Meghan shouted as soon as she saw him and ran into his arms. He half-hugged her back—he could tell she was already popped.

The whole night Meghan and her friends were hanging onto Shawn and Cage as if they were a couple of rap stars. Shawn was no stranger to drinking, but these kids could drink like neither of them had ever seen before. They were sloppy drunk and still calling for more shots. As promised, Meghan bought everything Shawn wanted at the bar.

At one point Meghan and her friend Anna started tonguing each other down and rubbing on each other's breasts, right in the booth. Shawn and Cage looked at each other with a knowing look but didn't say anything. Meghan was the definition of a "party girl" getting "white girl wasted."

By the end of the night Shawn was drunker than he had ever been. They all stumbled toward Cage's truck.

"Can we get in?" Meghan asked. Shawn opened the back door and let her climb in. Her friend Anna went up front with Cage.

"We're going to be in the car Meghan," her other friend, who was the designated driver, said and then kept walking down the street.

"I had a good time tonight," Meghan said and then started rubbing on his leg. Shawn just nodded, trying to keep his eyes open.

Meghan reached over and started to unbuckle his pants. Before he knew it she was giving him a hand job, trying to get him hard.

Damn. She bold! he thought. But as interesting as this all was, Shawn wasn't really feeling it and he was too drunk to even think about sex. He wanted to pass out and couldn't help but thinking about how many men Meghan had probably done that same thing to after her drinking binges at that bar.

When she reached down to put her mouth on his manhood he stopped her.

"Naw, naw, another time," he said to her surprise and dismay.

"I can make you hard, just give me a minute," she said and tried to go back in.

Shawn pushed her head away roughly and zipped up his pants.

"What you don't like me or something? Look at this." Meghan pulled her shirt up, revealing two surgically enhanced breasts. One looked a bit less perky than the other. She started playing with her nipples.

"I'm just tired," Shawn said and shook his head as he ran his palm over his sweaty face. "Cage, you ready to roll brother?"

By then Cage was already getting head from the girl with him in the front seat. He didn't say anything for a while but then pulled the girl up.

"Yea man, let's roll."

The drunken girls weren't happy until both Shawn and Cage agreed to meet up with them soon for a trip to Atlantic City.

"I been with a white girl before, but those were just some sloppy broads," Cage commented on the drive home.

"Yea, I couldn't get into it," Shawn agreed. "Hope that chick don't start blowing up my phone."

Chapter 13
Nuts

Shawn had been attending school for three weeks and doing well. He passed all of his quizzes and homework assignments with at least a B grade. His teachers liked him and treated him like the teacher's pet.

But the school had a strict attendance policy—three absences and you were dropped from the class. Three latenesses from one class equaled an absence. Shawn had already missed one full day of classes and was late twice for his morning class, messing around down the way.

Even though he was going to school, he still did a bit of slang-ing on the side to have a few dollars in his pocket. His school refund wasn't coming through for at least another week. So Shawn made his way down to the block after classes as usual that day and posted up. Within a few minutes he had already made $50—it was near the first of the month and the block was buzzing.

Everyone was happy because they were making money and already making plans for what they would do for the weekend. Just then, a black sedan screeched up next to the store and three men jumped out.

"Task force!" someone shouted. Everybody groaned. There went most of their weekend plans.

The officers made everyone put their hands up on the wall and searched them thoroughly for drugs. One by one, each of them started to get bracelets and led away to the paddy wagon that had pulled up behind the sedan.

When an officer finally made his way to Shawn, he was the picture of coolness. He even laughed a little.

"Ay that tickles!" Shawn taunted as the officer ran his hands down and around his entire body and rabbit-eared all his pockets. "Let me find out, I got a girl you know!"

The officer wasn't amused at all, and decided to do another thorough check. He was surprised to find nothing and was forced to let Shawn go.

"Clear the block!" the officer shouted at Shawn and the few other brothers who came up clean. "I better not see you here again tonight or I'll lock you up just for the hell of it."

After the paddy wagon left Shawn laughed and lit up a cigarette.

Q, one of the only other brothers who hadn't been carrying anything that day, couldn't help but ask Shawn how he had pulled it off. Shawn looked around to make sure Ron or any other possible snitch was around.

"I'm just a lucky nigga!" Shawn said in low tones with a wink and grabbed himself. "Plus I got a real special hiding spot he ain't gonna look, even though I'm sure he probably want to!"

* * *

"Almost got locked up today baby," Shawn said to Kay on the phone, hoping to get some sympathy. They had made up, as usual, after their huge fight on July 4th. And strangely since then hadn't had one argument—it was as if they had released a lot of burdens.

"Again Shawn? What, over child support court again?"

"Naw, something else," Shawn said with a chuckle. "I'll tell you when I see you. When you coming down here again?"

Kay sighed. "I thought you said you were done with that bullshit Shawn, you're supposed to be in school now."

"I am in school. Don't worry 'bout it Kayby, I got this."

"Yea that's what you said about that child support situation and now I got my credit card company coming after my ass," Kay said.

"Don't worry 'bout that Kay, I'm gonna break you off when my refund check come," he assured her. "I got you."

"I hope so, we're behind on the mortgage you know."

"I know, I know."

"So I found a little gig," Kay finally said. "Somebody hired me to do an illustration for an ad."

"Word?"

"Yea, something small it's just $250, but it's something," Kay explained. "And I might have a lead for a data entry job. Found it at one of those temp agencies."

"Cool," Shawn said but his heart dropped. If she found a job out there it was even less likely that she'd come back to Philly. She also wouldn't be able to come out as often and spend days hanging with him.

"And Shawn stop playing on my phone!" Kay said, changing the subject. "You left me 12 fucking messages last night and all these text messages!"

"What I say?" Shawn said, the smile returning to his face.

"All kinds of crazy shit," Kay said, shaking her head. "You left them you should know what you said!"

"That wasn't me."

"Who was it then?" Kay said, twisting up the corner of her mouth. "SB?"

"Probably," Shawn said. "Either that or one of your boy-friends."

"Don't start Shawn, I don't have any boyfriends."

"That's right you got a *fiancé*, right here, so bring your ass home!"

"I gotta go Shawn! Call me later!"

"Yea whatever, you better pick up the phone."

"Please be safe and smart if you go out tonight!"

"I will if you bring your ass home!"

Chapter 14
Schooled

Because he stayed out too late and couldn't pull himself up out of bed at eight in the morning, Shawn missed his morning class at school a third time and was in danger of being dropped from the class. If he didn't maintain a certain number of credits he would be in danger of losing his GI bill funding and certain grants to register for the next semester.

But on a positive note he was expecting his refund check for $3,000 within the next couple of days. He was daydreaming so deeply about what he would buy when he got it that he didn't see Meghan coming down the hallway. He had been trying to avoid her, because she was starting to act a little bit like a stalker.

"Here, I got something for you," Meghan said and held out a bag as she walked up to him.

"What's this?" Shawn said and couldn't help but smile as he grabbed it.

"Just look!"

Shawn pulled three tagged Polo shirts and a Fossil watch out of the bag.

"Gotta look good for school and be on time!" she commented, pleased that he looked pleased.

"Damn! Thanks," Shawn said, never one to turn down a gift. By the gifts and all the money Meghan had been throwing around at the bar the other night it was obvious that her family was well off.

"So you're still going to Atlantic City with us this weekend right?"

"I don't know, gotta get back to you about that," Shawn hesitated.

"We got a luxury hotel suite and you can gamble all night long, on me. Just come on, it'll be fun!"

"I'll let you know," Shawn nodded. "Gotta go to this meeting with my counselor. Thanks for the clothes though."

Meghan reached up and gave him a hug before going on her way.

When Shawn walked into the counseling office his eyes were immediately drawn to a cute slim brown-skinned girl sitting in there waiting. He sat across from her and stared her down the entire time with a smirk on his face. She finally giggled. He knew he had her without ever saying a word.

When Shawn left his counselor's office his mood had turned sour. His counselor basically said that one of his teachers had marked him down as "withdrawn" and he would have to appeal it with her. She said that if he got dropped from just one more class he might be disqualified from his GI bill and grants for the next semester.

As he left the building, seeing red, he saw the brown-skinned girl from earlier sitting there pretending to read a book. She looked up when she saw him and smiled, obviously hoping he would come over and say something. And of course he did.

"Hey pretty girl, what you readin'," he said and sat down right next to her, forgetting his problems for a moment. He figured if he was going to have to start dating again best to get himself another college girl.

"Biology. Got an exam coming up," she answered sweetly, pushing her hair behind her ear as it blew in the wind. "You go here?"

"Yup, at least for now," he said with a little laugh to hide his frustration and then a sigh. "What's your name?"

"Blake, and you?"

"Shawn. Ay, you busy? What you about to do now?"

"Nothing, just go home and do some homework."

"Why don't we go up the street and get a drink or somethin'?" he offered.

"Alright," she quickly agreed. "Do you drive?"

"Naw, I take the bus up here. You?" he asked as they started walking.

"Yup, we can take my car," she volunteered.

Shawn was so involved in his conversation as he walked to Blake's car that he didn't notice Meghan standing in the doorway of the school eyeing them both down...

Blake took Shawn to an Irish pub near their school to have a few drinks. They ordered the happy hour special—a pitcher of beer—and a few shots. Blake immediately went digging into her purse and pulled out a $20 bill to pay for the drinks, but Shawn stopped her and put his own money down first. She protested even while the bartender was putting it in the register.

"No really, it's okay. I don't mind paying for the drinks," she told him. Shawn looked troubled.

"What type of dudes you be dealin' with? On a first date a man's supposed to pay for his lady," he schooled her. "Only a sucka ass nigga would ask you out then let you pay his way."

Blake nodded and tried to relax. "Okay."

Blake's father left her, her mother and two siblings when she was just two. She hadn't seen or talked to him since. At 22, she had never had a real boyfriend and whenever she had the attention of a guy she did everything in her power to keep him around, even if it meant paying for everything or driving him everywhere. Problem was they still left her eventually.

After drinks, Blake drove Shawn all the back to his mother's house. He had to handle some business in the city the next day so figured he would take advantage of the free ride home.

"This where you live?" Blake asked when they were parked in front of his mom's house.

"Naw, this my mom's crib."

"Oh okay, can I meet her?"

Shawn looked at her as if she had lost her mind. His mother rarely liked any of his girlfriends and he wouldn't hear the end of it if he brought some new random girl into her house. Especially when she thought he was still engaged to Kay.

"Naw, she probably ain't home," he said shaking his head. "Thanks for the ride, I'll probably see you at school Monday."

"Okay, maybe I'll see you this weekend."

"It's possible," he said as he shut the door.

* * *

Shawn was upset when he learned that his refund check still didn't come. He had been counting on that money to take care of bills and ball out a bit that weekend. He had gone all the way up to the house to check the mail for nothing.

But he saw a letter from child support court about an upcoming date and brushed it off.

"Catch me if you can I'm the gingerbread man!" he said and crumbled it up. He was tired of getting called up to court hearings when they knew he didn't really have any money or a steady job yet. This school money was the first bit of cash he would have in a long while.

Meghan had been blowing up his cellphone ever since he saw her on Thursday—all that night and then that morning. He knew what she wanted. She wanted him and Cage to come with her and her friend to Atlantic City—they were supposed to be leaving that night.

Shawn plopped down on the couch and tried to figure out what he was going to do. He sorted through his pockets to see how much money he had on him. $22—barely enough to make it back downtown and get a few beers at the bar.

Just then Meghan called his phone again. He looked at the screen for a while and bit his top lip in quiet contemplation. He thought about how she said he could gamble all he wanted on her dime. The thought made him pick up the line.

* * *

On the drive down to the shore, Meghan and her friend Anna were already wilding out. They blasted a mix of rock music and rap music the whole way and flashed a few people on the road. It was as if they were going out of their way to fit a girl's gone wild stereotype and to impress Shawn.

Shawn sat in the back laughing and guzzled straight from a bottle of champagne that Meghan bought him when they visited the liquor store before leaving the city. He was feeling good and having visions of all the money he would win using Meghan's chips.

When they arrived at the hotel Meghan kept her promise— she kept Shawn laced with chips and they made their rounds throughout the casino. Shawn tried to dip on them on more than one occasion because they were being "extra" and drawing attention to him. After a few hours Shawn had broken even and was starting to realize it wasn't his night.

"Baby, let's go up to the room," Meghan pleaded with him. She was tore up along with Anna and had finally had enough of running around the casino acting silly.

"Alright, alright, just let me do one more run. Gimme like 50 and then that's it," Shawn said.

Meghan reached into her pocket and grabbed $100 worth of chips and handed it to him along with a key to the room. "Okay, we'll be upstairs. Room 1052."

An hour and a half later Shawn finally went up to the room. He had played, won a bit, then lost it all.

He slid the card key into the slot for room 1052, still holding his Grey Goose and cranberry drink from the bar. When he came in he saw Anna and Meghan lying there together, butt naked on the King-sized bed, asleep. Anna's head was resting on Meghan's stomach as if she had been down there for a while. It looked like they had started something but didn't quite finish, probably waiting for him to come in for a threesome.

He tiptoed into the room and quietly made his way to the couch. He put his phone on silent and then started texting Kay—he knew she'd probably be up late.

>*hey bae*
>>*what's up?*
>*down in ac for couple days*
>>*oh yea? you having fun*
>*yea, but down here with this rich white chick I met at school. she wilin*
>>*messing around with the white girls now huh lol*
>*well you know, she offered to pay for the trip. tryin to win me some money*
>>*how's that working out*

>not so good lol

>>well that's what u get, using that girl for her money

>she got money to burn. i ain't gonna say no

>>you a mess

>I think her and her friend was trynna do a 3some or something lol

>but I ain't fuckin around that's how they got kobe

>>lol

>when u coming back to philly

>>prob next week sometime. call me when you back in the city

> aiight. love you bae

>>love u too bro

By 2pm the next day Meghan and Anna were drunk again and back to the same tricks. Shawn walked paces behind them on the boardwalk as they drank from their water bottles filled with vodka and... more vodka. He was starting to feel like Driving Miss Daisy, escorting the two girls around everywhere.

When they got back to the hotel casino, Anna was stopped by one of the security guards, who asked her for identification because she looked too young for the casino floor and was very drunk. Anna tried to bribe the security guard by flashing one of her tits, which was a bad move.

Shawn immediately stepped away from them and called Kay, who picked up on the first ring.

"What's up bro?"

"Kay, help," he said and then laughed nervously.

"What, what's going on?" she asked.

"Still down here in Atlantic City with these white girls," he told her. "They acting a fool, gonna get me in some trouble!"

Kay just laughed at him.

"Kay I thought me and my boys were bad. These bitches is crazy!" Shawn said as he watched the security guard escort them both to the elevators. Meghan was getting loud and unruly about the whole thing—she was of age but Anna was not. "They see a black man with these two drunk young white girls you know who gonna take the heat."

"Look bro, lay low and stay away from them if you have to," Kay advised him seriously. "Just be cool. Be smart about it, you know. I ain't tryin' to come down to AC to bail your ass out."

"Alright I'll be smart. You got any cash though? I'm broke down," he admitted. "Lost all my money last night."

Kay sighed as she ran a few figures in her mind. "I can only spare like 50 bucks."

"Aiight, that's cool. Thanks bae," he said. "Can you wire it though?"

"Yea, but now it's like 40 bucks."

"Aiight let me know when it's there."

As promised, Kay wired him some money and he immediately went down to the casino to change them for some chips.

Within an hour Shawn had $300. It was like his luck had changed overnight. He played one more hand and won another $150. He was about to place another bet when his cellphone started buzzing. It was Kay.

He looked at the cell phone screen, then at the table, then back at the screen.

"Nah, I ain't gonna push my luck," he said, smiling to himself as he gathered his winnings and headed for the clerk to change them for cash. After that, he hopped on the express bus back to Philly without saying a word to Meghan.

Chapter 15
The Beginning of a Beautiful Friendship

"Top three," Bob the Barber said.

"Hmmmm... I'll take Rihanna, Halle Berry and Kim," young Mike commented.

"You putting a white girl in your top three Mike?" Bob asked.

"Well she bad. Yo SB what you think?" Mike asked.

"You can keep all the white chicks," Shawn replied, thinking about his crazy weekend with Meghan. "I'll take Gabrielle instead. I like me a nice chocolate sista."

"Word. And I seen some sistas down the way that would put *all* those Hollywood broads to shame," Bob commented. Shawn gave him a pound.

Shawn was in the barbershop getting a fresh shape-up. He was trying to look his best because Kay was due into town in a few hours. She had been hired for a new data entry job and was now earning enough to stay afloat with her bills. She and Shawn helped each other out—whenever one had a plus, so did the other.

"Yo Mike, when you start school?" Shawn asked him seriously. Mike had just turned 19 and had barely graduated high school.

Mike laughed as if Shawn had just told him a joke. "I ain't going to no school man. Done with that bullshit."

"So what the fuck you planning to do this year then?"

"I don't know, just hang out with the boys. Get me a couple big booty hos, you know!" Mike said.

"I know you ain't serious," Shawn said shaking his head. "Ya'll little niggas so smart ya stupid."

"What? I mean I can always go back to school later."

"You ever hear that saying, 'the idle mind's the devil's workshop'?"

"Naw."

"Young bul, that means you can't be hanging out on the streets all the damn time," Shawn explained. "Unless you want those streets to start hanging on *your* ass."

Mike nodded as he thought about it, then started making excuses. "Well I can't find no job though anyway."

"Drop the bullshit—you can get a job at your age. And even if you don't find a job you can go to school. Community college or those tech schools don't cost you nothin' when you get those school grants. You kids got all these benefits, but stay on some dumb shit. So smart ya stupid!"

"Ehh, I just really ain't feelin' school right now SB. But I'll think about it," Mike said with his mouth twisted up.

"Ay SB!"

Shawn looked up from his chair and saw one of his old heads, Lou, walking in.

"Lou." Shawn gave him a nod and Lou sat down to wait his turn.

"What's up young blood?"

"You getting' that reverse fade trimmed up today Lou?" Shawn teased and Bob the Barber chuckled.

"Keep laughin', you gonna be right here with me soon enough," Lou chuckled as he rubbed his bald head.

"Been asking 'bout you, they told me you started school," Lou commented. "That true?"

"Yea trynna get my shit together." Mike was listening—he didn't realize that Shawn was in school himself.

"I hear that. Ay SB, you know that nigga Huey still running off at the mouth 'bout you down the way right?" Lou said.

Shawn's expression didn't change. "Fuck that bitch ass nigga."

"Aiight, just wanted to let you know. You know that lil nigga don't got no damn sense," Lou put up his hand. "Just lookin' out for ya."

"Thanks," Shawn said as Bob brushed his shoulders off and removed his smock. "But I ain't thinking 'bout that pussy."

Shawn walked down the road toward Wilhemina's house looking so fresh and so clean with his shape-up. It was just starting to get dark outside. He had on one of the Polo shirts Meghan had bought him along with the new watch, a pair of dark khaki jeans and new chocolate brown Timberlands he bought with the money he had won in Atlantic City. It was starting to get chilly so he had picked up a black jacket as well.

In addition to the money he won that weekend, he finally got his check for his school refund. The first thing he did after cashing it was deposit $1,000 into Kay's account.

Shawn saw Cage pull up in front of Willie's house just as he turned the corner and made his way into the street towards the driver's side of Cage's truck.

Pop! Pop! Pop!

Gunshots rang out and Shawn immediately dove across the hood of the car right behind Cage's truck. He rolled over onto the other side and hit the ground. Bullets hit the side of the car and bust out one of the windows.

The car where the shots came from screeched down the street and turned the corner. Shawn didn't even have to see the occupants to know it was Huey or one of his people.

"SB, you aiight brotha?" Cage said and dashed around the back of his truck to help his friend up.

Shawn touched all over his body to check for bullet wounds. "Yea I'm good. Damn, they almost got me!"

"That nigga Huey?" Cage yelled as they both looked down the street in the direction the car went. They wanted to make sure they weren't planning on coming back.

"Probably," Shawn shook his head and then started laughing to release the nervous energy. It wasn't the first time he had escaped a bullet in his lifetime.

"Yo either they a bad shot or you made it out the matrix nigga, they was right on you," Cage said and looked troubled. "Bring your ass in the house, we gotta have a pow wow. Can't have them niggas busting off in front of my girl's house."

As they were heading to Cage's house Shawn's cellphone started ringing. At first he thought it might be Huey sending out some threats, so he got ready to go off. But when he looked at the screen he saw that it was Kay.

"Hey, where you at?" he said, trying to sound calm.

"Coming down that way in about an hour. You want me to pick you up?"

"Yea come get me now. I'm down at Cage's girl's crib," he said, trying to maintain his cool while watching his back as he went into the house.

"Okay, I'll be there soon. Oh and I saw that deposit you made today, thank you bro!"

Shawn hated it when Kay called him "bro" as in her brother. He knew she was only doing it to make it clear that they weren't together in a relationship anymore.

"You're welcome Kay, see you soon."

* * *

"Hey check out that moon," Kay said with a smirk as she pointed up at the sky. As soon as he looked up she switched beers with him, giving him the empty and taking his fresh cold one.

"Oh you think you slick huh?" he said, catching her red-handed. But still he let her have it.

They were sitting out on the porch, relaxing, talking and drinking Yuengling beers as they liked to do often on a nice quiet night at home when they were together. They talked about everything from Shawn's sometimes strained relationship with his kids to the trip they both wanted to take to Europe to see Amsterdam. Shawn was a world traveler because of his time in the military.

Shawn went into the house and retrieved another beer. When he came back he looked at Kay for a while.

"Niggas was shooting at me bae," he blurted.

"What??" Kay said and sat up straight, almost dropping her beer. "Who? When?"

"Earlier today. I got an idea who, but they ain't get me, I did my Charlie Brown on 'em. They couldn't touch me. I'm God's son!" Shawn said with a laugh and a smile. He didn't want to alarm Kay but he felt as if he should warn her about these things so that she would be prepared if something did happen to him.

"It's not funny Shawn." Kay was not amused. "Why don't you just stay up here at the house and stop fucking around!"

Shawn rolled his eyes but inside he was happy that she cared enough to get that angry.

"I told you Kayby, I don't run from my problems. I'll be aiight," he assured her, even though he wasn't really sure himself. He knew this was all probably far from over.

Kay shook her head and put her forehead in her hand. "There's always something new with you Shawn. I wish you would stay in the house."

"I shouldn't have even told you," Shawn said, feeling a strange mixture of delight and regret at her distressed reaction.

She looked over at him and a tear rolled down her cheek.

"You crying?" Shawn said and started to chuckle. His phone rang and he immediately hit reject when he saw it was Meghan calling. He then shut the phone down completely. "Aw girl. Cut that shit out."

"No, I'm just concerned about you! Shut up," Kay said and wiped her face. "It's not funny."

"I know I know. But don't worry bae. Brothers only get killed over money and trifling women. Right now I don't got neither," he schooled her.

Kay didn't look convinced.

"I have to be up here more because of school now anyways."

Kay was a little relieved. "How's that going?"

"Doing good on all my assignments, but I can't miss no more days," he explained.

"How many did you miss already?"

"Too many."

"Come on bro, you gotta do better!"

"I'm trying but I don't really like going there no more."

"Why not?"

"Them young girls be getting on my nerves bae! Ain't too many thorough ass niggas like me that go to that school and they on a nigga," Shawn explained. "I ain't even trynna sound conceited, but they on my dick!"

"I believe you," Kay nodded. Shawn was good-looking and knew how to talk to women. "But Shawn that still isn't an excuse to not go to school."

"I know baby. And I'm trying to make an example for my sons now. How can I tell them to do right when I'm still in these streets myself?"

"Right. They need to see you doing something positive with your life brother."

Brother. There goes that brother shit again, he thought. Shawn sighed and guzzled down his beer, except for the last swallow. He never drank a beer down to the very bottom. They sat for a while in silence, caught up in their own thoughts.

"Kay, I been thinking a lot about our relationship."

"Oh yea?"

"You know I put you on that pedestal as one of the greats in my life. But by me walking in your shadows all those years made me lazy," he started to pour out his thoughts. The more he drank the more he liked to talk, even though Kay didn't always know what he was talking about.

"You used to complain 'what kind of man are you sleeping all day and running the streets all night?' And as usual you made a good point. I try not to make the same mistakes now so I became a morning person. I'm trying to break that cycle of thinking for myself."

"Yea I noticed you're up early in the morning more these days, texting me," Kay said with a smile.

"If I'm not healthy and feeling uplifted within myself what kind of man can I be to a friend or family member?"

Kay nodded and listened.

"You know I never told you this, but I heard you crying one night asking God 'Why?? Why did I get mixed up with this dude?' It made me mad, but now I kinda understand where you were coming from."

"When was that?"

"It don't matter. When we met you gave me a rating from A to F like you was grading me. I always been a good student and so you kept me around. But I ask still to this day what you thought about me? What you seen in me? It's a thin line between slavery and freedom, love and hate."

Kay didn't answer because she wasn't really sure what he was talking about. The more he drank the more he started to talk in riddles. She could tell he had a lot on his mind that he had to get it off.

"Don't get me wrong, I really don't want to know! I got my own problems right now and this drink will only make it worse," he continued.

Damn, I gave her an exit and she didn't take it, Shawn thought. *She didn't agree. There's still a chance. But she still ain't told me what she really thinks about me yet. Damn, she's good! Playing it cool. Even when I try to play it off she wins. But trust me I'm gone play this shit to the end like Chucky!*

"Kay, I used to come home at night to get up early to go to work, have a drink, something to eat not in that order. I was trying to be responsible," Shawn went on. "But I feel like you were pushing my buttons on purpose."

That rubbed Kay the wrong way. "I was pushing *your* buttons? How, by asking you not to come in the house at seven in the morning? A woman can only take so much Shawn."

"You gotta be fuckin' kiddin' me! So that's why you left me? Why do you always act like I was stagnating you or something? You know what? I feel like everybody just be taking my kindness for weakness," Shawn suddenly snapped back and Kay could sense that his attitude was starting to change.

"Because you were Shawn. I had goals in my life and it's hard to accomplish them when you're fighting with somebody all the time," Kay started to get annoyed and started to collect her things as if she wanted to leave the porch.

Damn... Shawn asked himself as he watched her snatch her beer and head for the front door. *What the fuck just happened that fast?* He was trying to stay cool for once in his life. He didn't want to run her off again. But he didn't know how to say what he really wanted to say. Kay was on some "when a woman's fed up" shit and if he wasn't careful she was going to be gone from his life for good soon.

Shawn, you so smart you stupid, he thought.

"Baby, baby," Shawn said as he followed her into house. "You right. I'm sorry, I'll shut up. Give me a hug."

Shawn opened his arms up wide and waited for Kay to come make peace. She looked at him peculiarly, wondering if this was some kind of trick, and then finally got up from her seat on the couch and gave him a hug. When they finally let go Kay grabbed his arm and turned it up so that he could see his "Real Nigga" tattoo. Then she looked up into his eyes.

"Shawn, this isn't you. 'Niggas' don't accomplish anything in life. You ain't a nigga, so stop playing the part. You're a real man, act like it."

Shawn thought about what she said as he watched her flop down on the couch to watch TV.

"Well a real man need a real woman by his side," he finally answered and sat down next to her. He put his arm around her and she settled back into his chest.

They sat together in peace and flipped through the channels, drinking their beers. Kay stopped when she saw an old Biggie Smalls video playing on the music channel.

"It was all a dream. I used to read *Word Up* magazine! Salt 'n Pepa and Heavy D up in the limousine..." she started rapping along.

Shawn sat there in awe as he listened to Kay recite every

word to *Juicy* without messing up once. Even he didn't know all the lyrics and it was one of his favorite songs.

"How you know all that?" he asked her. Kay looked up at him and laughed at his expression.

"I've been with you for over four years and you really don't know much about me do you? I'm from New York, I grew up on Junior Mafia and real hip hop. Not this new school bullshit," she said. "Do you really think I lived in a bubble before I met you or something?"

It was so strange to Shawn that there was so much he was learning about Kay every day since she left him. They had been living together for four whole years and didn't really know much about each other. Only now were they starting to really bond.

More and more each day he was starting to realize that he really was in love with this girl.

Chapter 16
Stalkers

"Shawn! Why this girl coming up to my house?" his mother demanded.

"What you talking about ma," Shawn asked groggily.

"This little girl come up to my house asking where you at. Boy I'm telling you, you better check her before I do!" she told him. "And you know your sister will drag her up and down the block, we don't *even* play that!"

"What girl, what's her name?"

"I don't know Brenda, Betty or something…"

"Blake?"

"Yea, that's it! She came up here asking where you at. I told her she best to step right up off my porch!"

"Sorry 'bout that ma, I'll handle it," Shawn said shaking his head. He had a feeling it was a bad idea bringing Blake up to his mom's house on the first date. He liked her at first but now she was becoming a pain like all the other girls he had dated. She was desperate, calling his phone ten times a day even though he hardly ever answered.

"Where's Kay at?" his mother asked. Shawn hadn't told her that they split up yet. Rhonda had bumped heads with Kay a few times in the past when she first started dating Shawn, but as time went on they became close.

"She's chilling, why?"

"You haven't brought her by here in a while, ya'll doing okay?"

"We doin' fine ma, why you all in my business?"

"Shawn you ain't too old to get slapped all upside your head! I'm hanging up the phone."

It was a good thing Shawn's mother called when she did because he had to get up to make his first class for the day. He had already been withdrawn from his 9am class and was at risk for being dropped from his 10:50am class, but his teacher had tentatively agreed to let him stay in the class if he did extra credit.

When he arrived at school he took the side entrance, hoping to avoid Meghan or any of the other people who seemed to look forward to seeing him whenever he came into the building. It was like high school. If it wasn't Meghan or Blake it was somebody asking him to hook him up with some weed. He was already about five minutes late to his class and couldn't spend any time chatting with folks.

He sat in class and took down notes carefully. He knew he had to do well on the next few assignments or he was toast. At the end of the period, he put his notebook away and grabbed his book bag to leave.

"Mr. Karlson," his teacher called to him before he had a chance to leave the room.

"Yes," he answered as he walked up to her desk.

"Mr. Karlson, you were late this morning. That makes three latenesses and two missed classes. Technically I should drop you today."

"But you told me I could do extra credit."

"Yes, but extra credit will only help you so much."

"Ms. Roberts, I need this class to keep my GI bill active."

"Then you need to be here on time every day for the rest of the semester," she replied. "If you miss one more day it's an automatic drop. I'm just letting you know."

Shawn nodded his head solemnly and left the room, grinding his teeth. He could already tell there would be a problem in the future because he had an upcoming child support court hearing and it was almost impossible to move those dates.

"Shawn!"

He tried to keep walking to door, hoping to escape the inevitable. He could tell by the whiny voice that it was Meghan. She didn't even have a class on that day but would come up to the school trying to socialize with people and see him. She was a stalker.

"Shawn! I know you hear me," Meghan said again. "Talk to me!"

Shawn reluctantly stopped and turned around to face her. She tried to kiss him on the lips but he turned and it hit his cheek.

"Why do I feel like you're trying to avoid me since Atlantic City?" she asked.

"Naw, nothing like that," Shawn lied. "Just been busy is all."

"Well make time for me. Take me out to a bar tonight! It can be somewhere close to you," she asked.

"Can't. I got homework."

"Fuck homework, take me out!" Meghan demanded and stomped her foot like a child.

"Nope, not gon' be able to do it!" he said definitively.

"What is it really? That black bitch that you're seeing?"

"Wait, hol, hol, hol," Shawn said and shook his palm in her face. "Hold up! You way out of line Becky Sue. First of all, I don't have to explain nothin' to your monkey ass!"

"Oh but you can take my gifts and my money though right?"

"I don't need your little trinkets. That's your stupid ass

fault for givin' em to me," Shawn said and felt himself about to blank out.

"So then give them back then!"

"Give 'em back?? Why you little yuck mouth bitch..." Shawn started to go off but then caught himself and bit his bottom lip as he looked around the halls. The last thing he needed was for this white girl to turn on him and have him locked up. She could claim any number of things and those cops out in the suburbs wouldn't even care what his side of the story was. He would be sitting right in jail.

"I'll call you," he lied and left her standing there. He saw a white guy from one of his classes coming down the hall, slapped hands with him and started a conversation with him as he left the building to ensure that Meghan didn't come after him. If she did at least he'd have a witness. He was going to have to work overtime dodging her from here on out.

Chapter 17
Doin' Too Much

A couple of months after receiving his financial aid refund, Shawn was already flirting with broke again. He was down to about $100 and feeling like he might have to get back on his hustle if a job opportunity didn't come up soon. There was one thing he did right though—he had used some of his refund money to buy gifts for his kids and put them up for the upcoming holidays.

Blake called while he was walking his daughter home from school one afternoon and he finally decided to pick up the phone. Blake was happy to hear his voice.

"Don't be going to my mom's house no more," Shawn scolded her as he pushed Mya in the swings. "I'm only gonna warn you once."

"Shawn I'm so sorry, I didn't know, honest!" she exclaimed, playing the innocent role. "Let me make it up to you? Let me treat you to Chickie's & Peete's!"

When Shawn thought about getting down on some crabs, crab fries and shrimp at his favorite restaurant his mouth started watering and the next thing he knew he was telling Blake where to come pick him up in an hour.

"I've been thinking about you a lot," Blake said as she watched Shawn devour his meal. Shawn just nodded and took a sip of his beer before diving back in.

"You been thinking about me?" she asked.

"Excuse me boss," Shawn said to their waiter as he came around their area. "Some more tartar sauce."

"So I was thinking..." Blake said slowly. "Maybe we could go back to my place after this."

Shawn looked up at her and watched as she licked the rim of her fresh Corona seductively. Then she put her lips over the mouth of the bottle and sucked the lime up out of the opening. Shawn was turned on by the display and started to get a little excited, but he was also a little embarrassed. He looked around to see if anyone had seen her do that.

While he was glancing around, Blake slid her fork off the table in their booth and made sure that it hit the floor.

"Ooops!" she exclaimed. "Shawn can you please do me a favor and grab my fork? It fell under the table."

Shawn looked at her curiously. "I'll just get them to bring you a new one. Excuse me—"

"No, I *really* want that one. Please?" she begged. Shawn looked confused, but shook his head and maneuvered his way under the table.

The fork was way over on the other side next to Blake's leg, but that was the last thing his attention was focused on. He was more interested in the sight of her legs cocked wide open. She had a little skirt on and she wasn't wearing any panties.

As soon as Blake had Shawn in her small dorm apartment she started taking off the rest of her clothes. She had a nice body—Shawn could tell that she worked out regularly. Once she was completely naked she turned on some music and started to do a little booty dance in the middle of her tiny living room-dining room. Shawn laughed, took off his t-shirt and sat on her couch.

"You like that?" she said and bent over to give him a better view. Shawn nodded and smiled.

When the song was over Blake walked over to him and knelt between his legs. She unzipped him and started pleasuring him. After a while he finally pulled her up from his lap and lifted her up from her knees. He pushed her head down onto the small dining room table across the room.

A thought crossed his mind that made him pull out his wallet to retrieve the condom he kept there. He put it on carefully and then grasped Blake by her hips tightly. As soon as he started going to work, she started yelping out loudly like a scared pig. Shawn was certain her neighbors down the hall and around the corner probably heard—she would be the talk of the dorm the next morning.

* * *

Tino was celebrating news that he had a third child on the way with Elisha. He offered to buy his boys drinks all night, which wasn't a big deal since it was $2 Tuesday at the bar. Besides Cage and Shawn, Ron—who was at the bar when they arrived—managed to weasel his way over to them. They were doing shots and having a good time as usual.

"Beezy. Why the fuck you wearing those dark sunglasses inside the bar?" Tino asked.

Shawn didn't answer—he just took a sip of his free Hennessey and smacked his lips. His phone started vibrating in his pocket and he pulled it out to do a quick check. Blake's name flashed boldly across the screen. He pressed the reject button immediately.

"Who's Blake?" Cage asked, being nosy.

"That broad from school," Shawn answered shortly.

"Oh yea? I thought you said she was fine, wifey material?"

"Yea she aiight but I ain't really feelin' her like that," Shawn shook his head.

"Why not, she holdin' out on you?" Tino asked.

"Naw, the opposite. She gave it up too easy. That broad took off her panties and flashed me in public," Shawn said as he shook his head. Tino and Cage ooohed and slapped their hands on the bar loudly.

"So what's the problem!" Cage wanted to know.

"I like a girl who's sexy and freaky, but that's something you keep for your man you know? What if someone saw her?" Shawn explained. "She smart but wanna act like a ho. She doin' too much. So smart she stupid!"

By the end of the night Shawn was gone, tore up off the Hennessey shots Tino was buying all night. He stumbled his way out onto the block clutching his cellphone, walking toward a small gathering near Cage's house with his boys and Ron. He saw 10 missed calls; a couple from his boys and the rest from Blake and Meghan. Seeing not one call from Kay prompted him to call her. It went right to voicemail, enraging him even more. Although they got along for the most part those days, when he got very drunk and thought about her possibly being with another man he flipped out.

"So you just gonna send a nigga right to voicemail. You ain't shit! I bet you out there fucking with some baby huey looking college boy motherfucker. Ya'll deserve each other! Stanking ass bitch! Acting like your shit don't stink! I lived with you for four years I know it do!"

He would have kept rambling but got cut off. He had been calling and leaving similar messages on her voicemail all night.

The phone rang just as he was about to write Kay a nasty text message and he accidentally pressed the "Answer" button.

It was Blake.

"What!"

"Shawn, hey! I've been trying to get in touch with you all day, where are you?" she asked.

"I'm busy mindin' my bizness!" he told her as he tried to walk a straight line.

"Doing what? Can you come over tonight? I'll come pick you up," Blake offered. It was one o'clock in the morning.

"Girl I'll speak to you later," Shawn said and was about to hang up.

"Are you fucking other girls Shawn? Just tell me!" Blake shouted and all she heard was Shawn talking to someone in the background. "Man! I can't stand brothas like you, always trying to dog a sista out!"

Shawn heard her yelling and put the phone back to his ear. "Yo chill, I said I'll speak to you later. Bye."

"Don't bother! You fucking asshole! I can't believe I gave it up to you!" Blake screamed and started crying.

"Don't blame me, blame your hot puss!" Shawn shouted back at her. He was tired of girls acting like hoes then getting upset when they were treated like it.

"Please! Your dick game wasn't even all that!" she shouted.

"Bitch it must have been the best you ever had the way you been blowin' up my phone all fucking day. Get a life!"

"Now I'm a bitch? Oh ok. That's why niggas like you will never have shit and never be shit! Fuck you!" Blake shouted and then hung up.

"Fuck you too! Deuces!!" he shouted into the receiver and shook his head. "These fucking broads!"

"Man, they a trip," Cage said. Tino was a few steps ahead on the phone with his wife telling her his plans. Ron, as usual, was quiet and listening.

A few minutes later Shawn's phone rang again and lo and behold it was Meghan. *Damn, these young girls are really pressed,* he thought and hit the reject button immediately. When it rang again literally one minute later, he was all set to let Meghan have it over the phone too. But it was Les calling.

"What's up my nigga," Shawn said, putting him on speakerphone.

"SB, what up," Les said. "Look just wanted to give you a heads up. That nigga Huey down here at the Mirage talking all kinda reckless. He said he gonna hunt you down tonight."

"Tell that pussy come on then! And he don't have to drive by like a little bitch this time, come see me in person! Tell 'im come down the spot on Girard in 15 minutes, I'll be waiting," Shawn said emphatically as he picked up his pace. He had still been feeling that angry energy ever since Kay left and was finally ready to do something real stupid.

"Aiight, I'll tell 'im."

As soon as Shawn hung up with Les, the phone started ringing again—it was Meghan, yet again. This time, heated, he picked it up on the first ring.

"Bitch! If you don't fuckin' stop calling my number Imma give you something to call home about!" he yelled and then threw his cellphone down on the ground. It broke into several pieces. He stomped on it a few more times to make sure that it was dead.

Cage shook his head at the news—he already knew Shawn was talking about Huey. He got mentally prepared for some shit to go down. They had been talking about what they were going to do about Huey for a while and they would have to make a stand or it would only get worse.

"Ya'll stay up," Ron said, trying to pretend like he had been on the phone and didn't know what was going on. He put his hand up as he turned the corner sharply. "My baby momma been trippin' lately." Nobody paid him any mind.

"Yo lemme go get my piece from the crib," Cage said after some thought and they all went separate ways. "I'll meet ya'll there in a few minutes."

"Imma call Lift," Tino said and grabbed his phone. His mind flashed to his family for a moment but he shook it off, knowing that he couldn't abandon his friends. Deep down he knew that he had to eventually leave them alone if he was truly going to put his family first if they continued to attract drama.

Tino, Cage, Lift and Shawn were sitting in Cage's truck down the street from the place where a small gathering was going on, smoking cigarettes and getting hyped up. They were all strapped and ready.

"That lil' pussy gonna wish he never went to that party at all," Lift said nonchalantly as he felt for his glock. He loved drama and he was like a ghost when he did his dirt. He'd disappear and nobody knew where he went. Lift had no real loyalties to anyone on the streets, but he had respect for Shawn and his crew. On more than one occasion Shawn had stepped up when others stepped back.

"Can't stand these niggas, catching feelings over the most minor shit!" Shawn commented as he smoked his third cigarette in 10 minutes. He had sobered up really quick. "This nigga wanna shoot somebody cause he couldn't get in a fucking birthday party! Who do that?"

30 minutes later there still wasn't any sign of Huey or his boys. An hour later they finally decided to go into the gathering—Huey was a no-show.

* * *

154

"You know they probably gonna have a team of niggas up there already waiting," Huey's cousin Rick commented, but was really giving him a casual warning.

"I don't give a fuck, I got my team too," Huey told him. "Unless you want to bitch up now?"

"Fuck you nigga. When have I ever sat anything out?" Rick said, sounding insulted. "Here take this shit."

They were sitting inside of Huey's Impala doing an inventory of the weapons they had on them. Huey was high off of coke and had smoked some wet with Rick. Huey's other cousin Bennie was in the back looking like he was having serious second thoughts.

"Fuck wrong with you? Here B, take this shit," Huey said and threw an old dusty gun into the back seat. Bennie didn't touch it. Huey held a Crown Royal sack full of bullets back for Bennie to load up.

"I 'oun know 'bout this Huey. You know I'm on probation, they catch my ass with a gun, even if it's just in the car, I'm back in the clink, 10 years," Bennie shook his head.

Huey turned to look back at his cousin like the girl from *The Exorcist*. "So what are you trying to say?"

"I'm saying, you need to chill out and just let this shit go cuz!"

"Let it go? Nigga I never let shit go! *And* he challenged me? Naw, that nigga goin' down tonight!" Huey declared.

"Over a fucking party though?" Bennie asked, starting to get angry. "You gonna make me risk my fuckin' freedom over an argument about getting into somebody birthday party?"

"I can't believe this nigga!" Huey was amazed. "You really gonna front on your cousin for SB sake? That nigga's an asshole. Knowing how he roll he probably got a price on his head. If I get 'im might even get paid off this shit!"

"I 'oun care, that ain't no shit to go poppin' off over. We already went for 'im and he made it. He got the point, just dead this shit cuz!" Bennie reasoned.

"Nigga get the fuck out my car," Huey said.

"Yo Hue! Come on! Just dead this shit!" Bennie said as he leaned forward in his seat.

Huey pointed his gun right at Bennie's forehead. "I said get the fuck out my car bitch before I dead *you*!"

Bennie frowned, stunned that his cousin would go to those lengths. He leaned back and got out of the car without saying another word. Huey screeched off down the road barely giving him time to shut the door.

"Can you believe that nigga?" Huey said as he clutched the gun in his lap. He bobbed back and forth in his seat impatiently—he couldn't sit still.

"Yea, but hey what you gonna do," Rick commented.

"Fuck that nigga. Where Les say he's at? 12th?"

"Naw round 10th I think ," Rick said as he pointed. Huey darted over to make a turn on 9th street but didn't see the red pickup truck barreling down the other lane trying to make the light. The truck slammed into the back of Huey's Impala causing him to jump the curve and hit a pole.

A police cruiser sitting at the end of the block saw the whole thing.

* * *

Shawn and his boys had waited all night at the house party for Huey to arrive, but he never did. They found out the next day that he had been in an accident that killed his cousin Rick—Rick flew right through the windshield to his instant death. Huey survived but was locked up on illegal weapons possession charges. He was likely to do five to 10 years in jail.

Shawn was just glad he didn't have to put his boys into a precarious situation, but yet again they proved to him that they would ride for him if necessary. Those were his partners for real.

Ironically, the next day Shawn was up bright and early to go to school. Even though he only had about three hours of sleep, he arrived right on time for his class and found out that he had aced his paper. He worked well when under pressure.

As he walked out of the class looking at the huge A in red across the top and feeling accomplished, he didn't notice Meghan standing right next to the door, waiting.

"So I'm a bitch now huh!" she said getting up in his face and trying to sound "gangster."

"Little girl! If you don't get out my face," Shawn said and kept strolling down the hallway.

"I heard you fucked that bitch Blake!" Meghan shouted. "So you chose her over me?? You're with her now??"

"Who told you that?" Shawn shook his head and kept walking. He felt like he was back in high school dealing with these people.

"My friend Josie saw you go into her dorm room," Meghan revealed as she kept walking beside him.

"Well, your friend Josie a damn liar," Shawn lied as he pushed the door open and went outside. "But even if I did do it, one thing for sure and two things for certain, it ain't nonna *your* fucking business."

"Shawn, what's the problem? Don't you like me?" Meghan asked him seriously. "Come with me, I can take you home."

"Meghan, you a nice girl and all, but I ain't trying to date nobody right now," he told her as she continued to follow him out of the lot toward the bus stop. He started to get a little nervous as people started to stare.

"We don't have to date, we could just fuck! I'm fine with that!"

"Naw, go on and find you a college dude for all that. You too young for me," Shawn said as he looked side to side before crossing the busy road.

"I'm 21 years old!" Meghan pleaded. "You let Blake fuck you but not me and she's my age. Why, is it because I'm not black or something? Do you only fuck black girls!?"

"Go home Meghan."

Shawn made a dash across the road when it was somewhat clear. Meghan followed him and almost got hit by a car because she wasn't even looking.

"What the hell is wrong with you girl?" Shawn shouted as he jerked her by her hand out of harm's way.

"See, I knew you cared about me!" she exclaimed as she let him lead her safely across the street.

"Stop fucking around and go home."

"Please Shawn, just give me a chance!"

Shawn stood there and just listened to Meghan go on and on about how good she was in the bedroom and how white girls "do it better." She didn't even realize that she was turning him off more and more with every word. She probably really got around. Finally Shawn saw the bus coming down the road about a mile away. Meghan saw it too and her mind started to go a mile a minute.

"Shawn I know you're not going to just get on that bus and leave me…I want you to fuck me just like you fucked that black chick!" she said with a crazed look in her eyes. Shawn just shook his head at her.

Suddenly she jumped into his arms with her legs straddled over his torso and started kissing him all over his face and neck. She roughly dug into his pants and tried to grab his penis.

Shawn pulled her hand out and unraveled her legs from his body as he pushed her away. She fell backwards and almost hit her head on the concrete.

"Owww! Shawn why'd you do that!" Meghan screamed just as the bus pulled up. Shawn ran his hand over his head to wipe away some of the sweat that was forming.

"Girl you gonna get me in trouble!"

The driver hesitated to open the door and Shawn had to knock to get him to do so. The last thing he wanted was to be caught up there by the police tussling with a sex-crazed blonde girl in the middle of the street.

The driver finally let Shawn on. Meghan got up from the sidewalk and tried to follow behind him.

"Don't let her on boss, she trippin'," Shawn said to him in low tones before moving to the back of the bus. He had never been so happy to see another brother.

"No miss, sorry but I can't let you on," the black male driver told Meghan as he shook his head and held out his hand to stop her.

"Why not?? I have money so I can ride any bus I want!" Meghan shouted back.

"Because I saw you attack that young man and I don't allow fighting on my bus."

"You didn't see shit!" Meghan shouted. "If you don't let me on I'm going to call SEPTA and have you fired! I have your bus number."

"Do what you need to do miss," the driver said nonchalantly and started to pull off. Meghan had no choice but to back up. He closed the doors when it was finally clear.

* * *

Tisha's cousin Joy was at home, as usual, sitting in the window holding a glass of wine, waiting for her husband Travis to get home. Travis worked on Wall Street in the city, which is why they were able to afford such a nice home in New Jersey.

Joy just knew she had hit the jackpot when she met Travis two years before. They had a whirlwind romance and within just a year they were engaged. Six months later they were married. She didn't have to work and spent the majority of her day making their home comfortable. She knew that she was the envy of all her friends and loved the simple thought of it.

But now she wasn't so sure about her "catch." Travis would leave her at home alone well into the night, sometimes overnight, staying in the city. It was rare they even had a weekend together, as he was usually making some excuse to go to the office.

Joy sighed and picked up her phone to send him a text.

Will you be home tonight? she asked politely, trying not to nag.

Twenty minutes later she still didn't have an answer.

Joy woke up from her slumber when lights appeared in the driveway. She had fallen asleep on the couch waiting for Travis to show up. She checked the clock and it read 12:34. She quickly got up from the couch to check her face and hair in the mirror in the hallway before going to the door. As she opened the door Travis was walking up the steps.

"Hey baby," she said with a big smile. He looked up and didn't say hi back.

"What are you still doing up?" he asked shortly as he brushed by her with barely a kiss on the cheek. He smelled of gin.

"I was waiting for you. Didn't you get my text?"

"No."

Joy followed him up the stairs to their bedroom.

"You know you don't have to wait up for me every night. Just get some sleep. I know you have sooo much to do during the day," he said sarcastically.

Joy bristled at the insult but didn't bite back. "I just want to make sure my man is alright, that's all."

Travis went right into the bathroom, shut and locked the door. Joy sat on the edge of the bed and started to strip down. As she did, Travis' cellphone started to go off in his jacket, which he had left hanging on the chair.

Travis shot out of the bathroom, butt naked and clutching a towel, in a flash to go for his phone.

"Oh, it's my partner Will. I need some privacy," he said as left the bedroom just as fast. Joy looked behind him curiously.

She got up from her seat and went to the bathroom to do her nightly rituals before going to bed. As she brushed her teeth, she glanced over and saw Will's pants, shirt and socks on the floor. Minding her housewife duties, she put her brush down and immediately went to clean up after him.

She pulled his clothes apart to separate them into the white and colored hamper. His tightie whities were inside of the pants. When she pulled them out she noticed something red on the back part—it looked like traces of blood.

She was a little concerned but didn't think much of it. *Maybe he had a tough bowel movement*, she reasoned.

Later that evening as they both finally lay in bed, Travis with his back to her as usual and no physical contact, the thought of the blood in his underwear returned to her mind. As she was caught in deep thought and finally about to drift off to sleep, Travis let out a strange hollow-sounding fart that was loud enough to wake her back up.

Chapter 18
Be Safe and Smart

It had been over a year since Kay left and Shawn was starting to accept his new life without her as his fiancé. But they had somehow become the best of friends instead.

He dated a couple of young girls from the neighborhood and colleges nearby but they were so full of drama that he couldn't take it for long. He had been spoiled with a quiet hardworking woman for four years but didn't value the serenity of the situation until it was gone. He found out that the last young girl he messed with had been whoring around both in the neighborhood and on her college campus down at Temple for a long while before they met. He was embarrassed and disgusted.

Somehow he had managed to complete two full semesters of school and was already enrolled in the third. Ironically it was Meghan and Blake who ended up dropping out of school because they were too busy chasing boys to focus on their studies.

Shawn was in the bar hanging with Cage late one night. As was becoming usual, he had on his trademark dark sunglasses and refused to take them off. He knew it bothered people, which was why he kept doing it.

"I'm done with women," Shawn said and shook his head as he took his last shot with Cage. He was feeling tipsy and in the mood to talk.

"Yea right. I bet if Kay come back right now you'd change your mind," Cage teased and laughed. "You a sucka for love nigga."

"Fuck you Cage," Shawn said. But he couldn't deny that his friend was right. Even though he had been dating someone for a couple of months, he was still waiting for Kay to come back.

"Some of these chicks always got gossip, calling themselves a woman of God but stay drinkin' that malt liquor wine. Anything goes after three malt liquor wines."

"Nigga what you talking 'bout now."

"Every time I fuck with a new chick seems like she got some little friend in her ear talking shit. Fucking drunk, gossiping bird brain broads."

"Yea okay, I feel you."

"Don't ever invite a gossiping drunk bitch to drink with you, shit! They will be your best friend for life as long as you got that bottle!"

Cage just laughed.

"Bitch be like the genie in the bottle. Just open up a bottle and here she come, popping up from anywhere with some gossip to tell… 'Hey girl, what you need to know?'"

"Nigga you a fuckin' fool!" Cage said with a laugh. "Genie in the bottle bitches!"

"Yea leave those genie in a bottle bitches alone! Shit they even talk in code… 'hey girl am tired girl,'" Shawn went on. "That's code for you running out of malt liquor wine and I'm running out of things to tell you!"

"Ha! Tell me about it."

"She like 'got drink? Shit then I got some shit to tell you girllll'. Cock blocking ass broads!"

"Damn man, sound like you been through it lately. That's what happens when you fuck around with the young broads," Cage said as he took one last swig of his beer. "Look dog, Imma take my ass in the house early tonight. I think I'm in the dog house for some reason."

"You sound like a genie in the bottle nigga right now," Shawn said as he slapped hands with his best friend.

"Except you ain't paid for none of my drinks muthafucka," Cage said as he was walking away. "I don't got to tell you shit."

As soon as he got out of ear shot of Cage he called Kay and then started walking out of the bar himself.

She picked up after a couple of rings.

"Hey bro, how ya doing?" she asked.

"Alright, thinking 'bout you."

"Oh yea, something good or bad? Last message I got from you was a doozy!"

"That wasn't me."

"Right... you want to hear it and tell me who it was then?"

"I miss you," he said.

"I miss you too."

"So why don't you come home."

"You know why Shawn."

"No, tell me."

"I can't go all into that now. I'm on the train."

"Train to where?"

"Going out with my friends."

Whenever Shawn heard that it made him jealous and insecure. He knew she was out there meeting new guys and starting a new life. He didn't like it.

"Fine. Go out there tonight and fuck 100 niggas if you want, I don't give a fuck no more. You got my blessings," he said with an attitude and hung up in her face.

A few moments later he tried to call her back but it went to voicemail. He tried again and it went to voicemail again. He left another ignorant message until he was finally cut off. Just as he was about to try her again, he got a text message from her.

shutting down my phone. I love you bro, please be safe and smart.

Be safe and smart.

Kay always told him that. As he walked to the gas station down the dark block on his way to the El smoking a cigarette Shawn thought about how many times he had escaped death while running those cold Philly streets. The first time was when he was 15—he almost got caught in the crossfire while out hanging with the neighborhood hustlers. The second time was when he first started out hardcore slanging himself, after leaving the military. A rival group of drug dealers decided they didn't like the new competition in the neighborhood and shot at the store. After that a string of close-call incidents occurred that left Shawn feeling a little bit like the Miracle Man. But his mindset was starting to change. He wanted to get completely out of harm's way and live a different kind of life.

At the same time he knew he needed money. He needed to provide for his kids. He was always applying for jobs but nothing came back. His refund had been lighter that semester and ran out quickly. With the holidays coming up soon he felt like crap knowing that he probably wouldn't have the funds to give them everything they wanted. Just like that he started thinking about going back to the streets and selling drugs again, at least for a little while.

As Shawn turned the corner leading to the gas station he saw a couple of hooded figures lurking nearby in the darkness. One was drinking a 40 ounce bottle of Steel Reserve. When they saw him they became quiet and started to watch him. Shawn took note of them but kept walking down the block toward his destination.

He started to sense that they were following him and glanced back briefly to check. They were.

Shawn threw his cigarette down on the sidewalk and pulled up his jeans, getting ready to act if necessary.

As he predicted, one of them advanced on him quickly and tried to bash the beer bottle over his head but it hit his shoulder blade instead. Shawn was shaken but had been prepared to get hit and stayed steady. He turned around and immediately started swinging.

He hit the first hooded figure with a few body shots and then a cold cock to the forehead. He dropped him. The other one seemed a little surprised when he saw his boy get laid out on the ground so quickly and started using the broken beer bottle as a weapon. He stabbed Shawn in the stomach and the chest as fast as he could—Shawn grabbed his arm to stop him but he was kind of strong and managed to get a few more stabs in. Bleeding and feeling weak, Shawn twisted the stabber's arm and tried to get him to drop the bottle. The first attacker finally got back up and jumped on Shawn's back. By then Shawn could tell that these were two young kids, probably no more than 18. As he struggled to get the first young dude off his back, the other one started stabbing him again in rapid succession.

Shawn fell backwards, causing the one on his back to hit his head hard on the sidewalk.

"Go in his pockets!" The one on his back shouted and the stabber did so quickly before Shawn had a chance to get back up. Shawn was losing a lot of blood from his chest but still managed to get his footing and swing on the stabber again—he laid him out on the ground with a left jab and a right uppercut to the chin.

The stabber dropped Shawn's wallet but the other guy picked it up and ran. Shawn tried to run after him but was too weak at that point. The stabber rolled over a few times but then got his footing and made off in the other direction.

Shawn staggered his way down the block closer to the lights of the gas station. When someone saw him bleeding through his white tee and asking for help they called an ambulance. He finally collapsed to the ground.

Part III - Changes

Chapter 19
Miracle Man

Dear Jerome

It's me, your son Shawn, remember me?

Jerome! Jerome! I know you hear me! You can ignore me all you want, but I ain't no mistake.

See I am not like you, I am gonna calm myself down.

"High blood pressure is a bitch"—that was your favorite line to get out of trouble.

I am gonna chill out, I know what you're trying to do. You think you're slick, you almost had me breaking out my character. Real funny...

You ain't gone never change...

Damn Pop, you don't have to even talk to me and you still get under my skin!

Yah, I know you're my pop, don't kill your teacher, I know that line. I heard it every time you came home drunk arguing with mom. I knew you were wrong but I always took your side...

But don't get me wrong. It's cool, you're my pops—you can make mistakes. Hey guess what dad, I am old enough to know how babies are born now. By mistake? Not at all!

Jerome! I ain't no mistake. God don't make mistakes. I'm here for a reason.

Shawn woke up in the hospital days after being viciously attacked and robbed. The thieves were a couple of young knuckleheads from around the way who had been involved in a number of robberies around the city. They thought robbing Shawn would be a cinch since it was two on one, but didn't know exactly who they were targeting that night in the darkness. Shawn had been rumbling in the streets since he was 13 years old. Everybody in the neighborhood knew who did it because they had lumps and bumps all over their head. All they got away with was $80. They both went on the run soon after to escape the heat.

Shawn had been stabbed over 50 times all over his chest and stomach with that beer bottle but somehow walked out of the hospital with stitches. When he heard who did it—two young fools, one of whom was a cousin of one of his friends—he decided to let the situation simmer for the time being.

Shawn had escaped with his life, but because he missed days he was dropped from his classes at school, causing him to lose his GI bill eligibility for the upcoming semester. He also had a bench warrant out for child support for missing too many court dates.

"Why did they leave a piece of glass in there?" Kay asked as she inspected his scarred chest, stomach and arms. She came back to town when she got word of the attack. She was distraught and confused about the whole situation. She couldn't understand how someone could be so vicious over $80.

"Said I could have bled out if they didn't," he explained. "But it hurt like a bitch."

"Well lay back and get some sleep Shawn," she said as she prepared the bed for him. Shawn did as he was told. Inside Kay was going crazy with concern for her best friend. *Why won't he just stay his ass in the house!* she thought.

Kay sat down on the side of the bed and quietly watched Shawn lay there watching television. Finally he closed his eyes to rest.

After that latest close call with his life Shawn had officially become fed up with the lifestyle. He realized how much he didn't want to go back to running the streets on a full-time basis. He wanted more. He wanted to be a family man—reconnect with his sons and spend more time with his daughter.

Being separated from Kay for so long also gave him some clarity about their relationship and his problems. He realized the source of a lot of his struggles was getting high and drunk. He almost always got into a fight down in the projects when he was high. The drink made him just not care. The drugs made him hype and crazy. So he decided he needed to stop using drugs recreationally, stop drinking so much and get on a mission to get a real job, get his finances straight and finally get on the right track with his life. He just didn't know how to do that just yet.

* * *

"Tino you know I don't get on you too much, but we gotta talk," Elisha told him seriously as they sat in the car on the way to go shopping for the holidays. They now had three kids to shop for, including their new baby.

"Okay, let's talk then," he told her.

"I can't stop thinking about what happened to Shawn," she said and then paused. Tears started to well up in her eyes. "What if that happened to you? And what if you didn't make it? What would we do without you?"

"It's not gonna happen to me Lish. Don't worry."

"How do you know that? Shawn was just minding his business walking down the street!" she said. "The streets ain't safe anymore Tino, I don't want you down there so much anymore."

"Baby, you know those are my friends. I gotta go see them sometimes!"

"Why? They can come see you here if they want to hang out!"

Tino shook his head. "Baby I will be okay. Your husband is a smart man, remember that."

"I know you are love, but smart people make stupid choices all the time," she told him. "Your family needs you. That's all I'm going to say about that."

Tino bit his tongue and got caught up in his thoughts for the rest of the ride.

* * *

It was a couple of days before Christmas and Shawn was feeling down in the dumps. He was by himself. His body hurt so badly that he had to take pain pills just to get up out of the bed every morning.

Even worse he was broke and facing the prospect of not being able to give his kids anything at all for Christmas.

He was just about to get back into the bed and try to sleep through the New Year when he heard keys jingling at the door downstairs.

As he was slowly making his way down the steps to see who it was the door opened and in walked Kay.

"Surprise!" she yelled with her hands up.

"Bae! What you doing here?" Shawn said as a bright smile lit up his face and he continued down the stairs.

"I came to see you brother, Merry Christmas!" She gave him a hug and a kiss. "Let's go get a Christmas drink or something!"

The first stop Kay made was to the bank. When she came back out she handed Shawn an envelope with cash in it.

"This is for you brother, Merry Christmas," she told him.

"I had a little blessing and now so do you. And don't feel bad about not getting me anything for the holidays, you know how we do."

Shawn flipped through the cash in the envelope—there were several hundreds—and felt like he had just been given a boost of energy. He smiled and it was full of love for his best friend. She was right on time.

"Thank you bae."

They decided to go down to one of their favorite Mexican bars for happy hour to have $4 margaritas.

"Shawn why do you insist on wearing those sunglasses inside? It's the winter!"

"I don't know," he shrugged and winced in pain as he adjusted himself in his seat. "Habit I guess."

"I think you're being paranoid again Shawn. You look ridiculous," she said. "Don't let the crazy take over. Please, take those glasses off!"

Shawn took a sip from his drink and thought for a few moments. He finally put the drink down and reluctantly took the glasses off. His eyes squinted in the light.

"Thank you."

After having drinks they went to the mall and walked around just like old times, shopping for a few Christmas gifts for his kids, laughing and cracking jokes. Soon Shawn couldn't even feel the pain anymore.

* * *

Joy had had enough.

The holidays came and went and Travis hadn't spent any time with her besides the obligatory Christmas morning with his family. He left Joy at home to fend for herself on New Year's

Eve and didn't even care that she sat at home alone through midnight. Tisha had invited her to a New Year's Eve party in the city, but Joy bragged that Travis was taking her out to a five-star dinner that night. When the day came, he left to go hang with his boys instead—Joy was too embarrassed to call Tisha back. She sat at home alone drowning in champagne.

On Valentine's Day, Travis had a bouquet of flowers and chocolates sent to the house but he was nowhere to be found until two in the morning.

One lesson that Joy had learned in all her years was that the definition of insanity was doing the same thing over and over while expecting a different result. So today she was going to do something different. She was going to follow him and find out what he was doing in the city until midnight almost every day.

She watched Travis leave the house without kissing her goodbye, get in his car and drive off to the train station as he did every morning.

She let a few minutes pass as she pulled on her disguise and then jumped into the car she rented the day before. She parked it down the street so that Travis wouldn't know that it was hers. She drove straight to the city, knowing that even with traffic she would probably beat him to his office.

First, she sat outside of his office building with the blinkers on waiting to see if he went in. 20 minutes later, he did.

When she was assured that he was in the office, she parked the car in a garage for the day and walked around the area, shopping and checking out the scenery. He had never once invited her to his job.

Finally, around noon she settled into a restaurant across the street, which she assumed was a hot spot for the Wall Street workers in that area. She guessed right because just 45 minutes later Travis walked in with three of his colleagues—two male and one female. She had on a convincing wig and a pair of diva sunglasses that covered most of her face, so that he wouldn't recognize her.

She couldn't help but swoon a little as she watched Travis sitting there at the bar with his co-workers. All were wearing designer suits and expensive loafers, looking like masters of the universe. Travis tossed the bottom flap of his jacket back and put his elbow on the back of the chair. For a minute, Joy was nervous that he might look over and see her there pretending to read a book, but he didn't. He was engrossed in conversation.

Travis stayed at the restaurant for over an hour, talking and drinking. She could hardly believe they were going back to work after drinking so much.

The day blew by because before Joy knew it it was 6:30pm. She stood a block down from Travis' building watching and waiting calmly for him to come out. An hour and a half later she finally saw him emerge. He was still with the red-headed female co-worker who he had lunch with.

They hailed down a cab in front of the building and Joy panicked a little. She had assumed he would walk.

Knowing she didn't have enough time to go get her car, she hailed down a taxi on her corner and instructed him to follow the other cab. It felt like a scene out of a movie.

The cab driver expertly followed Travis' cab while maintaining a safe distance. Clearly, he had done this before. Finally, they stopped in front of a hotel in the meatpacking district. Travis and his co-worker got out and went in. Joy waited a few moments before following them in. Her worst suspicions were already coming true.

"Here for the party ma'am?" the doorman asked her when

she came in.

"Um, yes, where is that?"

"On the rooftop. Just take one of those elevators up to the top."

"Thank you."

Joy's heart was pounding with anticipation. She hoped that when the elevator doors opened she didn't come face to face with Travis.

When they finally did open she heard music playing and saw colorful pink and orange lights. There was a bar, a dance floor, an outdoor terrace looking out over the city.

She went to the bar for a drink and then went out onto the terrace. She was actually enjoying the scenery and the music as she glanced around to look for Travis.

After a little while she finally realized what was a little off about this party—there was a whole lot of men there and only a few women.

She came back into the main room and immediately her eyes fell on Travis sitting at a table with his female co-worker and a bottle of champagne on ice. They were talking and sitting very close. Joy burrowed her brow in anger.

Joy found a comfortable place to stand at the bar and observe the two without looking obvious. The co-worker kept leaning in close to Travis' ear and whispering to him. It took everything in Joy not to jump in and beat the breaks off of her right there and then.

She prayed that Travis was not cheating with this woman, who was average at best. Her only distinguishing attribute was the unusual color of her hair—Lucille Ball red. She watched them closely for over an hour, but Travis never kissed or even touched her. They just chatted.

Soon a couple of gentlemen came over to their table and

joined them. One of the men sat right next to the red head and put his arm around her waist. Joy breathed a sigh of relief—maybe this was the woman's husband and they had just been waiting for them.

Joy was starting to feel stupid. Maybe she had overreacted, going through all of this trouble just to find out what Travis was up to. She paid her tab and was about to leave the rooftop. She turned around to look back at their group one more time and her mouth dropped open.

Travis was shamelessly tonguing down the other man who joined them at the table. He was grasping his ears and really getting into the kiss. The red-head and her date were just sitting there talking and laughing like nothing was going on.

Joy's knees started to buckle and she had to hold onto the bar to keep her balance. She slowly creeped her way out of the room and to a bathroom. The bathroom was unisex and there was a short line of all men.

"Excuse me, is this a gay club?" Joy blurted out to the man in front of her.

"Well not really," he said with a nervous laugh. "I guess you can call it… 'gay-friendly' though."

Joy felt like her head was spinning. She turned around to go to the elevator but stopped in her tracks when she saw Travis standing there holding hands with his boyfriend. She stood to the side and waited for him to get in, then quickly pressed the button to call the next one.

The elevator doors opened just as she saw them leaving the building. She followed them—this time they decided to take a stroll on foot. Joy was in full stalker-mode by then, walking just paces behind them.

They turned a corner and disappeared into a dark-looking night club that didn't even have a sign at the top.

Joy tried to follow them in, but one of the security guards stopped her.

"Do you know a member?" he asked.

"Um, no…" she thought, wondering if she should have just lied.

"Do you have a password?"

Joy looked confused and it was obvious that she didn't.

"I'm sorry ma'am, but this is a private club," the security guard told her, then went in and closed the door.

Joy stood there with her mouth open not knowing what to do or say. Her husband had just gone into a dark private club holding another man's hand. Her first thought was to call someone. The only person she could think of who could handle this news was Tisha.

"Hey Joy, what's up?" Tisha said into the phone.

"Tisha!" Joy sobbed.

"What? What??"

Joy told her everything that happened and Tisha was floored.

"Go up in that bitch!" Tisha told her angrily.

"They told me I couldn't because I don't have a password or something!"

"Do you want me to come up there! Where's it at?"

Joy ran off the address and Tisha did an Internet search. Google revealed a few results but none went into detail about the location, so she did a specialized search of a database of businesses that they used often at her job.

"That's a swinger's club Joy. For gay men."

Joy was overcome with emotion. She was so distraught that she actually considered walking into traffic.

"Joy!" Tisha said, snapping her back into reality. "Do you want me to come up there?"

Joy thought about it for a while, but something told her that this was a battle she would have to fight on her own.

"No, I got this cousin. I'll call you."

Joy threw her phone into her purse and marched right back up to the door of the swinger's club. She banged on the door as if she was a mad woman.

"Open up this fucking door!" she yelled.

As soon as the fat security guard from earlier opened up the door she dashed inside, slipping by him with ease.

"Hey, you can't go in there!" he yelled after her.

"I'm going in there to get my husband. Don't try to stop me!" She frantically looked around for the entry and finally burst through another door before anyone could stop her.

After some searching she found the main area, where men of all ages were inside lounging, drinking, talking, kissing and smoking both weed and cigarettes. She quickly looked around for Travis, knowing that security was on her tail. She heard some moaning and carrying on going on in another room that was separated by a curtain. She snatched it open and it looked like a scene out of a rank porno movie inside. Everyone in that room was engaging in some type of sex act. It smelled like hot ass and sweat.

She looked around and saw her worst nightmare come true. There was Travis on the floor with his shirt off giving head to his boyfriend. The boyfriend's eyes were closed.

She hit Travis in the back of the head with her purse and he nearly choked.

"What the!" his boyfriend said in shock as Travis fell to the side and put his hands up defensively. Joy continued hitting him with everything she had until security finally came and carried her away.

"It's not what it looks like!" Travis tried to say.

Chapter 20
New York State of Mind

"Joy is getting a divorce," Tisha mentioned to Kay nonchalantly as they sat in the nail salon getting their feet done for the upcoming warm season.

"Huh?" Kay asked. "Really?"

"Yea, it's over. It's a done deal," Tisha said, shaking her head. "I don't even know if I should be telling you this to be honest."

Kay was quiet and watched the nail lady scrub down her feet. She knew that in time her best friend would tell all without any pressuring.

"She found out he was fucking men!" she finally blurted.

Kay's eyes almost bugged out of her head. "Wait, what??"

"He's on the DL. And he's a card carrying member of a male swinger's club. He was *hoing*!"

Kay's mouth hung wide open. Her mind immediately went out to Joy. As much as she didn't like her, she knew Joy was probably distraught. Her whole fantasy life had been shattered to pieces.

"How is she doing?"

"Not good. Now she's got to get tested and she's freaking out."

"Wow I didn't even think about that. How did she find out about it?"

"Woman's intuition. She sensed something was up when she kept finding suspicious shit around the house," Tisha explained. "She followed him and caught him in the act."

Kay shook her head. "Wow, are these men are really on the DL like that in New York? I thought that was just Atlanta?"

"You have to be careful of these high-powered guys who work in the city. Some of them are into some really shady shit because they have money," she warned her. "Joy just swore she had herself a catch."

Kay nodded.

"Kay that's why I always tell you, you should never let someone make you feel bad about being single or for who you choose to be with. Don't let people judge you. A lot of couples are just keeping up appearances and faking the funk."

They were both quiet for a long while listening to their massage chairs whirring as they got caught up in their separate thoughts. Kay thought about how Joy had judged her relationship with Shawn.

"I asked Shawn to come out here this weekend," she blurted.

"Where, to the city?"

"Yea, we're going to do the whole city thing. Happy hour and all that for his birthday."

"Sounds like a plan. So are you getting back together with him or what?"

"Naw, we're just chilling right now. That's my buddy you know? That's my homie."

"Whatever," Tisha said with a laugh. "I doubt that's how he feels."

* * *

Kay smiled when she saw Shawn come off the Greyhound bus. He was dressed to the nines in a pair of black slacks, black Kenneth Cole Oxford shoes and a black zip down sweater. She could tell he had a little bit of extra pep in his step, he was feeling himself and knew he looked good.

"Happy birthday babe! How was your trip?" Kay said with a smile as she let go of Shawn's strong embrace. Shawn groaned a little because his body had been hurting from sitting in the cramped seat for three hours.

"Fine, these muthafuckas over an hour late though! Sitting in traffic."

"Yea you know they don't hardly ever be on time. You look good bro!"

"So do you," he said as he looked her over mischievously. She was wearing a maroon dress that hugged her curves, sheer brown stockings and a pair of matching open-toed heels.

"Come on, we gonna go down to my favorite spot for happy hour first, then the club later."

They started to walk down the street side by side. Shawn immediately moved her to the right of him on the sidewalk so that she was on the inside—he was taught from a young age that you keep ladies away from the street when walking. You only keep a female on the outside if she's for sale.

Shawn started to look all around him at the sights of midtown Manhattan and listened to the sounds. People were rushing by as if they were blurs and he was standing still. He didn't tell Kay, but this was the first time he had ever visited the Manhattan that you only see in movies. It was completely different from downtown Philly, like a whole other world. He puffed out his chest a little and took a big breath full of the city air.

"It's right across there," Kay said as she pointed across the street at a popular happy hour bar.

A half hour later they were enjoying drinks at the bar, which was starting to get a little packed with folks coming in for a drink after work.

"What you been up to out there?" Kay asked as she sipped on her Courvoisier and he had a Grey Goose and pineapple juice.

"Just looking for a job. Got a few leads. I took those state tests and got a top score."

"Good, I'm praying for you bro, do your thing," Kay encouraged him. "You been staying up at the house more, staying away from those streets?"

"Yea, sure," Shawn said, lying. Even though he was on a job hunt he was still hanging down in the projects almost daily. It would always start and end the same way—with a friend offering to buy him a drink and him crashing down at someone's house.

"Yea, okay," Kay said, reading him like a book. It had come to the point where she could tell when he was lying or stretching the truth.

"What about you, how that job going?" he said, changing the subject.

"It's whatever, pays the bills you know," Kay said with a nod. "I'll leave you alone only cause it's your birthday. You getting old bro!"

"Yea, that's why I'm trynna get my life together Kayby, I just had enough you know? God put me here for a reason, I gotta make something happen."

"Well if you gonna do that you need to leave those streets alone though," she said.

"Thought you just said you was gonna leave me alone about that," he said with a chuckle.

"Had to get that last one in."

"Happy birthday Shawn," a voice said behind him.

Shawn looked up and saw the bartender standing there

holding a cupcake with a candle in the center. They both sang happy birthday to him and he couldn't stop smiling.

Later on Shawn and Kay hit up a small party spot downtown. They had a good time dancing and being wild together, just like old times. But they both had a little too much to drink and soon enough the tone started to change.

Some guy walked up to Kay and started dancing with her, trying to get her phone number. She quickly moved away and told him to go away, but Shawn had seen it. He clenched his teeth but didn't say anything at first—not until they both left the party and were walking to Houston Street.

"If I wasn't here you would have gotten that nigga number wouldn't you?" Shawn asked.

"Huh?" Kay tried to play stupid as she stumbled along. "Give me a break, don't start Shawn."

"Just answer the question!" he demanded.

"No, okay. He had a big ass head just like yours," she said and rolled her eyes as she put her hand up to hail a cab.

"You think that's funny?"

"Yea, it's funny," she said with a nod as a cab slowed and let her in.

"Okay, I see how you is!" he shouted as he got in the cab and slammed the door. The driver started to wonder if he should have even picked up the fare. "Truth is, you don't really give a fuck about me anyway!"

"Think what you want," Kay said and then told the driver the location of the bus station. She leaned her head up against the window to stop the dizziness.

"I don't want to go home. Take us to another club," Shawn demanded.

"It's 2 am, the last bus to Philly leaves in like a half hour so quit playing."

"I don't care, I wanna go to a club."

They continued to argue back and forth in the cab until they reached the stop. The cab driver was all too glad to arrive because their drunken discussion was quickly escalating.

"Shawn if you miss this bus we either gonna have to walk around New York drunk for five more hours or pay $300 for a few hours in a hotel! You got that to blow?"

Shawn finally just threw a $20 bill down on the ground for the fare and got out of the cab. He power-walked away to the station without saying another word.

When Kay finally got home she charged up her phone, which had gone dead hours ago. She was about to call Shawn to make sure he made it into Philly, but heard her voicemail indicator go off first. She logged on and there was one message. When she clicked the option to listen to the new message, she heard a song playing faintly in the background as if it was playing from a car radio...

Tell me what I gotta do to please you...

Baby anything you say I'll do...

Cause I only wanna make you happy...

From the bottom of my heart it's true...

Kay smiled as she listened to Joe's *I Wanna Know* play on her voicemail. She knew it was Shawn's way of telling her that he was sorry for tripping out. A few moments in she heard her text message buzzer go off.

> *just touched down. nite*

>> *aiight, love you bro. talk to you tmrw*

Chapter 21
An Idle Mind

"Kay!" Shawn said enthusiastically when she picked up the phone.

"What's up?" Kay said with a smile, sensing that he was in a good mood by his tone.

"Got a job!" Shawn said excitedly.

"For real? Congratulations babe!!"

"Good job, pays $21 an hour with benefits."

"Whaaat??"

"Yuuuppp," Shawn laughed. "I start Monday."

A few months after taking some tests downtown and going to interview after interview, the city finally placed Shawn with a job at the water company doing janitorial work. They told him to come down to fill out his paperwork the next day and get his uniform. Everything felt rushed but that was fine with him—he just wanted to get to work.

The first day on the job, Shawn showed up 15 minutes early for his shift and got right to work. His supervisor was impressed with how well he followed instructions and how thoroughly he completely his duties. Shawn was beaming with pride. He was finally a legitimate brother.

The second day he again showed up early and got to work.

Around 2:30pm his supervisor Bobby came to find him in the building where they were working that day.

"Hey Shawn, can I talk to you for a moment," Bobby said. By the look on his face, Shawn could already tell that it wasn't a good thing.

* * *

"I lost that job," Shawn said. He sounded so dejected that Kay's heart dropped into her stomach.

"You're kidding me, why??" Kay asked. "Some lady called me earlier asking for you."

"Yea I gave them your number for a backup. Said my drug test came back positive," Shawn said so low that Kay barely heard him.

"Huh? Well why the fuck didn't they check that before they hired you?!" Kay almost screamed. She was just as distressed as he was. She could feel his pain—he had been so excited about the new job and a new beginning. He figured he could finally get caught up on his child support payments, properly take care of his kids and help Kay with the bills.

"They were rushing because they had to hire somebody before the first to make their budget or whatever," he explained. "The drug test came back today."

"I don't know what to say. I'm so sorry Shawn, I know you wanted that job."

Shawn didn't say anything and for the first time ever Kay had the feeling that he might be crying or emotional.

"Shawn, it's gonna be fine. You just get that all out of your system and get back out there in a few weeks. There are more jobs."

Easier said than done, Shawn thought. It was instances like this that drove him to drink and act crazy.

"I know. I gotta go bae, I'll call you later," Shawn said.

"Okay, you know I love you bro," Kay said. "Call me later."

"I will. Love you too."

* * *

Shawn was fucked up. His pockets were light, he had just lost out on a major job opportunity, he no longer had his studies to distract him and his body was hurting really bad from a combination of his now-healed stab wounds and his lifelong back problems.

With Kay still out of town and nothing better to do, he of course found his way back down the way to his favorite bar. He sat down at the far end of the bar and drank from the afternoon on, thinking and avoiding phone calls; even from his boys. He just didn't feel like being bothered.

To his great dismay, in walked George's cousin Kev. Shawn still didn't like George, but since he was finally trying to get his life together he decided to let his beef with him go—at least for the time being.

"Sup SB," Kev said with a nod as he sat down just two seats away. He brought with him the strong odor of hydro. He ordered a Hennessey.

Shawn didn't acknowledge him—he just kept looking at the mirror behind the bar. His cellphone rang again and he pressed the ignore button.

"So SB, I heard about those young buls who shanked you, they still on the run?" Kev asked trying to make small talk.

Shawn didn't respond.

"So you ain't gonna do nothin' 'bout that?" Kev asked, being nosey.

"Look nigga, if I see 'em I'll deal with it at that time. I ain't thinkin' 'bout that bullshit right now," Shawn said. He was getting more and more annoyed. The incident had happened almost a half a year ago and here Kev was bringing it up again.

"Shit. If they pulled that shit on me I'd hunt them niggas

down one by one."

"Right," Shawn said and took a shot.

"Don't tell me you goin' soft on me SB!" Kev said and laughed.

Shawn clenched his lips together and glared at him as if to say: "You trynna start some shit?"

Kev held up his hands, reading Shawn's expression loud and clear. He ordered another double shot of Hennessey.

"And get one for my nigga SB here," Kev added. "Naw matter fact, make that a dacquiri with a little umbrella on the side."

Kev laughed heartily at the shade he had just thrown and got up to go to the bathroom. He slapped Shawn hard on the back playfully as he walked past him. Shawn snapped. This wasn't the first time someone had made a comment about him being soft after he decided to let the two young teens who stabbed him slide.

On instinct, Shawn reached forward and grabbed a bottle of cheap whiskey out of the bartender's rack. With one precise backward swing he hit Kev across the back of his head with the bottle. Kev fell forward onto the dirty bar floor. He started to shake a little before losing consciousness. The bartender and the few other folks in the bar just stood back and watched.

Shawn threw the rest of the bottle down on the ground hard so that it cracked into many pieces. He bit his bottom lip to deal with the pain waving through his own body from making such a quick movement. Glass crunched under his Tims as he went back over to the bar to grab his cell phone. As he was leaving he casually reached over and took Kev's double-shot of Hennessey, then walked right out of the door with it.

A half an hour later Shawn somehow found himself in

front of Kidd's grandmother Miss Sherri's house. He saw her out on the porch and she invited him in to eat some leftovers from dinner.

Kidd's grandmother was a down-to-earth older lady. She had done her share of dirt in her time as did her kids, but ever since her grandson was killed she mostly just stayed to herself. That had been her heart.

"You know Kidd really liked you Shawn," Ms. Sherri told him as she spooned some gravy over his steak. Shawn devoured the food as if he hadn't eaten in ages and tried to relax.

"I liked him too. He was a thorough brother Miss Sherri," Shawn said with a nod.

"And you know, Kidd was really talented as a youngster," she told him as she watched him eat. "We all thought he was gonna be an engineer or something. Always fixing stuff."

Shawn nodded.

"He missed his callin' you know. Couldn't leave them streets alone," Miss Sherri said and shook her head. "You know why they killed him right?"

Shawn shook his head no as he continued eating, but his ears were peeled.

"Some little girl told her brother Kidd was beating her up," she explained. "But come to find out she was pregnant and he just didn't want nothing to do with her. She got my boy killed."

"I ain't know that," Shawn said shaking his head. Everyone had assumed Kidd was killed because of a drug beef.

"Kidd could have gone to any school he wanted if he had finished high school."

Shawn nodded.

"How about you Shawn, what did you want to be when you grew up?"

Shawn thought about the question for a while. "Well, I

always liked to work with my hands and build things. Maybe own my own construction company. Or maybe become a chef."

"What stopped you from doing that?"

"I don't know. Slow money. Having my kids young. I just got off track."

"Well you know babe, the track still out there. You can jump back on it if you want, anytime you want," she told him as she got up and went into the kitchen to grab him more food. "Maybe if I would have told Kidd that more when he was younger he would still be here with me."

Shawn thought about the violent act that he had just committed in the bar and wasn't sure if getting back on that track was even a possibility anymore.

Shawn's phone had been blowing up all night long. Tino texted to tell him that Kev was in the hospital and hadn't regained consciousness yet. Everybody knew who did it by then. Shawn had so many calls and messages that he finally got fed up and broke his phone again. He hopped on the bus up North to the Badlands to get away from the drama. He went to a Puerto Rican bar where he used to go to sell and get free drinks. They knew him well around there.

"Hey papi!" the bartender said to him when he walked in. "You lookin' for Manuel?"

"Not really... but yea if he's around you can tell him I'm here," Shawn said as he sat down. "Let me get a Coors."

After a couple of beers, his old partner Manuel came from the back.

"SB!" he yelled out and opened his arms. He walked over and gave Shawn a bro-hug. "Where you been? I haven't seen you in a minute!"

Shawn smiled a little and was happy to see a friendly face.

"Hey papi, been on a mission."

"You don't look so good. You need something?" Manuel asked.

"Naw, I'm good," Shawn said but inside he wanted something to get his mind off of his problems. Manuel read his mind.

"Here, take this. No charge papi," Manuel said as he slid something in Shawn's jacket pocket so smoothly even he didn't notice at first. "Maria, give SB anything he wants on the house."

Shawn woke up the next day in someone's house. It wasn't familiar. He heard a baby crying in the next room.

He had gotten so tore up and high the previous night that he couldn't even remember half of what had happened. He felt as if he was falling back into an old routine. It was an old routine that he had vowed not to go back to, but yet here he was. He sat up from the rickety bed and held his head.

"Heyyy papi," he heard a voice say. He turned quickly and saw a Spanish girl walking around the room with only a pair of shorts on. Her saggy breasts flopped around and her nipples were pointed at the floor. She looked like she was strung out.

What did I do? Shawn asked himself as he watched her walk out of the room at a feverish pace. She came back in a few minutes later with a mirror with coke on it.

"You want some papi?"

Shawn watched as she placed the mirror in the middle of the bed and sat crossed-legged. She started preparing it with a razor.

"Naw I gotta get home," he said and started pulling his pants on. "What happen last night? Did we…"

The girl laughed. "Naw papi, you was knocked out as soon as you came in the house. You can go home to your girl with a clean conscience."

Shawn cracked a smile and put his fitted cap on his head. He thanked her for her hospitality and left the house without another word.

As soon as the sun hit his face he decided that he would have to face whatever had happened down the way. He jumped on the bus back downtown, got off at Girard and headed straight to Cage's house.

"SB," Cage said through the screen when he opened the door to see who it was. "What up nigga, I was calling you all night."

Cage briefed him on what had happened. Kev woke up but was going to be in the hospital for a while. He had suffered a concussion from getting hit with the bottle. Of course George wasn't happy about the whole thing, but as of that moment wasn't making any threats toward Shawn. He didn't like his cousin that much anyway.

"Let me use your phone," Shawn said and got up from his seat on the couch. As soon as he logged into his voicemail he heard that it was full. He started listening to each one and pressing the delete button after just a few seconds for each one, up until he heard Kay's voice.

Shawn I'm concerned about you. Your phone keeps going straight to voicemail and you're not answering my texts. Please call me as soon as you get this message!

A smile grew on Shawn's face. He immediately hung up the line and called Kay's number.

"Shawn," Kay said, picking up on the second ring. "What is going on, your phone isn't working."

"Yea I know, I broke it again. But I'm alright bae, what you doing?" he asked.

"Would you stop breaking your phones? How am I going

to get in touch with you? You had me worried."

"Sorry."

"Look I'm coming up there on Friday. Are you going to be busy this weekend?"

"Nope. I'll meet you up at the house."

"Okay, miss you bro."

"Miss you too."

Shawn walked out of Cage's house feeling a little better. Just as he was stepping down off the last step, his phone to his ear, someone ran by him so fast that he could barely make out the figure at first. He stepped back and looked—it was Ursula, his old customer. She was so thin and frail looking she could probably fit between the bars of a fence, but she could sure beat her feet like FloJo. She was being chased by an older man who was having a lot of trouble keeping up.

"Stop that bitch, she just stole my hubcaps off my car!" he yelled. Shawn cracked a smile.

"I'm gonna hurt you bitch!" the man yelled out behind her as he wheezed and held his chest.

Ursula continued her Olympic dash down the block, but didn't see a car coming. The car stopped short—she rolled right over the hood, landed on her feet and kept running as if nothing had even happened. She soon disappeared around the corner.

By then Shawn was cackling in laughter. His smile and confidence returned, washing over him like a baptism. Cage was behind him in the doorway laughing as well.

"What the fuck ya'll laughin' at," the man, now bent over holding his knees, asked.

"You must not be from 'round here. You ain't catching ole Urs!" Cage said.

"She gone with the wind!" Shawn said and started walking down the street again.

On his way down to the bus he heard a voice yell from behind him.

"Ay SB!"

Shawn turned around, wondering what else would be coming his way that morning. His face relaxed when he noticed that it was his young friend, Mike.

"Ay what up my man?" Shawn said as he slapped hands with him.

"Just doin' my thing. What about you?"

"I'm just a squirrel trynna get a nut."

"I mean that whole thing down at the gas station, I heard about what happened."

"Oh yea. Lil pussies almost kilt a nigga."

"Yea they two dumb muthafuckers. I heard they both got popped, trynna rob a couple old white folks down South Street."

Shawn shook his head. As 'bout it' as Lift had been to go for their heads, something in Shawn just said to let it go. They were just a couple of young idiots who were bound to go down on their own.

"So guess what SB, I'm starting school in a few weeks!" Mike revealed.

"Say word?" Shawn looked at him curiously and a smile started to grow on his face.

"Yup, I took your advice and start looking around at some shit. Saw this ad in the paper for free job seminars, so I went down there, met some people and they taught me how to apply for this special training program for high school grads and GED candidates," Mike explained. "Everything paid for, in fact they gonna pay ME for a work-study job. I'm going for computer technology."

Shawn's face was frozen in a smile—he was a little surprised that Mike had actually listened to him that one day in the barber shop. It got him to thinking about how important it was to talk to his own sons about their future—they were getting older. His relationship with them hadn't always been so great.

He slapped hands with Mike and gave him a bro-hug. "Proud of you young bul, I want to hear how it goes, aiight? Maybe I can work for YOU one day!"

Mike laughed. "Thanks man! I'll keep you updated."

Shawn slapped hands with Mike and then watched as he bopped down the block in the opposite direction.

Chapter 22
Played

"Cage, when you gonna take me down the Gallery?" Tanya, his West Philly girl, asked in her nasal voice as she sat on his back and rubbed him down slowly with baby oil.

"One of these days," he said nonchalantly as he flipped the channels.

"Why not tomorrow?"

Truth was Cage was finally getting bored with Tanya. He saw her less and less as the months went on. Young girls were only fun for a little while but then became more annoying than anything, always asking for money and complaining. And all they had to offer in return was sex—they all thought they had the golden ticket between their legs. But in truth Cage had a preference for older women when it came to sex—they were much more interesting and experienced.

"I can't tomorrow, I'm busy."

"Aw come on! You don't never buy me nothin' no more," Tanya whined. "I want a new bag, my shit lookin' rough these days. And I need my nails re-done. You don't want your girl walking around with chipped nails do you?"

"I'll give you a couple of dollars to get your nails done, but I ain't going down no mall tomorrow."

"Why you be acting like that sometimes? Damn all I'm asking for is a fucking bag!"

"Don't be raising your voice in my house girl."

"I ain't, but you be irkin' Cage. I don't ask you for much, but then I do ask you and you act like I'm always bothering you or something. Shit, I shouldn't even have to ask, you should just wanna give it, as much good pussy I be givin' you!"

"Good pussy come a dime a dozen," Cage let slip but meant to just think it.

"What the fuck do that mean?" Tanya said and slapped his back. "You got a whole lot of pussies on deck huh?"

"I ain't say that, shut up."

"Nah I ain't gonna shut up nigga! Tell me, do that mean you fuckin' around with other girls or sumthin'?"

"It mean whatever you want it to mean," Cage said and rolled his eyes.

Tanya came in front of the television to block his view with her hands on her hips. She was wearing a bra that barely held her D-cup breasts and a pair of booty shorts. "I ain't movin' til you tell me the truth. It's cool, I ain't gonna trip Cage."

"Don't start with me Tanya, I ain't in the mood for ya shit today. Come over here and sit your ass down or leave. Your choice."

Tanya's mouth flew open. "What? Oh okay, I see how you is nigga, fuck you!"

She started stomping around the room collecting her things. Cage watched as she jiggled around like jello and was amused—that, her attitude and her decision to leave was starting to turn him on.

"Come here girl and stop playing," he said, gesturing with his head.

"No, fuck you," Tanya said with her back turned to him as she pulled on her t-shirt and put her long dark brown weave into a ponytail.

Cage got up from the bed and smacked her on the behind hard.

"Ow!" she yelled. "Don't be doin' that shit."

He grabbed her roughly by her ponytail and tossed her over onto the bed. He pulled her shorts down to her knees so that she could barely move and pushed her forward more onto the sheets. He then pulled her hips up and entered her from behind. He usually wore a condom to avoid the possibility of getting her pregnant, but on the spur of the moment he chose to go with his impulse instead.

"Uhhhhh," she moaned in ecstasy. Cage knew she loved it rough. He grabbed her by her ponytail again and wrapped it up around his fist.

"Not my weave Cage," she complained and tried to hold his hand down. By then Cage was putting it down and she was enjoying every moment, so she eventually just let him have his way.

When Cage came, he tried to pull out but knew that some of it didn't make it out. He sighed and shook his head as he backed up from her. She lay there on her stomach with her butt up in the air. He let out a few more breaths as he gazed down at her body. He had conquered her.

"Okay, now you can leave," he said bluntly and went over to grab her clothes off of the chair. He threw them on her legs.

"What nigga?"

It took him another half an hour to be rid of Tanya, who ranted and raved her way all the way down the stairs and finally out of the door with a little help from Cage.

The next day he called Tanya to officially dump her.

* * *

Shawn had been hitting the Internet and the city hard applying for jobs but it was almost impossible after the recession hit. He applied for everything from janitorial positions to hard labor jobs, even though he knew his body wasn't up to speed after the stabbing. Most of them didn't call him back because he had to admit to his felony from years ago. A couple of hiring managers called him back but when they heard his voice and found out he was a black guy from the hood they didn't call back anymore. Other jobs required all applicants to be licensed—Shawn's license had been suspended for over a decade because of missed court dates and someone else was still racking up tickets using his name. Every time he tried to get the Philadelphia traffic court to fix the situation they just gave him the run around.

It was only a matter of time before he found his way back down the way, hanging out with the boys and looking to get into something.

That day Shawn was sitting out on the porch at his daughter's house watching her play. It was one of those bad days when his body was really hurting. He saw his old buddy Les walking up and winced a little in pain as he stood to greet him.

"Sup brotha," Shawn said and slapped hands with him. They started walking down the block a bit to talk.

"What's shaking," Les asked him.

"Not a damn thing just the change in my pockets," Shawn said with a chuckle. "Been trying to find me a gig. It's hard out here for a brother."

"So I found you at the right time. I got this thing going on. Quadruple your money."

Shawn scratched his chin. "Nahh, I think I'm gonna pass on that."

"Nigga if you bust down, why you gonna turn down a perfectly legit opportunity like this?" Les asked.

"I been knowing you for damn near 10 years Les, you ain't never had a legit scheme in yo life!" Shawn laughed and shook his head. He looked back at his daughter and his mind was made up. "I'll holla at you lata."

Chapter 23
Streets Keep Calling

Daydreaming...
She talking, I hear her but not really.
The respect I have for her...
Am listening very closely and trying to comprehend
every word she spit...
Don't get me wrong she have my attention...
Am listening, all ears.

"If you don't come back to me I'm gonna go out and get me a fat white girl," Shawn threatened Kay playfully as they sat in the living room watching television.

Kay laughed. "Do it."

"I'm so serious. She gonna be fat and sloppy with seven chins," he said and made a gesture to show how big she would be. "Rotund."

"Do it. I dare you," she said with a smile as she continued to type on her laptop.

It was late Friday night. Kay felt the urgent need to come into town after hearing about Shawn's mishap with the water department. She wanted to be there with him for moral support and to keep him on a positive track. She felt he was finally close to a breakthrough in his life.

Kay and Shawn were like two peas in a pod. They hadn't had an angry word to say to each other for a long time. They communicated more. It was as if their last huge fight had been a cleansing session for them both—they didn't have much to argue about anymore. There was an understanding between them—they weren't back together romantically, but they were still partners.

Shawn's phone rang—he glanced at it and put it back down. A couple of minutes later it rang again and looked at the screen longer as if he were thinking.

He reluctantly pulled himself up from the bed and headed down the hall to the bathroom to take the call.

Kay frowned. Whenever he left the room to take a call she knew it was probably someone from down the projects.

Confirming her suspicions, he came back into the room and started pulling on his Polo shirt.

"I gotta make a run," he said flatly.

"Shawn, come on," Kay said with a huge sigh. "They call and you come running."

"It ain't all about that. Just something I promised I'd take care of. I'll be back," he reassured her.

* * *

"This better work out Les, this my last bean 'til the first," Shawn said as he counted out $100. Les had assured him that he could make $400 within a couple of hours if he put into the pot.

Shawn really wanted to make some more money so that he could take Kay out to dinner and take her shopping to buy a new necklace for their anniversary that next week. She had mentioned wanting a small diamond encrusted name chain. They usually didn't celebrate their anniversary date anymore but Shawn wanted to surprise her.

"It's a guarantee," Les assured him as he tucked the money in his pocket. He gave Shawn a pound. "I'll call you in two hours, max."

Shawn watched him as he walked away from the front of the

bar and disappeared into the night.

* * *

"Shawn, didn't you say you had court or a meeting or something today?" Kay asked as she stood over him examining his greasy face like a CSI investigator.

Shawn was lying back in the bed with his arm draped across his forehead, eyes closed. He had come back into the house at two in the morning but went right to sleep without bothering Kay as she slept. He didn't start stirring again until three in the afternoon.

"Leave me the fuck alone Kay," he mumbled.

"No, answer me!" she demanded. "Do you have something to do today? It's almost four o'clock. I can take you there, but come on let's go now."

Shawn didn't say anything. Kay sat down on the bed next to him and lowered her tone.

"Shawn tell me the truth, are you on that shit again?"

Shawn opened his eyes in slits and gave Kay one of those old glares that used to mean some shit was about to go down if she didn't shut up and back off. She was pissing him off.

But that look only egged her on though because she was concerned—the last thing she wanted was for Shawn to revert to his old ways. If showing her concern meant that they had to have a major argument that day, that's what it was going to be.

Shawn literally bit his tongue and turned around to go back to sleep. He could finally see it from her perspective—she was just trying to help and it wasn't her fault that he had gotten played by Les. This was the first time Kay was staying in town for over a week and he didn't want to chase her away.

Shawn had waited at the bar that previous night for over four hours until it closed for Les to get back to him. He called Les' phone over and over but eventually only got sent to voicemail. Les had burned him and right about now Shawn was thinking of ways to go for his head.

Les would have never tried something like that in the past. Shawn was starting to believe that people down the way figured he had gone soft and that he wasn't as strong since the stabbing attack. He felt himself being pulled in two different directions even more strongly than ever—on one hand he was trying to get his life on track and on the other hand he wanted to maintain his reputation.

He knew that no matter what direction he went he was going to have to face the people from his old hood on some level—he would have to walk those streets. And the last thing he wanted was to become known as a bitch.

"Shawn you know what, okay I'm going to leave you alone," Kay said shaking her head. "But please, stop hanging out down there. Every time you go there you come back with an attitude problem."

Shawn just pulled a pillow over his head and kept quiet. He was really feeling like crap because he was broke and probably couldn't get Kay anything for their anniversary like he had hoped.

* * *

Shawn sat on the stoop at Cage's house, smoking a cigarette, waiting for a call. He was on a mission and needed some help from his various contacts around the projects.

Over the past few days Les was always conveniently nowhere to be found when Shawn was around and still wasn't answering any of his calls. Shawn decided that this was a battle of his choosing—Les was straight up disrespecting him and he had to confront him man to man. Les wasn't even a threat; he was the neighborhood hustle man. If he was going to be punking Shawn anybody would. $100 wasn't enough money to get killed over but now it was all about the principle of the matter.

Cage was making a few rounds around the projects in his truck trying to locate Les. He popped into all of the usual spots and tried to seem nonchalant. If someone saw Shawn with Cage someone would probably tip Les off.

Finally about an hour later Shawn got a call from Cage.

"Cuzzo," Shawn said, standing up and throwing the cigarette on the ground.

"Yo he down here at the store!"

"The Chinese spot?"

"He just went in by himself, you better hurry."

Shawn was already power-walking down the block with the phone to his ear.

"Bet. I'll be there in a minute, keep 'im in your sights."

Within minutes Shawn was standing right outside of the store against the brick wall waiting for Les to emerge. He kept his hands crossed in front of his waist patiently. Cage stayed close by in the car watching.

Les finally stepped out of the store laughing at whoever he had been talking to inside. Shawn stepped forward.

"Hey, say good night!" Shawn said then dropped Les with a one-hitter quitter. He caught Les so off guard and punched him in the eye so hard that Les did a little twirl. He stood there for a moment in a daze with his cigarette on his lip then dropped to the concrete and went to sleep. It was lights out!

Shawn's cell phone fell out of his jacket pocket and slid across the ground. He winced as a wave of pain shot through his own body starting at his back and ending at the stab wound in his stomach where the doctors had left a piece of glass. Cage, still sitting in the truck, covered his mouth in shock and amusement. He had expected Shawn to at least have a conversation with Les first, but nope. The brothers who had been in the store talking to Les came out to see what had happened.

"Oh shit! That nigga sleep!" one of them commented.

When Shawn finally recovered from his own pains, he reached down and pulled all of Les' things out of his pockets. To his dismay he only had about $80 on him and a bag of weed. Shawn took it all right down to the quarters, dimes and nickels, then threw the empty wallet back down on Les' chest. Cage couldn't contain his laughter inside the car.

"One 'Les' nigga. I'm cashin' out beeyatch!" Shawn said as he grabbed his cell phone off the ground. He casually strolled over to the passenger side of Cage's truck and jumped in, counting the cash. He gave Cage the bag of weed since he couldn't smoke anymore.

"Newsflash! SB still layin' mufuckas on they back!" Cage shouted out the window with a laugh as he pulled off down the street. "He still got it!"

* * *

Shawn's sister Rose had been invited to a party at Turquoise that night, a new hot club downtown. She invited Shawn to come by. He loved hanging with his sisters whenever he had the chance and was always concerned about them. They would get in free and have free drinks all night.

"What's going on with you brother? Seem like you got a lot on your mind," Rose told him as she poured herself some champagne at their table.

"Just trying to get off this Island bae," he told her. His hand was still hurting.

"I hear you," she said with a knowing nod. She knew better

than anyone how easy it was for her brother to get pulled back into the game. "I'm going to the bathroom."

Shawn looked around the table at all the guys posted up. "Want me to come with you?"

"Noo," she laughed. "I'm a big girl now. I'll be back."

"You better not give none of these knucklehead ass niggas the time of day. I'll fuck 'em up!"

He watched her until she was out of sight—always on big brother duty. Shawn looked back toward the club and saw Bennie, Huey's cousin, approaching his table. His guard immediately went up and he stood. He towered over Bennie so unless he was carrying something, he wasn't much of a threat.

Bennie put his hand up as if to tell him to calm down. "It's cool brother, I ain't on that dumb shit right now."

Shawn nodded his head but still looked at him suspiciously. "What you want?"

"Just wanted to holla at you for a minute. Can I sit?"

Shawn still looked at him suspiciously but gestured for him to have a seat.

"This might sound strange, but I just wanted to apologize."

"What? For what?"

"You know, 'bout Huey. That nigga don't have no fuckin' sense—none whatsoever. He always been like that since a kid, feel me?"

Shawn just rubbed his chin in contemplation and listened to him talk.

"And look. I'm the one that took shots at you that day on the block. Do you know that nigga Huey wasn't even in the car!" Bennie admitted. "He gonna send me on his mission over that dumb ass shit. A nigga just got outta jail, I ain't trynna go back!"

Shawn's facial expression changed when he thought back to that day, but he kept his mouth closed and continued to listen. He wanted all the details.

"And like a fucking fool I did it. I coulda been sittin' in jail for 20 years if I had stayed in the car that night he got locked up. 20 years. That nigga been dragging me down since we were 15!"

Shawn nodded but wanted to know his motivations. "Why you telling me all this shit right now?"

"Cuz I'm trynna get right. I been going to church more and I met a dude who trynna get me set up with a job in a trade. You know that union shit."

"So again, what that got to do with me?"

"He told me I should try to make right with the people I wronged. You one of 'em. On the real, I got no legitimate beef wit you SB," Bennie explained. "That was my cousin's issue. So I seen you in here and came over to say what I gotta say."

Shawn looked at him for a while and then nodded his head slowly.

"That's what's up Bennie. Appreciate that." He offered his hand and Bennie gladly grasped it in a man-shake. They both relaxed a little.

"And one more thing," Bennie said. "Hue might be getting out soon, so just stay on point. He still talking shit, talking 'bout he coming for ya neck."

Shawn shook his head and laughed. "That's all I need, more drama."

"I don't know if he serious or not, but just wanted to give you the heads up."

"Appreciate it, but I can't let that occupy my mind right now. Here, have a glass of champ," Shawn said as he poured Bennie a healthy glass and handed it over. "To a brand new future...and leaving dumb ass niggas in the past!"

Bennie chuckled and held up his glass. "Hell yea, I'll drink to that!"

Chapter 24
The Bet

"Shawn, why do you keep breaking your phones?" Kay asked as she watched him unwrap his new one.

Shawn just shook his head. This was his fifth phone in two months. The last time he broke it was after his incident with Les—ever since it accidentally fell out of his pocket it wasn't acting right.

"I got news. I got an offer to do some illustrations for this publishing company. The contract is for two Gs but it has exclusivity clauses. I'm not sure if I should do it..." Kay said out of the blue.

"What? Why you wanna act scary? Girl they gonna pay you to draw some shit? You better go for what you know!"

Kay ran her fingers through her soft curly afro as she looked at her laptop screen.

"Yea, but if I sign a contract they're probably going to want full rights to my work. I don't know if I like the idea of giving away the rights to my stuff. These things can get complicated," she explained. "Non-compete clauses and all that. And what if they want to change my drawings? I don't know Shawn, I don't really want to put myself out there like that. I don't wanna sell out and I don't wanna be a slave to their corporate bullshit. What do you think?"

Shawn looked at her like she was crazy.

"So basically, you gonna give up two stacks cause you scared? Far as I'm concerned they could take a dump on my page for that long as the check clear," he said and shook his head. "Girl you so smart you stupid. Always overthinking shit."

"Not all money is good money Shawn."

"True, and you right Kayby. That's why I fell in love you; you don't love money. But if you make a name for yourself you can use that to put out anything you want down the line. You feel me?"

Kay just looked at him.

"Bottomline, don't let fear of the unknown hold you back! You better get that money bae."

Kay was quiet as she thought about what he said. Shawn's chest puffed up a bit when he realized that he was actually getting through to her. She rarely if ever came to him for advice in the past, let alone followed it.

"Okay I'll think about it," Kay said as she got up to grab her purse and keys. "So we going or what?"

"Hell yea."

"Are you gonna spend an hour primping in the mirror again or what?" she teased.

"Shut up."

Within minutes they were headed out to the city to hit up one of Shawn's favorite pool halls in the Northern Liberties. It was a hood joint but a nice one—the $1 mugs of Yuenglings were the main attraction. They were both still pretty tight with money even though Shawn had reclaimed what was his from Les.

Shawn promised her that he would get her the necklace she wanted but it would take a few more weeks. Kay told him all she wanted while there was to spend time with her buddy and drink $1 Yuenglings. It made him smile. It was nice dealing with a woman who wasn't obsessed with money and material things.

"I'm going to bust your ass in some pool tonight," Kay teased as they drove down 95 with the windows down enjoying the warm summer air.

"We'll see," Shawn said with a nod. He already planned to let her win anyway.

"I've been practicing, be afraid," she said seriously.

"I've got to see this," Shawn said with a chuckle. "So I gotta tell you something."

"What?" Kay said, expecting the worst.

"It's nothing bad. I got a referral from my counselor at the VA to go to this rehab. I think I'm gonna go."

"Really? How long?"

"It's a 30-day program that can extend to 90 days."

Kay sat quiet for a long while thinking about what that meant.

"Then they said that can help me get a job when I get out."

Kay nodded. "That's awesome Shawn. You do what you gotta do bro."

"I'm trying," he said with a nod.

"You know Shawn I'm real proud of you."

"Thank you baby."

Shawn let Kay win the first two games and made sure the drinks kept coming. They alternated between shots of Southern Comfort and mugs of Yuengling.

"Why don't we make this interesting," Shawn finally said as he was racking up the balls for the next game.

"Like how?" Kay said as she sipped on her beer, feeling nice.

"If I win I get a kiss. If you win I wash your car early tomorrow before you leave."

"Hmmm, a kiss? Like on the mouth though?"

"Yes, on the lips. And I want tongue."

"You ain't getting no tongue, but I'll do the lips," Kay agreed, semi-confident in her pool skills, and they shook on it. "You better not be trynna hustle me though."

Shawn quickly finished racking up the balls and as usual Kay wanted him to break them up first. He did and about three balls went in immediately.

Five minutes later, Shawn was lining up his pool stick to hit the eight-ball. Most of Kay's balls were still on the table. She stood there with her hand on her hip. He looked up at her for a second and flashed his winning smile.

"You an asshole," she said and shook her head. Shawn broke out in laughter and then sank the eight-ball in the corner pocket with ease.

Shawn stood up and tried to look innocent, which was almost impossible. Kay shook her head.

"How you gonna hustle your best friend?" she asked. "You couldn't even let me get a shot in?"

"Hey, if it's about a kiss I'm not leaving anything up to chance. When I place a bet, I plan to win," he told her and then opened his arms as he walked around the table toward her. "A deal's a deal.

She kept her arms crossed as he grabbed her. She let her forehead rest on his chest for a minute, then closed her eyes and puckered up. He kissed her gently on the lips. It was a sweet, simple kiss and there was a comfortable energy flowing between them.

Shawn grabbed her into a bear hug and lifted her up from the ground.

* * *

Shawn stood outside of the house smoking a cigarette as usual. No matter how cold it was, he had to smoke outside— Kay's rules. He stood looking out at the street thinking of how beautifully they were getting along lately. He was truly starting to get to a place where he felt... happy. Just hanging out with his buddy made his day.

His phone buzzed and he figured it was Kay from inside. Instead he found himself reading a text message from Meghan, the white girl from his old school who had gone fatal attraction on him years before.

I miss u

"Random," he said to himself. He looked at the message and wondered what could possibly be going through her head to text him that after all that time. They never really hung out. They never really had sex. He hardly showed her any attention. He finally came to the conclusion that this girl had some serious daddy issues.

Without thinking much of it, he dialed her number.

"Shawn!" she said excitedly after picking up on the first ring.

"What's up Meghan."

"Ohhh, I"ve missed you so much Shawn, when am I gonna see you again?"

Shawn took a long puff of his cigarette and thought before he spoke. "Meghan, I'm getting back with my fiancée—I'm not going to be able to hang out anymore."

"Awwww, why not? Can't we just hang out as friends?"

"No we can't. But can I tell you something?"

"Yes..."

"You don't have to try to be something that you're not in order to get a man's attention."

Meghan was quiet on the other end.

"Guys like it more when you just be yourself, you know? And if they can't appreciate you for who you are fuck 'em."

"Mmmhmmm."

"I'm serious... do you hear me?"

"Yes, I do. You sound like my father," Meghan said with an eye-roll.

"And you too young to be drinking so much girl. Ease up. Calm down."

Meghan was quiet.

"You do those two things and I promise you, you'll find a dude one day who will make you real happy."

"Okay. I will."

"Take care of yourself and go back to school okay."

"Alright, thanks Dad," she said sounding a little sad, but content.

Shawn hung up, knowing deep down that that was the last he would hear from Meghan.

Chapter 25
Fearless

"So I was seeing this guy for a few months," Kay started as they sat at one of their favorite restaurants downtown having dinner.

"Yea."

"He would barely even call me twice a week," Kay said, shaking her head. "It's like he's waiting for me to chase after him or something."

"Oh yea. That's how these New York dudes are, you forgot?" Tisha said with a laugh. "They think they're God's gift."

"Yea well, they're not. And I'm not playing these little games anymore. So I dumped him."

Tisha laughed. "I feel you. But to be honest I think you push them away on purpose. You don't want to let go of Shawn."

"Push them away? Please. They push themselves away. Shawn was an ass sometimes but at least he knew how to treat a lady!" Kay said with a smile.

"Mmhm," Tisha mumbled.

"He calls or texts me every day. He bought me gifts and was ready to marry me after just a year. He even bought me a diamond ring. I'll be lucky to get a drink from these dudes out here!"

"You know damn well you still love Shawn," Tisha said nonchalantly. "You need to just go work that out."

"You know he's going to rehab."

"Oh yea?"

"Yea, for about a month."

"Well good for him!"

"Yea I'm proud of that brother he is really doing his thing."

The waiter came over with the check and Kay grabbed it immediately.

"I got this sis, you have been there for me so much over these past couple years. I don't know if I could have made it without you."

Tisha smiled and started to tear up. "You know I love you. And I know you'd do the same for me."

Kay had taken the exclusive gig and negotiated the contract so that it was less restrictive. She was now working as an illustrator for hire. A couple of publishers were referring her for children's books and also online comic strips. It was just what she needed to keep things afloat as she pursued her more serious art on the side.

* * *

Kay sat on the late train home thinking about what Tisha said. She had been treating Shawn more like a brother and best friend than her man for the past few years, but was that really what she wanted? Was she looking for reasons to break up with the guys she dated because she was biding her time waiting for Shawn to get it together?

As she was caught up in her thoughts a couple of young guys came past where she was sitting in deep thought. They doubled back when they saw her sitting there, legs crossed, looking nice in a white and yellow dress. They smelled like they were sweating gin and juice.

"Heyyy," one said and smiled. It was a smile that said he was up to no good. Kay didn't even know if anyone else was in the car with her at that point.

When one of them flopped down in the seat right next to Kay her antennas when up. He tried to put his hand on her leg and she slapped it away immediately.

Normally Kay's paranoia would flare up and cause her to immediately either try to get up to leave or scream and curse them out. But a voice within soothed her and said "Chill."

I be damned if I live in fear and let some lil nigga have me running away with my tail between my legs. You run from your problems you'll be running all ya life, she remembered Shawn telling her.

She looked at the young man with an intense stare. He was probably nearly a decade younger than her.

"Yo, what's a pretty girl like you doing all by yourself? Where your man at girl?" he asked, licking his lips and trying to sound smooth as his friend settled in the seat across from them watching.

"Living my life and handling my business, how about you?" she asked seriously.

"Uh, the same," he responded with a little chuckle.

"How old are you?" she asked, turning the conversation back on him.

"Um, 21."

"Damn, so nobody taught you how to talk to a lady yet?" she asked in a scolding voice. "Now that's a shame! How do you ever expect to meet a good woman if you approach women disrespectfully like that?"

The young man's expression changed. "I guess I ain't really thinkin' bout all that. I mean, I'm only 21. Give me a break..."

"No, give me a break lil brother. Our parents and grandparents used to get married when they were 16 years old and they made it work. If they didn't we wouldn't be here. So quit using that as an excuse. At 21 you're a grown adult, so start acting like one," she said sternly as she looked him right in the eyes. He averted his eyes, looking a little ashamed. Kay looked 18 years old, but by her tone clearly she wasn't.

"Oooh shit, she schooling you," the other older one chimed in and chuckled. "You better listen."

"You're older than him, you should be telling him this," she told his friend and he shut up. She turned back to the 21-year-old. "Remember this lil brother, you attract what you are. So if you go around acting like an ignorant fool, don't be mad when all the women you attract are the same way..."

Even though Kay saw he was uncomfortable, she kept telling him about himself, making him feel smaller and smaller with each word. Finally, the drunken young man stumbled up from his seat.

"You know you're right. Sorry to bother you ma'am," he said and then signaled to his friend to come on.

"Okay you have a good night then," Kay said and for the first time smiled at him.

"You have a good night too," he said and smiled back.

Kay watched them stumble away.

* * *

I'm pregnant...

Cage got the news from Tanya via text because he wasn't answering her calls. He had been trying to strengthen his relationship with Wilhemina lately. Watching his best friend Shawn go through it trying to get Kay back for so long made him see things a bit differently. He was also starting to sense that Wilhemina was becoming more and more detached from him. She barely even asked him where he was going when he left the house anymore.

Now his long-time jump-off from West Philly was claiming she was pregnant and he was the father.

quit fucking around on my phone, he texted back.

I ain't fucking around. I'm pregnant and it's yours! she told him.

ain't fucking wit you no more, don't call my phone no more

When she tried to call him again, he immediately rejected the call and went on about his business as if she didn't exist.

"Hey baby," Cage said as he walked into Willie's house uncharacteristically early. He saw her sitting on the couch with her kids on either side of her. She had a photo album open on her lap.

"Hey," she said nonchalantly and then looked back at her book.

"What you doing there?" he said and walked over to grab the book from her lap. It was her old portfolio of modeling pictures and headshots.

"Mommy pretty!" her little daughter stood up on the couch and pointed at the book in his hand.

"Yea, she was always a knockout," Cage said and flipped through the book for a while before handing it back to her.

"Mommy you should be a model!" her son said with a smile, beaming with pride.

"Mommy was a model bae," she said with a smile back and looked through them for a few more moments before shutting it closed.

"Anything to eat in here?" Cage called out from the kitchen.

"There's a plate in the oven. Just heat it up," she answered. "Okay kids up to bed, mommy be up to tuck you in in a minute."

The kids did as they were told and Wilhemina started tidying up around the living room. Cage set the microwave and came back out.

"What you been up to today?" he asked as he watched her mull around.

"Had off today, just chillin' wit the kids."

"Why you ain't tell me you had off, I woulda came home even earlier. I wasn't really doing nothin' today."

Wilhemina didn't answer, just gathered some cups and toys into her arms and started to head to the back. Cage grabbed her from behind and started to kiss her on the neck.

"Stop, I'm not in the mood," she said dodging his advances. She went into the kitchen to put the cups in the sink. Cage was a little surprised because Wilhemina had a sex drive like no other. Sometimes when he came home early they would get in a quickie in the kitchen right before the kids came in to eat dinner.

"You mad at me or somethin'?"

"Naw, I'm good, just tired is all. Enjoy your meal," she said as she headed to the kids' rooms.

Chapter 26
Smart Girls

Mya was over the house visiting while Kay was in town. They went to Dave & Buster's earlier in the day to play games. It was going to be the last time he saw his daughter before heading off to rehab. Shawn was getting a little too drunk and Kay had to chase him around Dave & Buster's to stop him from getting more shots of vodka. He figured if he was going to be going to rehab he might as well go out with a bang, but Kay wasn't having it—especially not while they had Mya.

Shawn had a policy with Mya. He would only be 100 percent real with her and didn't try to shield her from the truth. He didn't try to pretend to be something he was not around his daughter. He wanted her to be prepared for anything as she got older. He also knew that if he put her around the right people she would quickly absorb everything she needed to know about life from them. As a result, Mya had grown up pretty fast—at 10 years old she was a smart girl who was quick on her feet and absorbed knowledge like a sponge. Regardless of how her father acted she still loved him more than anything.

"So you gonna write me while I'm up there right?" Shawn asked her as they sat in the kitchen. He was cooking up his famous fried chicken wings with some macaroni and cheese and string beans. Kay had made a run to the store for cereal for Mya in the morning.

"Daddy you act like you're going to prison! It's only the rehab place!" Mya said and shook her head at her father.

He laughed. "Yea I know but it feel like it. When your report card coming out?"

"Next week, I think."

"I better see some As. And your mom gonna send it to me. I will break outta rehab and kick your ass if I see anything lower than a B. Ow!!"

Shawn shrieked comically as some of the chicken oil popped up and hit him in the face. Mya laughed at him.

"It's all As and Bs Daddy," Mya said confidently.

"Okay then. The last thing you want to be is a dumb little girl. Dumb people have really fucked up lives."

"I know Daddy, you told me."

"What else I tell you?" he asked, testing her.

"Uh… don't trust nobody. Especially not boys cause they dirty," she said after some thought.

"What else?"

"If a boy ever hit me hit him back 10 times harder!" she said enthusiastically as she sat up on her knees to watch her father flip the chicken.

"With a big rock if you got one. What else?"

"Smart girls get paid, stupid girls get played?"

"Give me five up top," he said and slapped hands with her. "That's my baby girl. Pass me that plate."

Later that night Kay and Mya were playing around on the computer so Shawn took the opportunity to go upstairs and call his oldest son. Shawn Jr. was 20 now, his brother Samuel 17, and they hadn't been on the best of terms for a long while, but lately since Shawn was getting his life together they were connecting more and more.

"Hey Dad."

"What up son. You know I'm going to this rehab tomorrow

right?"

"Yea I got your message."

"I'll be back in about a month."

"Aiight, that's cool. Proud of you Dad."

"Thanks son," Shawn said and felt a wave of relief wash over him when he heard those words. "How's your brother?"

"He aiight, just getting ready to graduate soon."

"Good. And you still thinking about going to that tech school I told you about?"

"Yea. Found out they do got that music production program. Those music producers start out making $100,000."

"Long as you 'bout something, I don't want you hangin' out in those streets no more. Look where it led me. I'm still tryin' to get my life together."

"I ain't in the streets, you know I got the baby on the way and all that."

Shawn had been ecstatic to hear that his first grandchild was on the way. He vowed that he would do whatever he could to help his son out in raising the new baby and make up for time lost.

"Aiight. You better tell me when the baby's coming, take my number down at the rehab center in case you can't reach me on my cell," he said and then ran off the digits.

"Okay Pop, I'll give you a call while you up there."

"Aiight, love you son."

"Love you too Dad."

Chapter 27
Living Fearlessly

Damn girl.... What are you reading my mind? I sit here listening, asking myself are we having a conversation or am I being taught a lesson?
As I think about how to play this situation, which I know could be a sip away from being a disaster...

"I know you dating somebody Kay. I was born *at* night, not last night!"

"Negro please! How do you even know you were born at night?" Kay laughed. "You always say that and I bet you were born in the afternoon. Be quiet."

"Don't worry 'booout it," Shawn said with a sly smirk and a wink as he drank another sip of his Coors Light. On the outside he was smiling but on the inside he was kind of hurting, because really he couldn't stand thinking about Kay being with someone else. She wouldn't say either way.

"Let me see your birth certificate then."

Shawn sipped his drink and glanced at her sideways.

"Guess what? I found a little regular side gig doing drawings. It pays about a G a month. Things are starting to pop off."

"What? Congratulations bae! I'm proud of you, you finally using your talents!"

"If you'd like to sign up for karaoke, now's the time! Karaoke, ahora el tiempo!" they heard Maria the bartender say over the mic in between serving drinks. They were in the popu-

lar Puerto Rican bar in the Northeast that Shawn liked to fre-
quent. It was karaoke night and the spot was buzzing. This was
the last time Kay would see him before he went to the rehab
center, which was over an hour and a half away.

"Why don't you sign up. I know you can sing," Shawn
said.

"Nawww, I only sing in the shower," she told him. Shawn
looked at her and gave her the screw face.

"Excuse me!" he said and put his finger up for Maria to
come over. "She wanna sign up for karaoke."

"What song?" she asked.

"Nooooo he's just playing around," Kay said with a laugh.
"I'm good."

"No she not, she can sing her ass off. Watch. Dancing is
another story but..."

"Shut up!" Kay said and punched him in the shoulder. "I
can dance asshole!"

"If you was on Soul Train they'd put you at the very end of
the line. Stop frontin'!" Shawn teased.

"I can't stand your ass."

"What song you want to sing," Maria asked as she put a
book of songs up on the bar. Kay looked up at her and then
back down at the book.

"What you scared of?" Shawn asked her. "Sing some Mary
J. Blige or some shit. Get out all that frustration."

Kay laughed nervously and grabbed the book onto her lap.
She chose one of Mary J's classics, *My Life,* and put in her order.

A few drinks and 20 minutes later, Maria came by with the
microphone and Kay's heart started beating faster. She couldn't
believe she was about to do this.

"Sing baby, sing," Shawn encouraged her. The familiar
tune started playing in the background. Kay closed her eyes.

"If you looked in my life and see what I've seen..." Kay started singing. "Life can be only what you make it...When you're feeling down you should never fake it..."

Shawn sat and watched her in admiration as she sang every verse at the bar in tune without ever looking at the karaoke screen. Clearly the lyrics meant something to her.

When she was done, everyone at the bar clapped and Maria smiled at her as she took the microphone. Kay felt like a million bucks even though her heart felt like it was pumping a million beats a minute.

"Can't believe you really did that!" Shawn said with a laugh.

"What do you mean, it was your idea!" Kay said and slapped his arm.

"No seriously, you did a great job bae. You conquered one of your fears," he told her.

"Yea I guess so. I think we're on the right track bro," she said with a smile and held up her drink in a toast. "To living fearlessly!"

"To living fearlessly," he agreed and they clinked their glasses together loudly.

Chapter 28
Made Me Go to Rehab

Shawn had been at the rehabilitation facility for close to two weeks. As usual he made friends immediately and everyone was trying to get next to him to be a part of his circle.

Most of the attendees were much older veterans who had decades-long addictions but a few were young guys who were just trying to get back on track.

Bill, a white guy who was staying in the facility, came into the common room and grabbed the remote control. He turned the channel as if no one was watching the current program.

"Yo what the fuck is you doing?" one of the older black gentlemen, Marlon, asked. "Did you not see us in here watching that?"

"You was really watching that wack ass sitcom? Seinfeld? Come on," Bill asked. By his accent he was clearly from Philly, probably South or Northeast. "Aw, I might have to pull your black card on that one."

The older guy stood up and came over to snatch the remote from the younger guy's hands as he laughed.

"You ain't never had a black card to pull dickhead," Marlon said.

Before Marlon had a chance to sit back down the white boy was up in his face screaming.

Shawn rolled his eyes and got up to break up the disagreement. That was becoming the norm—he was the mediator in a lot of the day-to-day issues between his peers in the program.

The other men, young and old, respected him. The group leaders were actually considering a move to make him a student-counselor at the facility.

That day Shawn was in a good mood and no one was going to mess it up. He was expecting Kay for a visit any minute. She had gone to the store to pick up a lot of supplies that he requested; mostly frozen dinners. The food at the facility was crap and didn't fill them up. It was up to them to buy extras.

Even though he was calming down, Shawn couldn't help expressing his asshole roots from time to time and causing a little drama at the facility. He planned to use the food Kay brought over to rub in their faces or as a bargaining chip. He would choose just the right moment to heat up a lasagna meal while everyone was in the rec room watching television with their stomachs still growling, then slowly eat it with the cheese stretching up from his fork...

"Karlson... someone here for you," the lady behind the counter came into the rec room to tell him, interrupting his thoughts.

Shawn jumped up and clapped his hands together. He got his stroll on to the elevator and took it down the ground floor. He peeked out of the elevator at the glass doors playfully and smiled from ear to ear when he saw it was Kay, standing there with a huge bag.

"Hey bae!" he said as he took the bag from her and gave her a big hug. "Why you ain't call me I would have helped you with this."

Kay took a good look over Shawn and was impressed. He was looking buff and refreshed as if he had been working out and living good. His body was stronger.

"We...well I got some more stuff in the car," she stumbled

over her words as she shot glances at his biceps, trying not to look too obvious.

Kay had brought him enough frozen dinners, sweets, drinks and books to last him the rest of his time at the program. He brought her up to the rec room, introduced her to everyone and then gave her the rundown on just about every person there.

"This nigga right here almost got me kicked out the program, because I was about to whip his ass," he said point right over at a skinny white guy who was watching television with his chin on his fist. "He tried to get me in trouble over some DVDs."

"What happened?"

"He wanted to watch one and I told him no. Suddenly they came and confiscated my shit," he said.

"Fucking hater," Kay said, shaking her head.

"You know? But I realized how people be doing little shit to piss me off and cause me to fuck up my situation."

"So what'd you do?"

"I had a one-on-one with the kid. At first he denied it talking all this shit, so I shut him down. Wasn't nobody talking to his rat ass for days. Then he come up to me one day and apologized."

"That was smart."

"Yea, I'm learning. You want to go down and get a cup of coffee?" he asked and Kay nodded. "Come on."

"I started writing you a letter," he said as they slowly walked down the hallway to the coffee machine. "It's supposed to be a letter of confessions—my counselor said it would help my recovery process. But I'm having a hard time with it."

"Oh yea, when am I gonna get *that*?" she asked.

"Soon, soon," he said with a nod. "But I got one confession I gotta make right now."

"What?" she asked, looking at him with a side-eye.

Shawn sighed deeply and then started chuckling nervously. Kay wondered what it could possibly be that she didn't already know.

"Remember way back when we used to fight all the time..." he started and then stopped, thinking if he should keep it to himself.

"Yes, and?"

"Well one time I was real mad at you, and..." Shawn stopped again.

"Spit it out, ain't no turning back now!" Kay's curiously piqued.

Shawn sighed. "I put Magic shaving powder in your shampoo."

Kay's mouth dropped open and she stopped in her tracks. "No you didn't!"

"Yea, I did." Kay punched him in the arm.

"Ow! I'm sorry!" he said with a chuckle. "Obviously it didn't work though."

"You know, one time I was about to wash my hair and the shampoo didn't quite smell right in my hand..." she said thinking back to that day. "It smelled funky, so I tossed it out!"

"Yup," he said and started laughing hysterically.

"You know you're lucky I didn't use that shit, I would have had to go get that pipe on your ass!" she said. "Give you two more lumps on the back of your head."

She and Shawn had a good laugh. He felt relieved, but there was so much more he wanted to say. He just didn't know how to express himself at the moment.

Chapter 29
I Be That Baby Pappy!

Shawn was beaming as he held his grandson in his arms for the very first time. It brought him back to the day when his own children were born—he was one proud pappy. Back then he had been so young, but now at 35 he was fully grasping the beauty of having a brand new extension of himself born into the world.

"He got your nose Dad," Shawn Jr., the proud new father, told him.

"Yea he do!"

Shawn had returned from the rehab facility that morning and immediately came down to his son's house to see his brand new grandson. He snapped pictures of his first grandchild and texted them around to everyone he knew. He was so proud.

As he left the house his two sons followed him out. He looked at them both and could hardly believe he had helped produce these two thorough, strong, good-looking young men.

"Ya'll better not be involved in that dumb ass shit I been hearing about on the news."

They both shook their heads no and looked away.

"Seriously, I will fuck you up!"

"Aaah, yea we know," Samuel said as if he wasn't convinced and rolled his eyes with a smirk.

"Boy I will still whip ya ass, you ain't too grown," Shawn said and started punching him playfully. They shadowboxed for a while in the street and their Dad showed them some new boxing moves until a car came, beeping for them to go back on the sidewalk.

Shawn turned serious again as he looked at his sons. "I know I ain't been in ya'll lives as much as I should have. But I love you and I'm here for you now, and I mean that. If you need something you call me."

"Aiight," they both said in unison.

"And ya'll need to stay in touch with your sister. Ya'll are blood, nothing more sacred. You'll learn that more as you get older," he told them. They agreed.

They all slapped hands. When he got to his younger son Samuel, Shawn leaned in close to his ear as he grasped his hand.

"I'm serious son, I love you man," he told him.

Shawn then turned to head down the street toward the bus. Ironically he was on his way down to traffic court to petition to get his driver's license back. The suspension was almost up and the folks at the rehab program told him all he had to do was get on a payment plan for past due amounts and request an occupational license so that he could get a good job. Kay was following her dreams to be an artist and she was inspiring him to go for his as well.

When he arrived downtown he stopped by a lunch truck just as it was about to close up and grabbed a hot sausage with peppers. He was almost finished with it before he even left the truck.

"Hey SB!" he heard a female voice say to him from behind. He turned his head and there was Tammy. The same girl he had dated all those years before but left after a few dates. She was pregnant and looked a little haggard, like life had given her a good beat down.

"Hey girl," he said slowly. Her name escaped him at first.

"How you been?" she asked.

"Doing good. How 'bout you?" he asked back, glancing at her stomach.

"Eh. Can't wait to pop this one out in a few months. This will be number four," she said as she rubbed her belly, trying to smile. "Just out here waiting for my cousin to come out of traffic court."

"Yea I'm heading down there myself," he said and looked at his cellphone. "Matter fact I'm late."

Tammy nodded and put her head down. Before it was as if she had a tiny glimmer of hope in her eyes, that maybe, just maybe Shawn would look past the fact that she was pregnant and they could pick up where they left off all those years ago. This was her fourth baby by a fourth guy who disappeared from the scene shortly after learning she was pregnant. She kept letting history repeat itself.

"Alright then," he said as he finished off his sausage and threw the foil in the trash can nearby. "See you around."

Shawn started to walk off and immediately felt a knot develop in his stomach. It got worse and worse with each step. He wondered if it was the sausage he just ate or maybe the piece of glass still lodged in his stomach.

Suddenly he stopped, turned around and walked back toward Tammy. He was surprised to see that she was silently sobbing. The knot in his stomach disappeared. The first thing that came to mind when he saw her crying, pregnant and looking miserable was "black girl lost." He wondered what part he might have played in that outcome.

Tammy looked up and was shocked to see him standing in front of her again.

"Hi..." she said.

At first he was going to say something. Maybe apologize for the way that he had treated her in the past. Maybe tell her everything was going to be alright. But instead he just opened his arms to give her a brotherly hug.

"C'mere," he said. She came to him and started bawling like a baby on his chest. He didn't have to say another word.

* * *

"Ay bae!" Shawn said loudly and obnoxiously into the phone when Kay picked up.

"Hey what's up bro?"

"Got my license!" he shouted.

"Whaaaaaaaaat."

"Got my fucking license Kay, holding it in my hand right now," Shawn said with a koolaid smile plastered across his face.

"No way! I got to see this!"

"And I might got a job!" he added.

"For real?"

"Yup, in a kitchen cooking. They supposed to call me back in a couple weeks."

"Whooo that's the shit Shawn!" Kay said excitedly. She closed her eyes and said a quick silent prayer that the new job would stick this time. "Congratulations, I'm happy for you bro!"

"Bae it feels so good. Can't remember the last time I had my license!" he said. "And I'm still coming out there for your birthday too."

"Can't wait. We got a lot to celebrate, time to party."

"Til the wheels fall off! We'll pop bottles," he said with his trademark laugh. "Gotta run though, I'll call you later."

* * *

"You ain't gonna believe this shit," Tino said to Shawn as they walked down South Street. They were going to the Adidas store and a couple of other shops so that Tino could get fresh for the weekend. He also had to buy his kids some new shoes. Shawn was tight on cash but still wanted to check out the latest sneakers and grab a hat.

"I don't even wanna know," Shawn waved him off and

looked in the shop windows.

"Sorry my dude," Tino said, and then told him anyway. "They talking about that nigga Huey getting out soon."

Shawn didn't say anything. Word though the grapevine was Huey had still been talking about how he was going to come get Shawn. Nobody could believe that he was still that pressed over getting slighted over a party.

"That dude clearly got problems," Tino said as they walked into the Adidas store. "He still talkin' 'bout that party."

"I told you, I don't even wanna know T. I'm rising above, then I'm gonna shit on all them niggas."

Tino laughed. "My fault, but I wouldn't be your boy if I ain't tell you… Yooo, check out these jawns!"

Shawn checked out the sneakers Tino showed him but his mind was occupied with thoughts of how drama kept pulling him back to square one. It seemed as if the more and more he made progress, the more negativity came in his life trying to set him back.

* * *

Wilhemina was ecstatic when she received the call inviting her to participate in a popular annual modeling competition down in Miami. She was a finalist out of over 2,000 girls. At the prodding of her kids, she had emailed in some recent photos of herself as well as a few from years back since she looked almost exactly the same as she did at 19, even after having two children. They called her back the next day.

Next to New York and Los Angeles, Miami was a big market for up and coming models. The exposure at this competition alone could help propel her into a serious high-fashion modeling career.

At first, Wilhemina simply felt vindicated to know that yes, she was still qualified enough to be a model. Going to Miami was a dream but impossible...

But then she got to thinking about what was holding her back from going to or even living in the beautiful city of Miami. She had a little money saved up. What was holding her back from starting a whole new life down there? What was holding her to Philly?

She went through the list of all the downsides of doing so and could only come up with one real answer to that question.

Cage.

On impulse, Willie picked up the phone and dialed her closest friend, Tino's wife Elisha. She had always been supportive and they babysat each other's kids from time to time.

"Hey girl! How you?" Elisha asked.

"Doing okay. Guess what?"

"What girl, spit it out! Spit out!" Elisha said impatiently.

"I got selected as a finalist for this modeling show down in Miami!"

"Oh word!!!? You're joking!"

"Nope, so serious! They want me to fly down there ASAP."

"Oh my God! Congratulations Willie! I can't believe this!"

"Yea, I wish I could go."

"What you mean you *wish* you could go?"

"Well, you know. I got the kids and my job. I don't know if I can do it. But it's nice to know I'm still wanted. I still got it," Willie said as she snapped her finger in the air. Elisha didn't respond—there was quiet on the line.

"Hello?" Willie said, thinking the line had gone dead.

"Girl you in irk-mode right now. I know you ain't seriously thinking about passing up this opportunity with that bag of excuses?"

"Lish, how Imma swing that though? My job ain't gonna wait for me. And what about the kids?"

Elisha was no dummy. "You mean what about Cage right? Because your kids are yours, you make the decision on where they go. You just don't want to leave Cage."

Willie was quiet, which was the same thing as admitting Elisha was right.

"Willie listen to me closely. You know why our mommas are unhappy and mean? It's because they tied their whole lives, their whole existences to men. Trifling men at that!" Elisha told her. "They gave up their opportunities to be great when they were young so that they could take care of trifling ass men who left them anyway. Now they old and bitter about it—you can't get those years back."

"You think?" Willie thought about her own mother and how she had doted on men, including her brothers, all her life.

"Girl I know. When you're young you have to pursue your dreams. This is the time to take your shot! Don't let Cage or any man hold you back from doing what you know you're good at! Girl you're a model. If you don't take your ass to Miami I am going to kidnap you there!"

Willie laughed.

"Hunny if I had that long lanky body you got I'd be right up there on the runway with you, givin' everybody the hand! Girl go for yours!"

Willie laughed. "Lish, that's why I fucks with you, you never been a hater a day in your life."

"What reason I got to hate on somebody? I love my life and I want the same for everybody who I love. You feel me?"

"Yea I do. To be honest you are the one I'll miss the most," Willie said with a little frown.

"I'll miss you too, but like I said you gotta go after your dreams! Do what makes you happy. I gotta run, love you girl."

"Love you too, I'll call you when I make my decision."

Chapter 30
Accepting Responsibility

"So what's the deal for this weekend?" Shawn asked Kay over the phone. They had been planning to go out for her upcoming birthday in Manhattan but both of them were having some cash flow issues.

"I don't know, we ain't really gonna be able to ball out or anything like we thought..." she said as she thought about it and counted some figures in her head. "I was thinking maybe we should just chill a little on the spending for a while. You know, 'til we get our money right and you get confirmation about that job."

"Oh alright. Well we can do it in a month or so," Shawn said, sounding a little disappointed.

"Ok. Maybe sooner."

They hung up and Kay sat staring at the wall for a few minutes, suspended in thought as if she were in a trance. She thought about how tight money was, especially since she had just paid off all her bills.

But then she thought about how much fun she would probably have hanging out with her best friend in the city.

Without thinking much more of it, she picked up her phone and called Shawn back.

"I'm booking you a ticket, come out this weekend bro. We'll make it happen somehow."

* * *

It was Kay's birthday. She stood on a busy corner in midtown waiting for Shawn to come walking down the road, as usual. He had come to New York several times since the first time and they always had an amazing time out running the streets downtown.

As she waited patiently her thoughts drifted to all of the progress that he had been making over the past few months. Shawn had finally received his license back after 15 years. She thought about how many job opportunities he had missed out on in all of those years just because he didn't have his driver's license. Most of the tickets he had on his record weren't even his, but the traffic court refused to remove them.

She thought about his time in rehab. Even thought he had gone back to drinking beers, he had finally given up drugs for good. He didn't even smoke weed because he was concerned about not qualifying for a job.

She also thought about how she couldn't remember the last time they had a serious fight. He treated and talked to her with the utmost respect at all times. All she ever heard from him was encouragement and love.

Is it time for me to give him another chance and go back to Philly? she thought to herself.

Half an hour passed and Shawn still hadn't shown up. She was starting to get concerned and pulled out her cellphone to call him. The phone rang, and rang, and rang until it went to voicemail.

15 minutes later she was really starting to trip. Had he even really caught the bus? Did he lie about that? Why wasn't he answering the phone? All kinds of thoughts entered her head as she started to revert into panic mode and started to call him again.

"If he stands me up I will…" she said to herself.

But before she could finish her thought she saw a figure in the distance with that familiar glide strolling her way from about two blocks away. She put her phone away and smiled. She knew it was him.

"Heyyy Kaybyyy," he said as he finally approached her, eating a hamburger. "You want some?"

"So you had time to stop and get a hamburger huh? I was waiting for your ass for almost an hour!" she scolded him, but was more relieved than anything that he was there. Shawn polished off the rest of his burger.

"Yup... mmm that joint was hittin' too! Happy birthday babyyy," he said and grabbed her into a hug, lifting her off of the ground.

"Uhhh! Thank you!" she said with a smile as he put her back down.

"You look good bae!" Shawn exclaimed. He crossed his hands near his thigh and examined her for a moment. She was wearing a black pencil skirt that hugged her every curve and accentuated her small waist with a pink sleeveless blouse and black slingback heels. She was finally starting to get back in touch with her sense of style. "Damn!"

"Thank you. You're looking debonair as usual. Man, you are one good looking black man! Mmm mmm mmm!"

"You gonna make me blush," he said with a grin. "I love you girl."

"I love you too. So let me see it!"

"See what?" he asked with a mischievous smirk and looked down at his crotch.

"Not that you pervert!" she said and slapped his arm playfully. He laughed. "Your license!"

"Oh! Hold up," he said as he went into his back pocket to get his wallet. He pulled out his license. It glimmered.

"Awww shit," Kay said as she looked at his cheesy smile on the newly printed card.

"Yup," he said with a nod. "Now I'm gonna go get my Caddy!"

Kay rolled her eyes and Shawn laughed again. He was so happy he could barely stay still. "You a trip! But I'm so proud of you brother."

Shawn chuckled. "Thank you bae, I'm proud of myself too."

"Let's go to this spot down the street I just saw," Kay said excitedly as she pointed in the direction.

"Whatever you wanna do birthday girl."

They walked down to the place but the happy hour didn't start yet and Shawn wasn't finished smoking his cigarette. They stood outside and enjoyed the last few moments of that sunny day as he smoked. He looked at Kay intently with an expression that said he had a lot on his mind.

"What's up? What you thinking about?" she asked him. She knew him like the back of her hand.

"I know I said this to you before, but I want to apologize to you Kay, for everything I did to you in the past," he said.

"I forgave you Shawn. Let's leave it in the past."

"But if it was really in the past you would give me another chance," he replied. "Right?"

Kay looked down at her feet and didn't say anything.

"You know Kay, I been dating other women. And they okay and all," Shawn started to say. "But for some reason I can't stop thinkin' 'bout you."

Kay looked at him and for the first time just listened instead of brushing him off.

"I realize that I'm still in love with you, and there ain't nothing I can do about it," Shawn told her. "I wanna be with you and I don't care how long it takes, Imma get you back. Imma get my shit together and show you better than I can tell you. I can wait. I *will* wait."

I love you too Shawn. Kay wanted to say so badly but she held herself back. She knew that if she revealed her true feelings he would want to get back together immediately. But she wasn't ready to go back to Philly and back to living with him. She didn't want to go back to worrying about Shawn possibly running the streets. She liked her freedom too much. So she held her tongue.

"I believe you Shawn," she said instead—and that was the truth.

The bartender came to the door and told them happy hour had started. Shawn put out his cigarette on the side of a metal garbage can and threw it away before they went into the bar.

They talked about what had been going on in their lives lately. Shawn gave Kay some advice about her business matters. She was dealing with a client who was taking her through the ringer.

"Certain types of people always gonna try to take advantage of you. If they can get you, they gonna get you," he was telling her. "It's on you to set your foot down at the beginning. Just be prepared for every outcome and move on."

Just as she was nodding his cellphone rang and he checked his screen.

"Excuse me," he said politely and went outside to take the call. "Gotta take this, it's about a job."

Kay watched him through the bar window as he stood there, head held high, back straight, talking on the phone like a business man. He looked confident and professional.

She continued to steal glances at him between sips of her drink and smiled when she finally realized what was going on.

He is a new man, she thought to herself.

After enjoying a few cheap drinks at the happy hour spot, they hopped on the subway downtown to hit up one of their favorite bars on the Lower East Side. They sat next to each other on the train and Shawn took the opportunity to look her up and down again. She was glowing, with her hair in a natural style with a flower behind her ear, looking better than he'd ever seen her. She laughed at him and they chatted as if they were in their own world. Other riders on the train watched them—it was clear that they were happy together. Like a happy married couple.

When they finally arrived at their destination, Kay grabbed his arm and he bent it as a gentleman would when he's walking with a lady. Of course, he made sure she was on the inside of him on the sidewalk.

They walked together slowly and enjoyed the scenery downtown. White hipster kids were standing outside smoking cigarettes and chatting. Shawn and Kay dodged careless taxi cab drivers. Shawn had that extra pep in his step that Kay only saw when he was out there with her in the city. His chest was puffed out proudly as he walked with his lady, laughing and chatting.

When they arrived at their usual spot, they immediately ordered a couple of drinks and then a bottle of champagne. Shawn didn't drink much, but Kay drank a whole lot. They laughed and talked until Kay fell asleep with her head on the table. Shawn snapped a picture.

At the end of the night they made it to a cab and rode together back to the bus station. Kay lay quietly on his chest sleeping as he watched the New York City blocks pass by. It was a complete contrast from the first time they spent time in the city together, when they fought the whole cab ride back to the bus station. He didn't want to go. Shawn was loving the city more and more each time he came—he wanted to live there more than anything but wondered how he could ever make that happen.

"Kay. Kay," he said, shaking her awake.

She got up and looked around. They had arrived at their destination. They paid the cab driver and dragged themselves out. Kay gave him a long hug and then started taking off her necklace, which contained a charm with a heart and a key.

"Here," she told him, slurring, as she wrapped the necklace around his neck. "This is yours now. You got the key to my heart Shawn."

Drunk mouths tell no lies, Shawn couldn't help but think as he looked down at the charm.

"Thank you bae," he finally said with a smirk as if he knew something. He stole a kiss and gave her a hug before heading off to his bus.

As soon as Shawn touched back down in Philly he felt a dark cloud fall back over him. Spending time with Kay in Manhattan was like going on vacation to a tropical island then coming back to a warzone.

It was very early in the morning and none of the buses were running. He was pretty broke and didn't really have anywhere he could go until a couple of hours. Instead of trying to make it to his mother's house he decided to go to the early morning service at a church nearby. He was surprised to see a few other brothers his age sitting in there that early too.

He sat toward the back listening to the church organ playing. It soothed his soul and he relaxed a little. Soon enough the church was erupting in music and dancing—the whole place shook.

The pastor made his way to the pulpit and laid down his bible. The theme of the sermon was "taking responsibility for your life."

"When something goes wrong, what's the first thing that people do?" the graying pastor asked the small congregation. Everyone looked around at each other.

"Exactly what you all just did," he continued with a laugh. "They start looking around for someone else to put it on. They immediately start looking for someone else to blame. They don't want that attention on themselves. Nobody wants to take responsibility these days."

A few people nodded in agreement.

"If something goes wrong in your life as an adult only YOU are to blame. You control you. Learn to accept responsibility for your own life my sister!! My brother!!"

Shawn felt a jolt as if the pastor had spoken right to him. His words had hit home. He glanced down at his "Real Nigga" tattoo and remembered what Kay had told him a while back.

Shawn, this isn't you. 'Niggas' don't accomplish anything in life. You ain't a nigga, so stop playing the part. You're a real man, act like it.

Shawn had played the blame game with everyone and anyone all his life. It suddenly dawned on him that he was responsible for all of the drama in his life. Everything. He was solely responsible for the choices he had made which led him to his current situation. From his child support woes to Kay leaving him to losing out on jobs to his numerous street beefs. Being a "real nigga" came with its consequences. Shawn lowered his head and started praying silently...

Forgive me for my sins Lord. I am a man and today I accept full responsibility for my life. I really want to move forward. Help me stay on my path. Amen.

Shawn woke up later that day to news that Huey was officially back out on the streets, but something told him not to be too concerned about it—at least not yet. Huey was stupid, but not stupid enough to try to shoot someone right after getting out of jail on parole.

He was more concerned about getting that job that the rehab program promised him. They were giving him the run around—on one hand they were telling him that going to the program for the full 90 days would make it easier to get a job and on the other hand they were saying that he couldn't re-enroll in the program just yet.

He tried to call his counselor, but got her voicemail once again. After leaving yet another message for her, he hung up the phone and started searching though his phone's contact list looking for the direct number to another one of his counselors from the program to see if she could help him out.

Just then he saw a call from his young niece Briana. She was a 17-year-old beauty who was on her way to college soon. They were really tight—she called him often to get advice and guidance about life. He picked up immediately, happy for the distraction from his problems.

"Heyyy love, how you doin'?" he asked her.

"Hey Unc!" she said. "Guess what?"

"What?"

"I got into Georgetown!"

"For real? Ain't that your first choice?"

"Yes!! I just gotta get my financial aid in order and I'm set."

"I knew you could do it Bri, congratulations!" he told her,

beaming on his end of the phone like a proud dad. "You need help with those financial aid papers?"

"I might. I'll let you know. Thanks for giving me those tips about my application."

"You're welcome," he said and his fatherly instincts immediately started to take over. "When you get there you better focus on your studies Bri, leave those little boys alone."

"Aw Unc, calm down. You know I ain't boy crazy like that," she said with a chuckle.

"Yea right, well I know they girl crazy! Mark my words, they gonna be scheming on you the first weekend you there. College boys prey on freshman girls," he told her. "It's a sport. You know I trust you, but..."

"But you don't trust them, right I know," she said, finishing his sentence for him.

"Keep being smart. I find out you messin' with one them lil college boys I swear I'll come down there, strip 'im and whip 'im up right in the middle of the school yard!"

"Okay Uncle, you trippin' now. Imma speak to you later!"

"You think I'm playing!"

"Love you!"

"Love you too Bri."

When he hung up, his phone screen went back to the address book. Ironically, Briana's name was listed right after the name "Blake," the girl he had dated briefly at community college. He thought about the conversation he just had, and how Blake was probably somebody's niece, or daughter or sister too. She probably went to college all bright-eyed and bushy-tailed, hopeful and anticipating the best but never expecting to get dogged out instead.

Shawn thought about how the last time he talked to Blake he was so mean. He had called her every name in the book.

Blake had tried to call him a few times after that night, leaving apologetic messages, but he always rejected her calls.

Now that he was in a different state of mind he could understand what probably made Blake tick. She was hurting. She was confused. He now knew what it felt like to want something sooo bad and not be able to get it, no matter how hard you try. He could understand her desperation.

Then he remembered how just giving Tammy a hug had helped her—he now talked to Tammy every now and again and heard she was planning a move to Maryland to start a new life.

Without thinking much of it, he dialed Blake's number. It had been over three years since he talked to her and he didn't even know if the number was still good.

But it was.

"Who's this?" Blake said with an attitude. Clearly she had deleted him from her phone after all that time.

"It's Shawn, remember me?" he asked. "From school."

She was quiet for a while. "Okay. What do you want?"

"Uh, I was just going through my phone and…"

"And what, you decided you wanna call me up after all these years for a booty call? Man please!" she snapped.

"No, not at all! I just was concerned about you," he said with a little bit of a screw face. Her voice was really dripping with anger and malice. She could barely allow him to talk.

"Huh?" she laughed. "Well I don't need your concern. So glad I stopped fuckin' with ya'll men."

"Oh! What that mean?" Shawn asked.

"That mean I'm strictly clitly now!" she announced. "You got a problem with that?"

"No, not at all," Shawn said with a thoughtful nod. "But can I ask you a question?"

"I got some time to waste, so go 'head."

"You doin' that cause you genuinely like women or cause you hate men?"

Blake was quiet for a moment. "I don't have to explain shit to you muthafucker. Bye!"

"Wait, hold up," Shawn stopped her.

"What!"

"I know you probably don't wanna hear this now Blake, but I just wanted to tell you that I apologize for everything I did to you in the past," Shawn said. "I was a real asshole back then, I was going through some shit, but that was no excuse for treating you like that. How I treated you was wrong."

Blake was silent.

"You a smart beautiful black queen and you deserve better. I apologize. Seriously," he said again. "You can hang up now if you want."

After a few more moments, Blake did just that.

Shawn took a deep breath, exhaled and put his phone down. He couldn't really blame her for being so angry. Women like Blake caught the shitty end of the stick all of the time—they did everything they thought was right and good, but still couldn't get any respect.

He got up from bed to go to the bathroom but stopped when he heard his phone buzz. It was a text message:

thank you.

was all it said. From Blake.

* * *

"Uh uh, that nigga ain't getting' away with this. You just watch."

Tanya sat in the passenger seat of the car wiping away

tears as her older cousin Towanna drove her down North to find and confront Cage. She knew that if Cage wasn't at his house in West Philly he would probably be somewhere in North Philly hanging out at that hour.

Tanya finally let go of her youthful pride and admitted to her cousin that she had been played. She told her cousin that Cage had gotten her pregnant and now he was ignoring all of her calls. It had been months and she was starting to show.

"These old ass grown niggas don't have no fuckin' common sense, messin' around with these young girls," Towanna mumbled mostly to herself. "Imma show you exactly how you handle these pussies."

Tanya's lip quivered and she tried to get a hold of herself. She really thought that Cage would be happy to learn that they were having a baby.

"And you dumb little birds, always ready to cock ya legs open for some old ass nigga you barely know!" Towanna scolded her cousin. "And now you done got me involved in your bullshit! Shit!"

"I'm sorry Towanna, I didn't know what else to do! You know I can't tell my mother," Tanya whined. "And he won't even talk to me!"

Ironically Towanna had five kids with five different fathers herself. She was a rough and tumble type of chick who was always ready for a fight, especially if it involved her family members. She was the type of mother who went outside with her kids to fight their foes right alongside them.

"Well you know we don't do no abortions up in this family, so get ready for a lifetime of pain!" she told her. "And baby daddy drama! Congratulations dummy!"

They drove down to North Philly and started their hunt for Cage's truck, which was easy to spot. It was black with green rims—his two favorite colors. They checked all of the stores and spots where Cage had taken Tanya in the past. He was nowhere to be found.

Finally, Towanna pulled the car over sharply and put it in park. "Call him."

"What? You know he ain't gonna—"

"I said call him got dammit!" she yelled. She watched intently as Tanya called his number on speaker phone once, then a second time and then a third time. Each time it rang and rang until the voicemail picked up.

Towanna was just about to give up and head back home as Tanya was calling him a fourth time... but this time someone picked up the line.

"Hello? Who this?" a female voice said on the other line.

"No who the fuck is this?" Towanna said as she snatched the phone from Tanya's clutches.

"Bitch you called *my* man's phone four times, now answer the question," Wilhemina said as she clutched the phone tightly. Cage was in the bathroom taking a shower before he went on his usual nightly adventures.

"Bitch? I'll show you a bitch, bitch! Your so-called man got my little cousin pregnant!"

"Who? You must got the wrong number. Quit playing on people's phones," Willie said nonchalantly and hung up in her face.

Of course, Towanna redialed his number immediately.

"Hello." Willie answered the phone calmly, sounding bored, as if she hadn't just talked to someone. Her approach was silent but deadly—she would keep her cool right up until the very moment when she could no longer do so. And that moment was approaching quickly—her heart was pumping with anger. If there was one thing she couldn't stand it was chickenheads.

"Ain't nobody playing on your phone bitch! Cage been fucking my lil cousin and got her pregnant. She barely 21 with his overgrown ass!"

"So what exactly you want me to do?"

"We down 5th and Girard and we wanna see his ass RIGHT NOW. This nigga ain't answered a phone call from Tanya for months!"

Wilhemina thought about it for a minute as she peeked down the hallway to see if Cage was still in the bathroom. She was quiet enough to hear that the shower was still running.

"Okay, come by here in the next five minutes. We'll get to the bottom of all this," Wilhemina finally said, sounding cool. She had learned since she was a child to confront her problems head on so that they didn't have much time to linger and get worse. She boldly gave them her address and hung up the phone. Then she went into the bedroom to get prepared. First she wrapped her hair up tight and put a scarf on. She took her earrings off and changed into some sweats. Then she slathered some Vaseline on both cheeks and around her neck.

She heard a knock at the door and was surprised at how quickly they made it.

"Hey Cage, could you come on out here!" she said as sweetly as she could as she went to answer the door. She swung it open, ready to pounce, but calmed down when she saw it was just Shawn.

"Nigga you was about to catch an elbow," she said as she opened the door wider and let him in.

"For what?" Shawn asked with a confused look on his face as he reached in to give Willie a kiss on the cheek.

"Never mind," she said as she glanced outside and looked around. "Cage!"

Cage finally came out of the shower clutching a towel around his waist.

"Cuzzo," he said to Shawn with a smirk as he gave him a quick fist bump. "I'll be right out."

"Hurry up," Wilhemina said as she glared at him intensely. "We expectin' company."

"Expecting who?"

"It's a surprise."

"Girl you know I don't like surprises," Cage said with his face screwed up as he went to the back to get dressed. Shawn sat there and looked confused as he scratched at his beard. Willie stayed near the door looking out the window as if she was in a scene out of the Malcolm X movie. She pulled out her cellphone and sent a text to Elisha.

> *girl don't you know this nigga side ho just called to tell me she pregnant!*

>> *what!*

> *can't talk for long, but if something happen to me use your key, get my debit card out my dresser n bail me out pls. pin's my son's bday*

>> *what? you want me to come over there? don't do nothin stupid willie! think about Miami!*

Willie didn't reply because she saw a car pull up. She snatched the door open and went outside. Shawn heard female voices talking back and forth and got up to see what the commotion was. He saw two women outside near the curb talking to Wilhemina in an animated fashion. Willie was standing with her arms crossed listening and tapping her foot.

"Ay yo Cage, who these chicks outside?" Shawn yelled back to his friend. Cage came back pulling on his button-down shirt. When he looked outside and saw Tanya standing there his jaw dropped. He didn't know whether to go outside to mediate or climb out the back window.

"...I don't care 'bout all that. This ain't about you," Towanna was saying with her finger flying everywhere as Tanya flanked her. "We wanna see Cage's ass! Right now."

"Oh, but you don't come to my house making demands," Willie said, shaking her head. "Uh uh. I call the shots over here boo boo..."

"There he go!" Tanya said and pointed when she saw Cage open the door. She ran toward him and he put his hand out to stop her from coming any closer.

"What the fuck you doing here?" he said through clenched teeth. Shawn stood by his side, slowly realizing what was going on.

"So you *do* know this little ho huh?" Wilhemina said as she started to walk toward them.

"Don't be calling my cousin a ho, ho!" Towanna told her and made the mistake of pulling Willie back by her arm. Willie turned around and got right into Towanna's face, literally millimeters away. She looked down at her menacingly. She was almost a full head taller and could rest her chin on Towanna's forehead. It was as if someone pulled the needle out of a hand grenade—there was no putting it back.

"Or what," Willie asked as she bit her bottom lip, daring Towanna to make a move. Towanna sized her up and decided she was just a skinny pretty chick who talked shit and tried to look tough.

"Or Imma kick yo ass!" Towanna finally said as she put her finger up against Willie's temple.

The rest went by in a flash—the next thing everyone saw was Towanna's face eating grass. Willie had her bun in a tight grip and was pushing her head down as she straddled her on the ground. She mopped her head into the ground then punched her in the face repeatedly.

"Willie chill!" Cage yelled out—he knew better than anyone how ferocious Willie could get when she was on a rampage. People always underestimated her because she was tall and slim. Tanya was more concerned with Cage than with her cousin getting beat up.

"Why you ain't call me back!" she screamed at him and started punching him in the chest.

Shawn immediately went over to Willie and tried to pry her apart from Towanna who was fighting for her life at that point. They all tussled around for a few moments and finally he got her to let go—but not before she brought Towanna's entire bun along with her.

"Say some more shit bitch!" Willie screamed and kicked as Shawn carried her back into the house. "Keep talking some more!"

Towanna lay on the ground holding the back of her head— she was missing a patch of her own hair. Cage followed Shawn into the house and had to roughly push Tanya away to escape her clutches. She almost fell backwards.

"I'm taking you to child support!" she threatened. She then went on to continue screaming outside of Wilhemina's house, drawing the full attention of neighbors. Shawn and Cage had to lock Willie in the bedroom to keep her from running back out and attacking them again.

"I hate you! I hate you!" she screamed when she saw Cage. She started slapping and punching him all about the head and chest as he crouched down, taking the blows. Shawn wiped at his cheek and saw some blood from one of the women scratching him. He went back out to the door where Tanya was still screaming at the top of her lungs for Cage to come out.

"Ya'll better get the fuck out of here, before the cops come! They right around the block!" he lied to get them to leave and slammed the door closed. Towanna finally got up—she had warrants—and started slapping and pushing Tanya all the way to the car.

"Where were you??" she screamed.

* * *

Kay came out to Philly for the weekend to see Shawn and help him with some of his plans. They both had a busy week ahead. They were sitting out on the porch as usual, drinking Yuengling beers and enjoying the quiet starry night. Porch talks had become one of their traditions.

"Willie really fucked that chick up," he said after telling her about the fight at Cage's girlfriend's house.

"Sounds like it. She should know better than to go up to someone's house like that talking shit!" Kay nodded with a laugh.

"She almost fucked me up too!" he said and touched the healing scratch on his face.

"Shawn I know this is gonna sound a little cold, but you really have to stop getting involved in other people's drama all the time. Don't let people drag you down."

"I don't really. But Willie was about to put that girl in the hospital. She probably would have gotten locked up."

"So let Cage deal with it. Just listen to what I'm saying Shawn, you have a big heart and you put yourself on the line for other people too much. I know because I used to be like that," she told him. "Just think about it—sometimes you have to mind your own business."

"I'll think about it," he agreed. "Did I tell you I love you today?"

Kay smiled and shook her head. "No but now you did."

"You love me?" he asked.

"You know I do bro," she said, making sure to add the "bro" at the end.

Shawn became a little frustrated. "Stop calling me your brother Kay. I'm gonna be your fiancé again. You watch!"

Kay just nodded.

"Do you regret getting with me?" he asked her.

Kay shook her head immediately. "Not all all. No matter what we went through I'm glad I met you. You're a good strong brother, and I have a whole lot of respect for you Shawn. Seriously."

Shawn smiled and laughed a little. "Aw, you gonna make me blush."

"Do you regret anything?" Kay asked him. Shawn thought about it for a moment and then nodded.

"Yea. I regret not spending more time with my sons. And not fighting for my license all those years ago," he said. "Of course I regret losing you. And I regret spending so much time in the streets because now I'm older and can't get my shit together."

"You'll get it together Shawn, you just have to take it one day at a time. And it's never too late to get back on track."

Shawn remembered hearing Kidd's mother tell him the same thing, but he still wasn't sure how to do it. Things weren't moving along fast enough. "Yea, I'm just gonna leave it in God's hands."

Shawn sat on the bed silently the next morning watching Kay as she packed up her bag. She turned around and saw him sitting there looking at her like a kid who lost his puppy dog.

"Why are you looking at me like that?" she asked with a smile and came over to sit by him.

Shawn just shook his head and looked at her. Whenever

they were together he felt such a feeling of peace and calm—a big difference from the chaos of the projects. He didn't tell her that Huey was out or any of his other problems. He didn't want her to worry.

"You know, I can stay another day if you want. I'll just take off."

Shawn thought about it, but then thought about all of the commitments he made that day to see people and run errands. He had put them all off the entire weekend.

"Naw, I gotta go down the way today anyway," he said and got up to start packing up his own stuff into a backpack.

"You sure? It's not a problem."

"Yea I'm sure.

Even though he had his license he still didn't have a car, and Kay took the bus in, so he had to take public transportation back downtown. After giving him the schedule times, Kay gave him a long hug on the porch.

"When you coming back up?" he asked.

"Soon, maybe even next weekend. You should come back to the city soon too," Kay told him.

"Bet. Aiight bae, love you."

"Love you too babe."

Shawn turned back around when he heard that. "You called me babe, not bro. What that mean?"

Kay laughed. "It means I'll talk to you later."

Shawn winked at her and flashed a quick smile before descending the steps and then down the street. Kay watched him right up until he disappeared from her sight.

Chapter 31
Miami

Cage sat back riding in his truck down Chestnut Street in West Philly listening to the late night quiet storm on the radio with all kinds of wild thoughts running through his head.

Ever since Tanya and her crazy cousin came to confront him at Wilhemina's house, Willie wouldn't even pick up the phone. She threw him out of the house and tossed all his stuff out in boxes. He was afraid to go by her house too soon because of her temper—and he didn't want to catch another beat down like Towanna did.

As the days went by he started to realize more and more how much he missed being around Wilhemina. Since he saw her last he felt like there was a hole in his life. He felt a little empty, sluggish and bored—bottomline, he felt like crap. Willie gave him a recharge that kept him going every day.

Her smile.

Her laugh.

Her gangster.

Her jabs at his style.

Her graceful model's figure.

Her smooth near-blemish-free complexion.

And she never hesitated to please her man in the bedroom, even if she was really tired after a long day at work.

Cage loved Willie, but like a lot of men he took her for granted. He knew that no matter what, she'd be around. She had suspected that Cage had a girl or two on the side, but she didn't question him about them. She was always trying to be the perfect woman for him, even if the cost was her self-respect. But one thing Wilhemina hated was for other women to throw her man in her face. It was the one thing that really set her off.

Then he thought about how Kay finally left Shawn and it had him messed up for years. Just then *When a Woman's Fed Up* started playing in the background on his car radio as if the universe was trying to tell him something. It was a sign.

"Shit...I gotta get my baby back!"

* * *

"Hey girl!" Wilhemina yelled into the phone excitedly.

"What's up Willie?" Elisha said, sounding groggy. "What's going on with you?"

"Girl you won't believe what I just did."

"What? What?" she asked. There was a long pause. "Tell me! You know I hate surprises!"

Willie laughed. "Yea I know I'm messing wit you!"

"Come on already!"

"I just gave two week's notice at my job and bought three tickets to Miami," Willie finally blurted out. Once she said it out loud to someone it made things even more real.

"Oh my God! Seriously?"

"Yes girl I did it. I'm going to Miami. I'm leaving this month!" Willie said as her heart pumped hard in her chest. She was still a little afraid of the unknown but excited about the possibilities.

"Yes!" Elisha shouted. She had been praying that her friend would make that call. "Oh wow, you did it!"

"I just have to take care of a few last details, like selling all my furniture, and then I'm out," Willie explained. "And listen girl, when I get settled I want you, Tino and the kids to come visit and stay with me for a few days okay?

"Bet, we haven't been to Miami in a minute!" Elisha agreed.

"But one thing—don't tell Tino just yet, because he's just gonna tell Cage and you know how that goes," Willie explained. "I just kinda wanna slide up out this bitch quietly you know?"

"Ughhh, that is gonna be so hard because you know we talk about everything," Elisha said. "But I will keep it quiet 'til you leave okay."

"I love you so much, thank you for everything sis!"

"Love you too. I can't wait to see you sprawled across a magazine cover!"

* * *

It was Valentine's Day and the community was having a rare outdoor barbecue that time of year due to the unseasonably warm weather. It was mostly about the kids, but of course all the usual suspects, whether they had kids or not, were out trying to get some of the free food and drinks. The community organization rented a bounce house and had games out for all the kids to enjoy.

Shawn brought Mya up to the party and watched as she played on the bounce house with her friends. He laughed when he saw her bossing other kids around and standing up for herself. He was a proud dad. Tino brought his kids by for a little while, but had to take them to their grandmother's house and get ready for a Valentine's dinner with his wife later on.

Shawn still hadn't heard anything about the job he was going for and was starting to get discouraged again. He called the veteran's office and asked if he could get back into the rehab program for the full 90 days and possibly work there, just so that he could get away from the drama of Philadelphia for a while. But they sent him through the ringer and tried to send him to some type of remedial program in the city instead.

"Uh oh, here come trouble," Ron said, always trying to instigate.

Shawn's eyes wandered to the right as he took a sip from his soda, which had a bit of vodka in it. He saw George and a couple of his friends approaching. Whenever George was around it was as if a dark cloud settled on the gathering. He didn't have any real reason to be at the community event except to see and be seen. Of course George had to come right up and stand near Shawn. Shawn couldn't stand the sight of him—each time they came across each other the more and more tense it became.

Everybody knew by then that Shawn was trying to become a changed man and leave the streets alone, but not everybody liked that. They were crabs in a barrel—if they weren't going to make it out the hood they didn't want anybody else to either.

Cage was on the phone, calling Wilhemina for the 10th time that day. She didn't pick up the phone again, so he left another voicemail message professing his love and wishing her a Happy Valentine's Day. Shawn felt bad for his friend, but was feeling just fine on his end. For the first time in years Kay had agreed to be his Valentine, even though they couldn't be together that weekend. He sent her a quick "I love you" text, just because.

George and his friends started laughing about something and talking loudly—loud enough for Shawn and Cage to hear.

"...Valentine's Day niggas. Showing so much love to these bitches. Man please," he heard George's friend say right after Cage hung up the phone.

"Sendin' em chocolate hearts and shit," George laughed along with him.

Shawn tried to keep his mouth shut and ignore the obvious taunts, but he was so disgusted by George at that point that taking the high road was almost impossible.

"It must be nice to have your boyfriend with you on Valentine's," Shawn took his jab and stared George down until he finally looked his way.

"Oh look who it is, SB! The college nigga. The rehabbed reformed hustler. How that rehab program work out for you my nigga?" George taunted — word traveled fast in the projects.

"It worked out real well," Shawn replied with a nod. "I'll give you the number, maybe they can help you kick your nasty habit."

George turned up his nose at the comment because he knew it was true. Shawn could tell he was upset so as usual he went in for the kill.

"Oh how that nigga Kev doin' by the way? He out the hospital yet?" Shawn said trying to look concerned, but it didn't last long because he broke out in laughter.

"He aiight," George said with a nod. "Was wondering if you might wanna go for that same trip? Cause that can be arranged."

"I already got my passport stamped beeyatch," Shawn said obnoxiously as he lifted his shirt, revealing all of his scars from the time he was stabbed.

"Well there might be one more trip left," George threatened. "And it's a one-way pass."

"If that's the case, I might have to take you with me then," Shawn said seriously.

"I doubt you'll even have a chance."

"Don't ever doubt me. I stay with something up my sleeve," Shawn replied as he pulled one of his coat sleeves up.

He and George continued to trade threats until Cage came

and pulled Shawn away, knowing how easily talk turned to action those days.

"Come on Shawn you gotta chill. That nigga ain't got nothin' to lose right now but you do."

"Fuck that pussy," Shawn said and threw the middle finger up at George.

George nodded and made a gesture for his waist as if to say he was strapped and ready. The days of throwing hands in a good old-fashioned street fight over petty disputes were long gone.

Chapter 32
Too Little Too Late

Shawn did his little Charlie Brown dance in the middle of the living room and laughed as he held the letter that held the key to his future. It was a letter from a state department office deep in the suburbs telling him that he was hired for a job in a kitchen serving other employees. Cooking was one of his favorite things to do. It paid $19.50 an hour and could go up to as much as $35 after five years.

Although he still got a little tipsy from time to time, Shawn had been clean for months—he didn't even smoke weed. He passed his last drug test with flying colors.

After he finished celebrating, the first person he called with the news was Kay.

"Hey bae!" he said in an upbeat voice when she picked up. "What's up?"

"I got that job. We movin' on up!" he told her. "Pays $19.50 an hour with benefits."

"For real, for real? No bullshitting this time?" she asked, reserving her excitement for a moment.

"No bullshit bae, I passed all the tests, went for the interview, everything is set. I start on Monday."

"That's that shit baby!!" Kay said and erupted in laughter. She couldn't stop smiling.

"And that ain't it. I won four Gs down Atlantic City! Baby, we set!" he told her.

"Four Gs? Well damn Shawn!"

"Hell yea, and you know Imma break my baby off with some of that."

"That's what's up," Kay said with a smile. "Thanks Shawn, you're always right on time."

"Look I gotta run, but I'll call you tomorrow aiight?"

"Alright, proud of you Shawn. Be safe and smart."

"I will."

Shawn ran upstairs to take a shower. He took the necklace that Kay had given him off for a moment and hung it on the door. In his haste, he forgot to pick it back up before he left the house.

* * *

"...so I just came to this realization, you know? It's time for me to settle down for real Willie. I want to move in here, sell the house in West Philly. All that."

Cage was standing on Wilhemina's porch holding a single red rose. He was still trying to figure out why she hadn't yet invited him inside. She was just standing there holding the door open looking at him as if he was a door-to-door vacuum salesman making a pitch. He initially tried his keys in the door but they didn't work, so he ended up having to knock until she answered.

"Here's a rose for my rose," he said in a sing songy voice, holding out the gift.

Wilhemina examined the rose carefully. One of the petals was falling off—he hadn't even bothered to get it properly pruned. Willie just continued to stare at him.

"Well ain't you gonna take it?" The expression on her face said *hell no*. "Look bae, I fucked up. I know. But I can make this right... I just need you to give me a chance to make it right."

Another chance… She thought of all the years she had spent with him, taking care of him, making him comfortable, taking him to court when he got into some trouble and even lending him money for bail. And this was all he had to offer, after all the mess that he had put her through with the young girl Tanya. Not even a marriage proposal—all he was proposing was to move into her house.

"Are you done Romeo? My kids waiting for me."

Cage looked amused. "Come on Willie, quit fooling around. You know we been through worse than this basic shit. We gonna be together no matter what, we were meant for each other. You my Bonnie, you know that."

"Well not anymore Clyde. I'm more like Columbiana these days, playing it solo."

Cage looked into her eyes for a sign that she was just playing around or just looking for a challenge. There was nothing there but nonchalance and boredom. His worst fears had been confirmed—Wilhemina had moved on.

"I know you're not gonna try to play me like this Willie," Cage said shaking his head. "Not now with all this shit I got going on. I need you, you my rock."

Wilhemina shrugged and started to close the door. "Sorry but my give-a-fuck meter's been on the fritz lately."

"Wait, hell no," Cage protested and pushed the door back open. He decided to try a different, more aggressive approach. "Now what the fuck's your problem for real?"

"What is MY problem?" Wilhemina shouted suddenly. "Your monkey ass goes and gets some young smut pregnant, coming in my house every night on some jo shit, laying up in my bed and you got the nerve to ask me what my problem is?"

"I know, I know bae, I was wrong. But you know this relationship's worth fighting for! Right?? We been ridin' together for too long!"

Wilhemina had heard it all before.

"Now all of a sudden you want to fight? After all these years?" Wilhemina said and her nostrils flared a bit at the thought. Cage opened his mouth to say something but she stopped him and put her finger up.

"Uh uh, shut up. You had your opportunity to talk and ain't saying nothing! Ya'll niggas put us through the most shit, and ain't about shit yourself. You act like you some kinda king and I'm supposed to bow at your raggedy ass ashy feet all my life! Why, just cause you a man? Hell no! What have you done for me?" Willie ranted.

She stood and waited a moment for an answer but Cage couldn't come up with one quickly enough.

"I mean, who the fuck is you though Cage, really? What the fuck have you done for me and my kids except sit around here and eat up all our food? Sleeping in my warm bed!"

"You know I give you money sometimes!" he declared.

"Fuck your little pocket change muthafucka! I work 10 hours a day, six days a week making my own money. Your little $20 here and there is not needed nor helping with shit."

She closed the screen door in his face and he slapped it angrily with his hand. She was just about to close the main door, but stopped to say one more thing.

"Oh and by the way, me and my kids moving out the city. So don't come by here anymore Cage or Imma have to pop the trunk on ya."

Wilhemina slammed the door closed and locked every lock. Cage stood there silently with a confused look on his face, still holding the sagging rose. *What just happened?* He didn't expect it to go down that way at all.

Chapter 33
Choices

"I'm putting some cash in your account tomorrow bae, I know you need that," Shawn said to Kay over the phone.

"Thanks bro. What you up to this weekend?"

"Nothing much, just gonna be mostly in the crib. But I'm definitely putting that in the account tomorrow morning aiight?"

"Uggh Shawn, don't say definitely, I hate that word. Whenever you say definitely it never happens!" Kay said with a laugh.

"I know I know, okay well for sure then. When you coming up here next?"

"Probably next weekend, I got that assignment to finish up then we can hang out there."

"Aiight bet! Love you bae."

"I love you too."

Shawn was at his mother's house visiting with his family. All his young nieces and nephews were there and the house was buzzing. He came to give everyone the good news about his new job and all his plans. He was set to start the job that Monday and wouldn't be able to hang out down the way too much more. They were excited for him. He was relaxing in the kitchen and cracking jokes with his sisters when he got a call from Tino.

"Yo, SB, we down at Tina's party tonight. Even Cage is comin' out, and you know he ain't been outside since Willie dumped 'im," Tino said with a laugh. "You comin'?"

When Shawn thought about all the money in his pocket some of his old self came back. He became excited at the thought of tricking it up a little at a party down the way. He had always loved flossing. This would be kind of like a going away party—if he was going to stop hanging out in the hood so much after Monday he figured at least he could go out with a bang.

"Yea I'll be there, come scoop me from my Mom's house," he said and looked at the time on his phone.

"No, he ain't comin' down nowhere!" Rhonda yelled loudly in the background. "Don't be coming by my house!"

Shawn shook his head and gestured for his mother to be quiet. "Pick me up in a half hour T."

"Shawn I really wish you would stay away from those people!" Rhonda said as soon as he hung up the phone. "They don't mean you any good!"

"What people? Those are my people ma, calm down," he said and put his hand up.

"Boy don't tell me to calm down!" his mother snapped. "You know exactly what I'm talking about, those people don't mean you well! They don't really care about you! You just got this good new job and still wanna be in the streets!"

"You don't know what you talkin' about ma in the first place. And you need to stay the fuck out my conversations in the second place!"

"Ooooo! Jesus be a fence! Cause Imma need one to stop me from strangling this boy!" Rhonda said and lunged for his neck, but Shondra got in the middle and Rose pushed her brother out toward the door.

"Brother you need to chill. She just concerned about you, we heard about George and Huey."

Shawn shook his head and pulled out a cigarette. "Ya'll should know by now not to worry about me. I got things under control."

They sat outside the house smoking and chatting for a while. Soon enough Shawn was feeling bad about snapping on his mother and decided to come back in to make things right.

"Ma," he said quietly as he watched her making busy work in the kitchen, washing dishes and putting things away. "I'm sorry ma."

"Don't be sorry. I can't stand a sorry person," she said without looking at him.

"Well then I apologize," he corrected himself. "I don't want you to worry about me ma, but I appreciate your concern."

"You're hard-headed and stubborn Shawn, always been since you were a little child," she said and shook her head. They heard a beep outside and knew that it was Tino.

"I got it honest," he said with a smirk and then reached in to give his mother a kiss. He put a $50 bill on the counter. "I love you ma, call you in the morning."

"Love you too son, call me soon as you get home!"

Shondra stopped her brother at the door and looked him over. She put her hands on him as if to put a blessing on him. Shawn just stood there and watched her curiously, not knowing the purpose, but not stopping her either. She gave him a hug and then they watched him bound out the door to Tino's car.

* * *

"You worried about Huey showing up?" Tino asked Shawn as they stood outside the Chinese store smoking like old times.

"Not even a little bit," Shawn said as he took a leisurely pull from his Newport.

Down the street Ron was on the phone talking to someone.

"Yo, that nigga SB down here right now," Ron said into the phone. "Down here at the store.... only got Tino wit 'im.... okay, I'll watch 'im."

George hung up the phone and directed his cousin to drive to the store. Shawn was spending less and less time down the way so it was rare to catch him. George had some beef to settle with Shawn and now was the time.

Shawn never liked Ron and that was why he picked on him so much. His suspicions were on point—Ron had always been a snitch. He snitched to everybody who would listen, especially someone looking to pay for some information. He had snitched to the hater who wanted Kidd dead for a $100 pay day and knew that it was coming in advance. He didn't like Shawn either and secretly wished for him to get cut down to size somehow. He had hoped Shawn would get popped right along with Kidd that day in front of the store, but he left early. Now was Ron's chance to finally get his wish.

Shawn and Tino were laughing about something when George rolled up with his car speakers pumping a beat with heavy bass. They got out of the car just as Shawn turned to look. Ron, the rat, joined them and smirked as if he knew something as he walked up behind George like a groupie.

"Ay SB, ain't seen you around these parts in a while!" George said with his arms wide open. His gun was clearly on display on his waist. Shawn immediately went into defense mode plotting a way to get control of the situation.

Shawn looked down at the gun and then started laughing as if he didn't have a care in the world. He had cheated death on plenty of occasions and he wasn't about to start running scared today. His laughter made George nervous. Tino just rubbed his chin and eyed George closely.

Before any words could be traded a cop car rode up real slow and parked right across the street from the store.

Saved by a cop, Shawn thought. *Ain't that a bitch!*

George took note of the police car and closed his jacket.

"I'll catch you later nigga," George said and went on into the store as if he was just going to get a beer.

Right then and there, Tino decided that this would be his last time hanging out in a very long while. Elisha was right—he was pushing his luck. His family needed him more than anyone. If he was to get killed on those streets nobody would come to his family's rescue.

"Yea we'll see about that," Shawn said. He took another long puff of his cigarette and stared at Ron with his free hand tucked under his arm. Ron's face twisted into a wince. Tino and Shawn continued to eye him down with a knowing look as they made their way back to Tino's car. Ron instantly knew he wouldn't be safe anymore. Word about traitors traveled fast. *Karma's a bitch.*

"Yo, maybe you should call it a night SB," Tino said once they were in the car. "I'll drive you up to the crib."

"Naw, I'm celebrating tonight T. Ain't about to let some ole bitch and a snitch ruin my flow," Shawn said even though his better judgment was telling him otherwise. He waved Tino on to drive down to the party.

* * *

Shawn, Tino, Cage and a group of their friends were at Tina's party having a good old time, just like the old days when things weren't so bad down in the projects. Everyone was playing cards, eating, drinking, smoking and enjoying good company. Tina had a spread of fried chicken, soft-shell crabs, macaroni and cheese, greens, potato salad and cornbread.

Shawn had a few drinks but not enough to get really drunk like he did in the past. He paid off a few old debts and played a few rounds of cards, but then stopped when he started to lose. Though he had had a few nice pay days in the past, he lost a whole lot more than he won. He had lost so much money over the years gambling that he cringed at the thought of how he could have better spent that cash.

Cage was finally coming to accept that Willie was gone from his life. She had left Philly with her kids on a red eye flight, early in the morning while the city was sleeping. She left almost everything behind—the only people she gave details about her plans were Elisha and her boss. If she had tried to tell her family they would have tried to convince her to stay, mostly out of jealousy and "crabs in a barrel" syndrome. The first week Willie arrived in Miami she was signed to a local agency and booked for two more shows. The agency was covering her first couple of months in the new city—with her amazing natural features and height she was going to be a consistent money maker for them.

Cage called and visited her house every day but she refused to speak to him right up to the day she left. She was on her way to becoming a top-rated International model and he had taken her for granted for years.

Shawn saw his boy sitting on the couch drowning his sorrows in a 40-ounce bottle of Steel Reserve, looking just like he looked when he lost Kay all those years ago. He went over and sat next to him. He didn't know what to say at first, so just waited for Cage to talk. Shawn remembered back when Cage was sitting in his place, telling him what he should have done with Kay and how it only made him angry.

"I lost her man," Cage finally said. "She left. She gone!"

"Yea, I know how you feel bro, you know what happened to me."

"That was my heart. I don't know what Imma do without her," Cage admitted as he shook his head. "Can't stand these other little bird-brained broads out here. I want my Willie. What was I thinking?"

"That's our problem, we don't think 'til shit goes down. So smart we stupid," Shawn told him. "But it ain't the end of the world. She might call you one day brother. Me and Kay closer than we ever been."

"You think?" Cage asked and looked at him.

"Yup," Shawn said with a nod. "But you gotta make the effort. Show her you a changed man if you want her back."

"Yea, I know. I ain't shit," Cage said and shook his head. They were both quiet for a while. "Do you know I ain't seen my son for over four years?"

"Well it ain't never too late to make that right, long as you living and breathing," Shawn said.

"You right. And now I might got another one on the way," Cage sighed. "I gotta get my shit together."

Just then Brian, the stink-breath neighborhood hater, walked into the party uninvited. No one liked him and after just a few minutes Tina made her boyfriend go tell him to leave. When he started to make a drunken scene Shawn, always the mediator, came to try to calm things down. But unfortunately he just fueled the fire—Brian was still pissed at Shawn for beating him up in the bar all those years ago and for generally doing and looking better. Also, Shawn wasn't aware that Brian was Towanna's cousin twice removed.

Niggas all in they feelings.

"C'mere," Shawn said to Brian, trying to pull him to the

side. "Let me tell you something."

"Nigga I don't need you to tell me nuffin!" Brian drawled. "Bitch ass muthafucka."

Shawn decided to let it slide and go back to the party, remembering how Kay told him to stay out of drama that didn't involve him. Someone else would handle it.

Finally, after realizing that he was outnumbered at the party, Brian backed his way out of the door. After he left, Shawn cracked a joke and everybody laughed along with him—he could always make the party lively. They all went back to enjoying themselves as if nothing had happened. All the bruhs and the sisters, most of whom Shawn had known for decades, were in the place. They were a tight-knit family—the gathering felt like home.

Finally, after another hour Shawn looked at his watch and decided that it was about that time.

"Yo Tino, Cage, I'm about to get up," he told them and slapped hands.

"Nigga, it's only midnight!" Tino yelled at him.

"Yea, I know but I think Imma go catch that late bus up to the house. Got things to do in the morning."

"You want a ride?" Tino asked.

"Naw, ya'll enjoy yourselves. I'll holla at you tomorrow."

"Aiight my nigga, stay up." Cage said and Tino nodded at him.

Shawn walked out of the party laughing and cracking jokes as usual, all the way out of the door. He walked towards the corner and patted his pockets instinctually to make sure his cash was still there. He couldn't wait to make that deposit into Kay's account—he knew it would make her month and give her some breathing room.

When he looked back up he saw Brian and his friend

standing there by a car talking.

"Here go this bitch ass nigga again," Brian mumbled. Shawn crossed his arms, swaying a bit from the alcohol.

"Ya'll enjoying ya'll little date? How precious. No wonder they call you dick breath," he said with a laugh.

Brian's anger flared up at the insult. He had always had a very thin skin, just like Huey, especially about his bad breath.

"You know what SB, I know what your problem is," Brian said as he stood up and walked toward him. "You think you better than the rest of us niggas. Right? But nigga, youse a sorry ass muthafucka who ain't never gonna be shit, just like the rest of us."

"Nigga *you* might be a sorry ass muthafucka, but I ain't," Shawn replied as he waved him off and kept walking. Brian stood in his path. It was then Shawn realized that Brian had something in his hand tucked under his sleeve.

"And yo, I heard you the one who caused my cousin to lose her hair," Brian commented.

"What? Who your cousin?"

"Towanna nigga!" he yelled impatiently. "They told me it was you that fucked her up."

"Well they a motherfucking lie," Shawn became angry, quickly flashing back to his old self. He got into Brian's face. "I ain't lay a finger on *her*. But fucking *you* up is a completely different story!"

"You know what, I should just stab the shit out your disrespectful ass right now," Brian threatened.

"Do it then pussy! Go 'head, I dare you!" Shawn spat in his face, calling his bluff. He was never one to back down from a fight, especially when threatened, and he wasn't about to start today. "Go 'head, do it then!"

Shawn felt something on his chest that felt like a very hard punch at first, but after a few moments his whole body became engulfed in pain. His body went into shock so that he couldn't even move his hands for a moment.

Brian yanked his knife from Shawn's chest and Shawn looked at him with a confused look. Brian had an expression of pure evil in his eyes. He smirked, looking satisfied as if he had just had an adrenaline rush, then took off down the street with his friend, disappearing around a corner.

Shawn had looked into the face of death.

He looked up at the dark night sky and clutched his chest tightly, trying to come to terms with the intense pain he was feeling. He had been stabbed right in the heart.

He winced and slowly started putting one foot in front of the other, trying to head back toward the party. Even with blood pouring out of his chest he still managed to make it back to Tina's front yard, where Cage, Lift and a few other familiar faces were standing outside smoking.

"…damn, he got me," he said weakly. He clutched his chest tightly as he struggled to make out his last few words. Blood spurted out from between his fingers and stained his white polo shirt. "That motherfucker Brian stabbed me."

Everyone rushed toward him. Tina came to the door and looked on in horror as he dropped to the ground and slowly rolled down the hilly sidewalk.

"Somebody call an ambulance, quick!" someone screamed.

Blood stained the concrete and grass. He was in a lot of pain and it showed on his face.

"God…" Shawn said.

"Beezy!" someone yelled. By then the voices were starting to fade and Shawn was losing his hearing. They all soon became muffled sounds in the background. He closed his eyes slowly and his life started flashing in front of him.

The first vision he saw was his father Jerome. Shawn was

10 years old and his father tackled him in the snow. Then he mercilessly rained snowballs on him. That was Shawn's favorite memory of his father.

The next thing he saw was his friends and his cousins as they all stood out on the corner politicking, smoking cigarettes and drinking. They kept him lively.

The next person he saw was Kay. She smiled at him, soothing his soul, as they sat out on their porch under the stars. That was his rock.

The next vision was of his mother, sisters, nieces, nephews and family at the house earlier that day, laughing and loving each other. That was his foundation.

The next vision was of his sons and his daughter when he attended one of their graduation ceremonies. He loved when his kids were all together in one place. They were his inspiration to do better.

Shawn could still faintly hear voices around him crying and shouting. He felt a warm light envelop him and suddenly the pain went away. He didn't feel a thing.

The last vision he saw was his father again. But it was more than just a dream or a memory. Jerome was smiling and gesturing for his son.

"Hey Pop!" Shawn said in amazement, still not exactly sure what was going on.

"Come on son," he said. "Been waitin' on you!"

Shawn smiled; that bright white smile that could light up a whole football stadium. And then he went on with his dad.

Epilogue –*Letter to Kay*

Kay was going through the tough task of gathering up Shawn's things and sorting through all of his paperwork. It was hours after his funeral and she was reeling after seeing her best friend lying in a box. As dangerous a lifestyle as Shawn was living she never once pictured him lying there. Not there.

They had plenty of evidence to convict his killer. Everyone from the neighborhood came out to see Shawn off and when the time came to take him to the limo, countless brothers who knew him, including Cage, Tino, Lift, Young Mike and all of his cousins ran to assist in carrying him. Shawn had his haters in life but he was more loved than anything. He left the earth with a big smile on his face—it fit his personality perfectly.

One of the first things Kay found back at the house was the necklace she had given to Shawn hanging on the door. She immediately broke down in tears when she saw it. She assumed it had been confiscated by the police or lost.

As she was sorting through his paperwork she pulled out a notebook and was about to throw it in a pile for possible shredding, assuming it was from Shawn's short stint in college, but something made her flip through it for a moment.

There was only one page with writing on it. It looked like Shawn had started writing a letter, but as usual it came out more like a poem. She sat down for a moment and took a deep breath as she started to read…

We meet

She listen

She Febreze me

I cooked

She listened

She showed me life

I provided things that can't be sold, brought, or explain

I gave you me

You look at me and laugh at me

I love to see you smile

I smile…

And what you thought about me I been figured out and I dare not blame you

I respect you always, encouraged you to keep moving no matter what

You showed me what being a real man is all about….

- THE END -

SO SMART YA STUPID
by J. GAIL & EL WIL

If you enjoyed this novel, please go to Amazon and Goodreads to add your review right now, while the story is fresh on your mind.

Your continued support and reviews are what keep authors motivated to write. Thank you.

MORE TITLES BY J. GAIL:

GRITTY URBAN TALES THAT INSPIRE AND EXCITE YOU

BEST SELLER IN URBAN FICTION

A 3-PART SERIES

Find all of J. Gail's titles
at Amazon, BN.com or
JazoliPublishing.com

Request them at a bookstore or
library near you!

Sign up for J. Gail's newsletter to receive updates on
upcoming titles, events, offers and more!

http://www.jazolipublishing.com

Contact the Author:
jgail@jazolipublishing.com
@Author_JGail

Parental Guide

This book is highly recommended for adult readers **18 and older** due to adult situations throughout. However, if you're a parent, here is a guide to pages containing very adult content.

Page 24
Pages 29-30
Page 40
Pages 45-46
Page 52
Pages 70-72
Pages 121-122
Pages 123-124
Page 136
Pages 149-150
Pages 154-155
Page 158
Pages 165-166
Pages 176-178
Page 188
Page 191
Pages 197-198
Page 204
Pages 253-255
Page 277

Thank you for supporting this work.

NEW SITE !

HotUrbanBooks.com

Get recommendations and news on HOT urban books from black authors.

Subscribe for updates and become a member today!

HotUrbanBooks.com